LAZYTOWN

STEVE SHEPPARD

COPYRIGHT

Copyright © 2025 by Steve Sheppard

All rights reserved.

No part of this book may be reproduced in any form or by any electronic or mechanical means, including information storage and retrieval systems, without written permission from the author, except for the use of brief quotations in a book review.

❈ Formatted with Vellum

WHAT PEOPLE SAY ABOUT THE DAWSON AND LUCY SERIES

"If Terry Pratchett wrote James Bond, then this would be it."

"Steve Sheppard is a gifted comic writer with a knack for clever plotting and thrills." *Greg Mosse (Author of The Coming Darkness and many murder mysteries)*

"A curiously magical thriller with suburban subterfuge and sparkle." *Helen Lederer (Comedy author and Founder of the Comedy Women in Print Prize)*

"This is a thriller, a chase, a buddy story and a mystery which rips along at a hectic pace." *Adrian Magson (Author of Hostile State and 25 other spy thrillers)*

"A very entertaining read which kept me guessing all the way through. Skillful storytelling and a sense of fun." *Imogen Matthews (Author of The Hidden Village and other World War II novels)*

"Love the characters and humour that permeates the whole book. The twins and their dialogue are hilarious." *Julie Hamstead*

"Witty, raucous, clever and intriguing. A very funny,

hapless lead with lots of strong women characters." *Onia Fox (Author of Enemy Closer and other comedy thrillers)*

"A fast-moving, roller-coaster of a light-hearted spy thriller. An action-packed, fun read." *Sue Clark (Comedy author of Note to Boy and A Novel Solution)*

"The pace is frenetic. Quirky characters appear, disappear and reappear (though called something else). Huge fun." *Julie Anderson (Author of The Midnight Man and four other thrillers)*

"A rollicking good read. It's like finding the fantasy child of James Bond and John le Carre. Steve's tongue-in-cheek (often laugh out loud) characters marry perfectly with a thrilling, finely-tuned plot." *Jackie Green (Co-Author of Quota)*

"A fun, page-turning thriller that kept me enthralled and chuckling. Lucy and Dawson's interactions with friends, foes and each other have a wonderful sort of sophisticated goofiness reminiscent of Nick and Nora Charles in The Thin Man. I couldn't put it down." *Steve Powell (author of political thriller, Term Limits)*

"It held me spellbound. Masterful storytelling and an intricate plot. Each twist and turn kept me eagerly anticipating what would happen next." *L Powers*

"Steve is so good at creating amusing names, funny situations and crazy murders, all delivered at breakneck pace." *Justine Gilbert (Author of Daisy Chain and Montecatini)*

LAZYTOWN

DEDICATION

Idleborough does not exist. Let me be quite clear about that. If you think differently, particularly if you happen to live in a village in West Oxfordshire, then that's simply your imagination at work. Of course, if it did exist, then this book would be affectionately dedicated to its wonderful, occasionally eccentric but always friendly inhabitants.

1
SUNDAY 14TH JULY
FOUR PUBS AND GRANNY'S BOBBINS

'The pub's shut!'

The voice on the other end of the phone sounded outraged. Mind you, this wasn't necessarily an accurate harbinger of doom, Banjo having a habit of sounding outraged over the smallest of things: the village shop running out of his favourite scotch eggs for example. Or his TV remote control needing a new battery.

'Which pub?' I asked in what I hoped was a calming voice. It was an important question, Idleborough currently boasting four such establishments. For a village of fewer than two-thousand residents, this seemed an inordinately large number of public houses, although my late grandad reckoned he could remember when there were thirteen of them dotted up the High Street and around the Market Square. And that was before the new estate had been built. It must have been quite hard work for the drinking inhabitants of Idleborough to keep thirteen pubs in business and inevitably they had eventually failed to do so as one by one the pubs had closed, leaving just four. And maybe, if Banjo was to be believed, three.

'The Farts,' replied Banjo, plaintively. I started to pay more attention. If true, this was quite serious. Whilst there were, as I say, four pubs still hanging grimly on in this third decade of the 21st century, desperately fighting a losing battle with cheap supermarket booze and annual hikes in business rates, The Farts was, to most of us, the best pub left. No, of course, it's not really called The Farts. In reality, it's The Three Pigeons but Clem, the landlord, feeling a few years ago that the place needed to rubber-stamp its identity, decided to commission a new pub sign, the old one having been rendered completely indecipherable for several years by a combination of wind, rain and non-existent upkeep. 'Bad for us business,' Clem had said when asked why he was commissioning a new sign and after we'd explained what the word commissioning meant in this context. 'No'un knows we's a pub, does them?' Whether its name was obvious or not, it looked more or less like a pub to the rest of us and if business was passing it by, it would have had more to do with the rubbish sacks permanently piled up by the Snug door and the absence of any food except Smith's Salt and Vinegar crisps from a large case in the cellar, which Clem purchased for a tenner from a taciturn man in a van five years ago and which he's been trying, mostly unsuccessfully, to flog ever since.

Anyway, where was I? Oh, yes, Clem's new pub sign. Now Clem's a great one for giving work to local tradesmen, indeed Bernie the Bookie runs his entire business out of the public bar. Trouble was, as Clem discovered, there were no village tradesmen proficient in the business of painting pub signs. Finally, Percy Pocock, from his old stool in the corner by the non-working jukebox, had been awarded the contract, having claimed to have once won a drawing cup at his primary school. When we saw the result of his efforts, we could only surmise that pigeons had not been the subject of his prize-winning schoolboy endeavours. The sign had been unveiled to great local fanfare on a Saturday night with all the local great and good in attendance, including Exhausted Ena, the editress of the village rag, the *Idle Eye*, and Squire Jonty from the Manor, who usually frequented The Trout at the far end of the village, the pub that boasted carpets, a garden and actual, edible food, but who had been persuaded to slum it for the occasion.

Percy was sitting there on the big night in his best shirt, the red and yellow one he'd bought from C&A in 1977, proud as punch, a pint of Old Bedstead in his mittened hand. Clem had brought the new pub sign down the stairs, covered in an old sheet, and made a rambling speech, something about encouraging new, young local talent to flourish. None of us was sure about the young bit: Percy was seventy-five if he was a day.

Finally, Clem called upon Squire Jonty to whip off the sheet, which Jonty did very carefully with the ends of a finger and thumb, surreptitiously wiping them on his mustard cords afterwards.

There was silence for quite a long time while we carefully scrutinised Percy's artistic creation. Finally, Postman Pat coughed slightly and said in a small voice, his brow furrowed, 'What the flickering fuck is that, then?' We all nodded solemnly at these words of wisdom. OK, the large splodge of green in the background could, if you were being generous, portray a tree of some description; but the three smaller browny-grey splodges in the foreground looked nothing like pigeons. The pesky blighters are virtually shoulder-to-shoulder in the Market Square so the whole village knows what a pigeon looks like. Not so much Percy though, it seemed.

Finally, Squire Jonty, with his reading glasses perched on the end of his nose, and peering closely at the sign, said, 'They look more like sparrows.'

So Percy started hurrumphing into his Old Bedstead and Clem, who didn't want to upset his oldest customer, said, 'Nome, me booties, them's def'ly pigeons. Anys ways, young Scooby's comin' round farst thing in t'mornin' with him's cherry-picker to put him up on bracket, so all's good. First drinks on me, boys.' The offer of a rare free drink from Clem was enough to put the thought of Percy's artwork out of our collective heads and the next day, Scooby had come and hung the new sign up and the pub became known by the local populace as The Three Sparrows, which inevitably soon became The Three Farts, as in sparrow-fart being colloquial for dawn; and finally just The Farts.

Which was, according to Banjo, now closed.

'How?' I asked. 'What's happened to Clem? Not just gone on holiday, has he?' Clem had not been on holiday in the last ten years to my knowledge, so he was undoubtedly due one.

'Grapevine has it he's retiring. Seems his missus has been pushing him for ages and he's had an offer from a developer.'

'Missus? What missus? Do you mean a wife?' I asked. I'd known Clem, been going to The Farts, since I was knee-high to a knee, and I'd never known he was married. It didn't seem likely. Clem didn't look like the marrying kind. No, make that the marriageable kind.

'Yeah, you know, small woman, thin, mousy hair, glasses stuck on top of her head all the time.'

I knew who he meant. 'What, Maeve? I thought she was his cleaner,' I said.

'Cleaner? Does The Farts look like it gets cleaned?' This

was undeniably true. It was clean inasmuch as there were virtually no mice wandering around the bar areas but only because they couldn't walk freely through the dust and dirt on the uncarpeted floor. "Original Polished Wood Floors," proudly proclaimed the pub flyer we'd found once, dated 1970. Remove the word polished and that still held true.

'Are you sure it's shut?' I asked. 'It's not just a nasty rumour, is it?' I'd long-since learned not to trust any information spread on the village grapevine.

'Standing outside now, mate. Big note on the door. "Closed until further notice", it says. Well, what it actually says is "Closed to father notice", but that's just Clem, isn't it? Proves he wrote it. It's the same note he stuck up when he was in hospital with his septic toe.'

I preferred not to be reminded of Clem's septic toe, which he'd taken to smearing with antifungal cream in the public bar on his return from hospital. 'Right,' I said. 'War Council. I'll be down in a jiffy. Anyone else with you?'

'Usual crowd, you know, Mucker, Billy, Daisy, Daisy's Dad, Dick; one or two others.'

'Right,' I said again. 'Bull, ten minutes, put the word out.'

If The Farts was less than prepossessing inside, where even the bar that Clem liked to call the Snug was little more than a store room filled with a wondrous collection of old tat, from disused computer monitors to a treasure-trove of no-longer-required solid glass ashtrays, then outside it was more depressing than prepossessing. It was an old stone building, vaguely Cotswoldy but long since painted an obscure shade of mouldy white, and which lacked any architectural note. It could be called picturesque only if the picture in question was *The Scream*. It looked a bit like an old barn dotted with small, grimy windows and bedecked with a string of elderly Christmas lights strung up at first-floor level that were never switched on, even at Christmas. Parts of the roof were invisible through the meandering mosses and clumps of small weeds that were doing their best to claim it for their own.

Clem was aware of all this but he simply didn't care. 'It'm not about the outside, it'm the insides what countem,' he'd say. And when someone had the temerity to suggest that, if that was the case, why didn't he consider sprucing the inside up a little, he'd add, 'Ah, no, it'm not about thems fixtures an' fittings. Nome, it'm about thems people, thems clientelly.' And it was indubitably true that the place was busy enough most nights of the week, especially when the Pigeon Fanciers Granny's Bobbins team was playing at home.

Granny's Bobbins? Ah, yes, well, if you don't hail from around these parts, you may not be aware of this traditional pub game, which is specific to within an approximate fifteen mile radius of our nearest proper town, Stockford. I don't believe it's played anywhere else in the country. Now don't ask me to explain how it works, I'm not an expert, although I quite like a laugh at the participants' expense on a Tuesday or Saturday evening in summer. Summer only, because it's an outdoor sport, and I use the term sport with tongue firmly in cheek. I guess it's best described as a cross between quoits, skittles and rounders. Despite witnessing hundreds of games down the years, I can't say for sure what all the rules are. I'm pretty certain some of them are made up on the spot, usually with a home bias. I'm more of a cricket man myself, a game which is much easier to understand. But it's taken seriously round here. Two of the other three pubs in the village also have teams and there's a league of twenty teams based in other pubs and clubs in the area. The bobbins themselves are made by a firm in Stockford itself. They have to be hand-carved and left to dry in a specially constructed kiln for upwards of a month before they're ready to be used. Mad, but there it is, and it's not much madder than many another rural custom in the English shires, Morris dancing for one.

2

SUNDAY 14TH JULY
TRIANGULAR SQUARES AND WELLINGTON BOOTS

These days, Idleborough found itself something of a backwater. Once a town of some importance, as the "borough" part of its name suggests, with a prosperous past built on the wool industry, it was now more usually referred to as a village, when it was referred to at all. And when it was, it was generally called, by both residents and outsiders, Lazytown. Whilst this epithet was more a reflection of the "Idle" part of its name than the working habits of its residents, it seemed somehow apt. It was well over fifty years since Dr Beeching had removed its railway station and rather more recently that the County Council had done likewise with its last bus service. There were few local businesses to speak of. Apart from Bernie the Bookie, there were the four pubs, plus three shops remaining like sentinels on the corners of the triangular Market Square: a butcher, the local general grocery store (more a subparmarket than a supermarket), which was somewhat bizarrely called Mrs Bee's Bazaar, and a hardware shop that somehow never managed to have in stock the piece of hardware you were looking for.

Not really in the home counties but hardly in the Cotswolds, Idleborough existed in a sort of geographical no man's land. No longer a town and yet too big to be a true village, it nevertheless boasted both a town hall and a village hall, the former Victorian, hideous, like a poor copy of an oversized Methodist chapel, the latter post-war austerity built out of homely red-brick, but too small for any of the purposes that a village hall is usually designed for. These competing edifices bookended The Bull.

Nine minutes after finishing my call with Banjo, I pushed open the heavy oak door of the pub. Ten people were propped up at the bar and, as one, ten pairs of eyes turned and looked at me. A collection of more sombre faces I had rarely seen.

'Cheer up, guys,' I said. 'It's not the end of the world.'

'That's what I told them,' boomed the ninety-decibel tones of Big Brian, the Yorkshire-born, hail-fellow-well-met landlord of The Bull. 'I said to them, I mean I said to them, no Farts, you can come here instead. Always welcome, I said always welcome, even southern softies like you.' And Big Brian honked out a huge laugh and exited cellarwards.

'Well we could if the beer was better,' murmured Billy glumly.

'And the wine,' added Daisy, shaking her curly head so forcefully that her round spectacles lurched precariously down to the tip of her nose. She held up her glass. 'It's supposed to be a white Sauvignon, but it's never seen the inside of a fridge. And it's got sediment.'

'So, what do we do, Sam?' asked Banjo, still employing the plaintive voice he'd used on the phone. I'm Sam, by the way, and despite assumptions to the contrary, I'm not Banjo's elder brother, although he's been treating me like one ever since I first introduced him to the pleasures of The

Farts two years ago, having found him standing aimlessly in the High Street by a bus stop that last saw a bus three years before that. Apparently he'd hitched a lift in Bristol, trying to get to London, and had been dropped off in Idleborough by the driver who had managed to convince him this was South Kensington. Banjo is not his real name. That would be Tim, but Tim is not the sort of name that any self-respecting regular of The Farts can possibly be known by and as he was carrying a banjo when I found him, that was what we called him instead. He can't actually play the banjo, he just carried it around to make him look cool. It had not had the desired effect.

'Well, first things first,' I said, after buying a pint of lager from Big Brian, back from his visit to the cellar with a crate of dusty Britvics under his arm. I don't often drink lager but The Bull's choice of real ales was limited to just the none. 'What do we know?'

'The pub's shut,' said Banjo, thus returning us neatly to where we were fifteen minutes earlier.

'Apart from that,' I said as patiently as I could. 'Has anyone seen Clem?'

'Not since last night,' said Daisy's Dad, Dick, a huge man who always wore an old Rolling Stones T-shirt. I hadn't previously realised that T-shirts with that many Xs before the L could be purchased. We hoped he had a stock of them and wasn't just recycling the same one day after day, but didn't like to ask. Daisy claimed she could once remember him wearing a proper shirt with a collar, but it didn't seem very likely. Mind you, she's known him for twenty-two years, which is all her life, so it wasn't impossible.

Well, we'd all seen Clem last night, in the then-open Farts, when he'd thrown us out the door at midnight with his usual cheery, 'Now fuckem off an' go home.' He'd seemed his usual self, in other words rude, clumsy and slightly the worse for wear and hadn't mentioned that he was thinking about shutting the pub, selling to a developer and retiring. It seemed unlikely that it would have slipped his mind, so given that the pub was definitely not open today and he'd taken the trouble to pin up the "to father notice" notice, I surmised that he had just been too embarrassed to tell us to our faces.

'So who told who about him selling up?' I looked around at the sea of unhappy faces. None of them answered; they just peered at each other questioningly. Finally, Big Brian boomed across from the bar, 'Well, Postman Pat told **me** this morning, so I rang The Farts and got mousy Maeve, who confirmed it, I say she confirmed it. Seems young Clem's up in t'Big Smoke today signing papers and what not.'

"Young" Clem was at least twenty years older than Big Brian. Also, I wasn't entirely sure what Brian meant by the Big Smoke . 'What, London?' I asked. 'And what papers?'

'Nay, lad, not London, don't be soft. Stockford, at t'brewers. Leastways, that's what Maeve said, I said that's what she said. Very pleased, she sounded. Said she's tired out running the pub all this time, so they've got a week booked in Benidorm and when they get back they'll be talkin' to some developers who've been sniffin' round.' I couldn't quite work out what might have tired Maeve out, given the lack of cleaning duties. And she certainly never served behind the bar.

Stockford was a sleepy place of barely ten-thousand souls, so it could hardly be classified as the Smoke, big or otherwise. It was, however, home to Downwycherley Brewery, where Clem got most of his real ale. He had long ago managed to negotiate some sort of exclusivity deal with them, which was why we couldn't get Old Bedstead or any of its sister beers at The Bull, or indeed at the other two pubs in Idleborough, The Trout and The Fleece. Again, whilst The Trout is that establishment's genuine name, The Fleece is more correctly The Waggoners, but gained its soubriquet by dint of a former landlord who was best known for ripping off his customers. The present host of the place merely shrugged and said he didn't mind what anyone called it, as long they visited it occasionally.

'So, Brian,' I said, 'did you know Maeve was Clem's missus?'

He looked surprised. 'Course I did, I say of course I did,' he said. 'Who did you think she was then, young Sam?'

I said that I'd always thought she was the cleaner and Big Brian laughed so much he nearly fell back down the cellar steps.

I turned to the crowd of Farts regulars, now looking more than a little lost in the alien surroundings of The Bull. Mucker was experimentally running his Wellington-booted feet up and down on the carpet as if he'd never seen or felt one before. It was quite good of Big Brian to let him into the pub in his wellies but Brian was aware, like the rest of us, that they were the only footwear Mucker owned. There were no secrets in Idleborough and, as if to emphasise the fact, the main reason why that was so chose that moment to push open the oak front door and enter. Ena Mackenzie had a tired look on her face and a pencil stuck behind her left ear. These were two givens as far as she was concerned. Her sixty-year old, permanently grey, permanently creased face always suggested that she and sleep had been strangers for years. Banjo, with the experience of a man who has been to Glasgow once, reckons that is a not uncommon look amongst Scots women of late middle age. Whatever the reason, she is always referred to as Exhausted Ena and as the editress and, it has to be admitted, sole employee of the *Idle Eye*, she evidently felt that the pencil behind the ear was a sort of badge of office. She never used it. She always wore a tattered old spiral-bound notebook hanging from a chain round her neck with a biro clipped to it that she utilised when the sniff of a story assailed her nostrils. It appeared that something had brought such a sniff to her attention now.

'Thought I'd find youse here, boys,' she started, collecting the double Bells that Big Brian had produced for her as she passed the bar on her way to our not-so-little group sat around the big square table in the bay window. 'So, Clem's a dark horse then, kept that little secret under his hat. Or more likely, under pain of death from Maeve. Hidden depths, that one.'

'So, did you know Maeve was Clem's wife then, Ena?' I asked desperately.

'Everyone knows that.' Ten heads nodded in unison. 'Anyway, went to the wedding, didn't I? Surprised you weren't there, Sam.'

'Wedding? What wedding? When was that?'

'Oh, I don't know, winter, six months ago, January perhaps, wouldn't you say, Dick?'

The big man shook his head, along with his jowls. 'Nah, Feb'ry, it was. The same week Nelly Richardson fell in the weir and drowned.'

'You're right,' said Exhausted Ena, pursing her lips consideringly. 'February. They had to put Nelly's funeral back a day because Vicar was double-booked with the wedding.'

None of this made any sense. Apart from Dick, I'd been

going to The Farts longer than anyone and I'd been to Nelly Richardson's funeral. I remembered it distinctly. Indeed, I'd sat next to Clem in the church, a Clem who had had no Maeve with him and who had completely failed to drop the subject of his apparent nuptials the previous day into the conversation we had had whilst waiting for the coffin to arrive.

I decided to let the mystery lay and returned to the matter in hand. 'So, are you planning to run this story in the *Eye*, Ena?' I asked.

'Yes, of course, if there's room but fewer and fewer local businesses are advertising with us so I'm not sure if I'll have the money for more than four or five pages of editorial, and it's filling up already. I'll have to make room for some Duck Race pictures and a report too.

I should explain here that the Annual Idleborough Duck Race, whilst originally like any other duck race in any other English village, in other words comprising a fleet of yellow plastic toy ducks floating higgledy-piggledy down a river, is now rather more individual in nature. Five years ago the powers that be decided in their infinite wisdom to dredge the River Stock, with the result that its minor tributary, the already rather less-than-mighty Idlebrook, which flows through the village, slowed to a meagre, muddy dribble. So we had to think outside the box as it were. Which, with major input from Exhausted Ena and, I have to say, myself, we did, coming up with a human version with villagers dressed originally as ducks, but now pretty much anything with feathers (we even had a feather duster this year), flapping around the village in groups of three, bound to each other with ropes around the ankles – well, it seemed a good idea at the time and, for comic value at least, still does – on a route that includes not only the four current public houses but every other house that used to be a public one, which you may recall comes to a total of thirteen, at each of which half a pint of ale has to be consumed by each contestant.

Villagers can either enter a sweepstake for the winning trio of "ducks" or take part in the entirely illegal betting operation run by Big Brian.

And yes, the posters do advertise it as having "been running for countless generations" but that's just artistic licence.

I brought my mind back to the current predicament. 'Presumably you'll have one fewer paying businesses now too,' I said to Ena.

'Yes, that's true enough, although Clem wasn't exactly one of our better payers.'

'Oh? When did he last cough up then?'

'1997.'

'I see. I wondered why the ad for The Farts hadn't been updated recently.'

'That's right,' piped up Daisy. 'It's still got the old sign in the picture – you'd think the pub was called The Three Pigeons.' Daisy's dad laughed and a couple of others cracked a smile.

'Yeah, and it still claims to have been recently refurbished,' chipped in Banjo.

'So why are you still running the ad?' I asked.

'Got to put something in and Maeve keeps saying she'll pay soon. And she's the one in charge of the money after all.'

'Would that be as well as being in charge of the cleaning?'

'Cleaning? Don't be daft, mon. What makes you think that? Clem sacked the cleaner in 2009. Doubt if it's had a dusting since. Another thing. As you know, we've only recently published an edition of the *Eye*.' I presumed that was the Royal We. 'Normally we try to get it out every three months but the next one could be a Christmas edition the way things are going.'

'Christmas? That's five months away. This story needs getting out now. The closure of a pub is serious.'

'You're assuming I meant Christmas this year.' But Ena was smiling as she said it, so I supposed it was a sort of Scottish joke.

'Bloomin' 'eck,' boomed Big Brian, beaming from behind the bar. 'Looks like The Farts isn't the only village institution in trouble then.' He seemed to be enjoying himself as only a man viewing the prospect of a significant increase in his weekly takings can.

I ignored him. 'So we can't rely on local publicity to help,' I said.

Ena pursed her lips and looked thoughtful. 'Well, I could have a word with young Mallory.'

'Mallory? Who's he?'

'Not a he, a she. Mallory Fillery. She's the local reporter for the *Stockford Spectacle*.'

'The *Specs*? Is it still going? I haven't bought one of those in years. Can't say I've seen one for sale either.' Several of the heads around the table shook in unison, along with Dick's jowls.

'It's part of some huge group now, isn't it?' suggested Daisy.

'Well yes,' said Ena, 'the Wessex Wayfarer Newspaper Group, which is part of something even bigger. Point is though, you can still get the *Spectacle* in the Bazaar, although it's usually covered up by copies of the *Daily Mail*, so you might not have spotted it. And I believe Mallory is keen to get more local content in to try and encourage sales hereabouts. Some weeks she gets a whole page to play with. She might have space. Although we'll need to give her more info before we call her. The headline, "Pub closes while owner goes to Benidorm on holiday" isn't likely to have the general public massing at the newsagents.'

'But we know there's more to it than that, don't we?' said Banjo.

'Do we now?' asked Ena. 'Really? I mean, Maeve may have told Postman Pat they were selling but after a week in the Med with only her to talk to, Clem could easily come back and just open up again as if nothing had happened.'

These words had the effect of cheering most of us up a little, so I bought a round which had the effect of cheering everyone except me up a little more.

'Even accepting that,' I said when I'd sat down again fifty quid poorer. 'I think we need to form a sub-committee to investigate and see if we can make sure The Farts is kept open.'

'I'm not sure you can have a sub-committee if there isn't a committee to start with,' said Exhausted Ena, 'but I agree that some sort of action group should be formed. Just in case as it were.'

At that, I had a rush of blood to the head, possibly caused by the new lightness of my wallet. 'I'm happy to be Chairman,' I said. That seemed to go down well. One or two people even applauded. 'Ena, you'll be part of this won't you?'

'Oh, laddie, no, no, no. I'm far too old and far too tired. And in case you havnae noticed, I don't actually drink in The Farts unless duty calls. I'm no' that keen on my shoes sticking to the floor.' It was true, that was an occupational hazard of the place. 'No, I'll get in touch with Mallory and see if she can come to your first meeting. Let me know when and where that is.' And she drained her second Bells, waved a sketchy farewell and left.

Big Brian lumbered over. 'You can always hold your meetings here, lads, I say you're welcome here,' he said. He clearly considered Daisy to be one of the lads, and she didn't object.

'Well, that's very kind of you, Brian,' I replied. Kind had nothing to do with it; he wanted the extra business. 'But I think we'll hold the meetings round mine. Nothing against The Bull but we don't want prying ears, I'm sure you understand.'

'And the beer's better at Sam's too,' muttered Billy darkly into his gassy pint as Brian returned to the bar.

'I'm not sure if ears can pry, can they?' asked Daisy, doubtfully. 'I think that's probably just eyes.'

I looked at her. 'You're in, I take it Daisy? Perhaps you could be secretary,' I added, in a not entirely unsexist way. I knew that Daisy owned a laptop and wasn't sure that anyone else around the big table even knew what a laptop was. Not Mucker at any rate.

'Of course,' said Daisy obligingly. Daisy didn't have many original thoughts, but she was reliable and conscientious and would make an excellent secretary.

'Who else?' I asked, which prompted a general averting of eyes. 'We don't need too many,' I added, encouragingly. 'Small committees are always more effective than big ones.'

'In fact, quite often, a committee of one person is most likely to get things done,' piped up the small voice of Jeremy Jeavons from the corner. 'Sorry,' he added. Jeremy is not the most confident member of our group, and usually feels the need to apologise on the rare occasions he ventures an opinion. There was, however, some truth in what he'd said, but I was damned if I was going to fight The Farts closure on my own.

Seeing a look of annoyance cross my face, Banjo sighed expansively. 'Count me in,' he said. 'I feel it's sort of my fault.'

'How do you work that out?' I asked, genuinely confused.

'Well, I found the notice, didn't I? I could have just ignored it or taken it down. Then this might never have happened.'

The logic was lost on me.

An hour later, an action group comprising Banjo, Jeremy, Daisy, Daisy's Dad, Dick and me had been formed and we agreed to meet the next evening, Monday, at my cottage to come up with some sort of hard-hitting name and an Action Plan.

3

MONDAY 15TH JULY
SLAUGHTERHOUSES AND RED HAIR

I have lived for all my thirty-five years in Slaughterhouse Lane, Idleborough, which is not so much a lane than a long, thin pothole with unkempt verges. It leads in an apologetic sort of way down behind Bob Baker the Butchers' and yes, my house, cottage as I like to call it, is in fact half of the old abattoir itself. The other half is owned by Bob, whose garden abuts the back of his shop, which makes it a conveniently short daily commute. The abattoir was closed about fifty years ago, which is when my parents, both no longer with us, sadly, as they emigrated to New Zealand ten years back, bought it. They still own Number 1, Slaughterhouse Cottages, but they allow me to live there for a peppercorn rent. At least, they refer to it as a peppercorn rent but as I am now solely responsible for the upkeep and maintenance of the property, which is old and not especially crepit, the peppercorn in question seems to have grown to award-winning girth. Yes, I know I'm lucky to have a roof over my head and a faintly picturesque cottage holding that roof up, but bear in mind that my address is

1 Slaughterhouse Cottages. I'm not fond of putting that on official forms.

As a sort of jobbing writer, I manage to work by and large from said 1 Slaughterhouse Cottages, except when I'm out prospecting, or more usually begging, for work. This Monday was no exception, so I was sitting in my comfortable swivel chair, gazing out at what I had once hoped would be a thriving vegetable patch and drinking coffee when the front doorbell rang. That was unexpected as Mucker had broken it a week ago with an over-meaty right paw, and I hadn't got around to mending it yet.

Broken or not, I put my coffee down and went to answer it. A tall, willowy, red headed young woman rather distressingly dressed in double-denim stood on the step.

'Hello, Mr Bryant?'

'Yes, that's me,' I concurred, as I couldn't see any good reason to lie and the young woman was after all tall and willowy, and it was always possible that the red hair came out of a bottle. 'How can I help you?'

'My name's Mallory Fillery,' said the woman. Ah, I thought, the reporter from the *Stockford Spectacle*. I hadn't immediately realised this as she didn't have a notebook strung around her neck and I couldn't see a pencil stuck behind her ear, although the tousled red hair did rather obscure the view, so I couldn't be certain. All in all, she was quite a spectacle herself.

'Would you like to come in, Miss Fillery?'

'Sure,' she replied. I couldn't help spotting something.

'You're American, Miss Fillery.' It was a statement but it should have been a question.

'Call me Mallory. And I'm Canadian.'

'I'm sorry.'

'Don't be. I'm not. Who the heck wants to be American,

especially these days?' I stood back to usher her past me into the tiny hall. 'Cute,' she added, nodding at the house name by the door as she entered.

'It could be worse,' I replied, smiling. 'I could live in Catgut Terrace. And I'm Sam.'

'Really?'

'Yes, really, that's my name.'

'No, I meant really, Catgut Terrace?'

'No, not really.'

'Didn't think so.'

'No, Catgut Terrace was pulled down ten years ago. It's sheltered housing for the elderly now.

'Okayyy,' she said musingly. 'I'm not sure if you're joshing me or not, so I'll let it go. I came about your closed pub, as I imagine you're aware. Ena Mackenzie asked me and I owe her a favour, so here I am. A little off my beaten track though.'

'Not too far off, surely. Idleborough's on your beat, isn't it?'

'Well, I guess so, but I won't lie to you, Sam. I've never been here before. Bit out of the way, isn't it?'

'Out of the way is the way we like it. No Idleborough news caught your eye since you've been here, then? Not even our world-famous Duck Race? And I take it you're not the Granny's Bobbins reporter?'

'Granny's who?'

I was beginning to think there was something odd about a local newspaper hack, Canadian or not, who didn't seem to know very much about the neighbourhood on which she was reporting, but I decided to let it go for the time being.

'First things first,' I said. 'Coffee?'

'Sure,' she said again. 'None of that decaf crap though.'

'I'll do my best. Have a seat and I'll try to brew up something as caffy as possible.'

Back in the living room with coffee, I found my visitor standing at the window looking out at the non-vegetable patch and scruffy lawn of my garden with her back to me. I had to admit that her back was well worth looking at despite the expanse of denim covering most of it. Even her hair looked more golden than red with the sun shining through it. 'Proper caffy coffee,' I announced, holding up the two mugs. I sat down and invited Mallory to do the same. She did, taking the proffered cup in one elegant hand as she did so.

'I was expecting you at the meeting tonight,' I began. 'Exhau... I mean, Ena texted me to say you'd be coming. You're about eight hours early.'

'Yeah, sorry about that, but I can't make this evening after all. Something came up. Still, a story's a story, so I thought I'd head on over, check out the lie of the land and get some intel from you in advance as it were.'

'How did you know I'd be in?'

'I thought it was a fair chance. You know, writer, freelance, works from home, light-hearted scribbling for various zines and stuff. And if you weren't, well, nothing lost, at least I'd have had a chance to check out Idleborough. Background, you know.'

'And what's my shoe size and blood type?' I asked, since she'd obviously been doing her homework on me.

'Come again?'

'I was just wondering what else you've found out about me in less than twenty-four hours.'

She was completely unfazed. 'I like to know something about the people I'm interviewing.'

'Is that what this is, an interview?'

'Sure, why not? You seem a bit defensive, Sam. I've been asked by a friend to cover a story that on the face of it doesn't seem to add up to much. I've been given your name, you're running this action group or whatever it is you've set up to save your local pub, but now you seem surprised to see me. Trust me, I'm happy to hightail it back to Stockford. Got lots of other stories I could be working on.'

She was right of course; I was being defensive. There were a number of reasons for that including her apparent lack of local knowledge and the fact that she'd rung my broken doorbell without checking first whether I'd be in. There was also the not inconsiderable matter of the immediate physical attraction felt by the party of the first part, me, towards the party of the second part, Mallory Fillery. An attraction that the party of the first part doubted was shared by the party of the second part. It had quite thrown me off my game.

I embarked on a recovery mission. 'I'm sorry. It's good of you to take the trouble to come. What do you want to know?'

'Well, first off, this pub that's closing. Where is it? I've driven round the town three times and I've found, let me see...' she whipped an iPad out of a denim pocket and tapped it, 'a Bull, a Waggoners, a Three Pigeons and a, er, Trout, but not a Farts.' She looked up. 'I know I'm not a native but isn't that a slightly rude name for a pub?'

Exhausted Ena, so used to calling The Three Pigeons by its newish local alias, had obviously not given Mallory the real name. I ran through a potted history of the pub's change of identity and she had the good grace not to laugh, although it felt less funny than childish in the telling.

'I see,' she said finally. 'Yes, I did spot it then, and you're right, whatever those are on the sign outside, they sure as hell aint pigeons. Seriously though, it's a bit of a dump isn't it? Or am I missing something? What's so important about it? What does The Three Pigeons offer that these other three places,' and she held up her iPad, 'don't.'

It was a good question so I gave it some thought. What about the nine other pubs in Idleborough that had closed since the war? Presumably they had all had something about them, some specialness, that made each of them unique. Presumably their demise, one by one, had been mourned by someone. Lots of people, I expect. It hadn't been enough to save any of them. Had petitions been drawn up to try and stop any of the closures? Had action groups been formed? If so, they had all failed and the nine buildings that had once been loud with laughter, or argument, or music were now owned by well-to-do incomers to the village, some of whom were doubtless unaware of the history of the houses they now occupied. Were we wasting our time trying to save The Farts? Why couldn't we all just raise a glass in memory and decamp en bloc to The Bull and persuade Big Brian to get in some proper beer; or to the Waggoners with its flock wallpaper redolent of an Indian restaurant; or to the Trout with its cartoon fish covering one wall of the bar?

She could see me thinking and sat patiently waiting for my reply. When it came, it was feeble. 'It's hard to explain.'

'Try. I'd like to know. I'm interested, truly.' And maybe she was. Or maybe she was just a reporter, despite my earlier misgivings.

'It's history, I suppose,' I started uncertainly. 'And the people. Not just the people there now either, the ones you know will be there when you open the door, waiting for a yarn or a moan or a laugh. But all those who used to be there. My dad, for example. He introduced me to the place and when he and mum emigrated to New Zealand, he said The Farts – The Pigeons as we called it then – was the biggest reason he could come up with not to go. It's the smell of the place, the feel, the atmosphere, the ghosts if you like. And it's the way that Mucker and Jeremy Jeavons can share the same bar without either of them feeling out of place.' I knew that Mallory hadn't the slightest idea who Mucker and Jeremy were, but she nodded thoughtfully all the same.

'Now **that** I get,' said Mallory. If there wasn't a tear in her eye, I believe there may have been one in mine.

4
MONDAY 15TH JULY
SPECTACLES AND ALLOWANCES

I'd considered Pop crazy when he'd put me on the payroll of this crummy little throwback broadsheet in Stockford two months ago, and I still don't know what I'm doing here. *Talk about learning on the job. I'm a fashion designer, at least I am by inclination, although none of my designs have seen the light of day beyond a few I've had run up for my own benefit. Back in Toronto I was merely an Executive Assistant in the family firm and after doing that since Uni I still have little idea what an Executive Assistant does, or at least not one whose surname matches that of the President of the Company. Not that it does, not these days anyways. I stopped using Stamp for both aesthetic and moral reasons just as soon as I put foot to tarmac at Heathrow. I should have done it earlier; I'd long since got bored by the witless attentions of other Executive Assistants, mostly (but not entirely) of the male persuasion and not in possession of the same name as the one over the front door.*

So I jacked it in, much to Pop's displeasure, and hightailed it across the pond to little ol' England. Pop threatened to disinherit me and I told him to jump off a very high building, whether he owned it or not and he sure does own a ton of very high build-

ings. Not the wisest thing I could have said but the money didn't stop rolling in, which got me thinking that Pop hadn't finished with me yet. And I was right.

'How's it going, Princess?' came Pop's less-than-dulcet tones down the phone back in May. 'Got a job for you.'

'Go to hell, you old bastard,' I replied, 'I don't work for you anymore.'

'Yeah? Fashion business going great, is it? Guess I can stop that useless allowance now, can I, Princess? Didn't think so. Small job, won't take long, do a bit of digging for your dear old daddy, you can be back in swinging London by the fall.'

The bastard had me. 'Where?' I'd asked, not unreasonably as he'd said it was out of London. I'm a Big City Bright Lights kind o' gal and I have no desire to live out in the boondocks. And boondocks doesn't even begin to describe Stockford in the county of Nowhere-shire – or Oxfordshire as I discovered it was called when I Googled it – where I share a couple of offices which still boast wood panelling for chrissakes with Jim Simkins, who may well be the oldest newspaper editor in the world. Nice guy and all that and maybe he was a big cheese back in Fleet Street once upon a day but all Jim does now is sit in his little office out back puffing on his pipe as if he hadn't heard of the ban on indoor smoking, and getting me typing up the same old drivel about hatches, matches and dispatches and local sports results every darn week. I can do that okay, I did my MBA at Joseph Rotman after all, but until Sunday I was wondering what the hell I was doing at the Spectacle, *which it turns out is part of some piddly group called Wessex Wayfarer which Pop owns. Newspapers! Who knew? Possibly not even Pop until he had need of it.*

So that's how I've been wasting my first summer in England, and two months down the line I was none the wiser about why I'd been shipped out to the back of beyond. Until yesterday that is, Sunday, when the phone rings again and dear old Pop's back on the end of the line, clearing his throat, asking how I'm doing and trying to sound cheery. He always had to work at that and the lessons hadn't been a success. 'Bored witless,' I'd replied. 'What the hell am I doing here?'

'Really? I heard it's kinda pretty out there, trees, rivers, lots of sheep.'

'Yeah, well, I'm not a shepherdess, if you hadn't noticed. Does nothing for me.'

'Well, not for long now, then you can get back to Notting Hill and start sitting on your useless ass again, Princess.' He wasn't great at compliments, my old man. 'I want you to go to a small place called Idleberg or some such, a few miles away from where you are. Spy out the land, in particular some old bar called The Three Pigeons.'

'Why?'

'Just dig out what you can find. It's of interest to me, that's all.' It didn't seem like a big deal. It would get me out of the office and away from Jim's pipe smoke, which mostly smelt of used knickers. So I said, yeah, I'll go tomorrow and let you have A Report, a phrase I made sound as sarcastic as possible. Anyways, I had no choice, not with the allowance thing and my desire to get back to my pals in London.

Whatever the old man had in mind for this bar I was pretty darn sure it wouldn't be in a good cause. The words Good Cause don't figure highly in the raison d'etre *of the family business and although helping to put bucks in Pop's back pocket might help me in the long run, it was the short run I was more interested in right now.*

As it happens, I'd heard of Idleborough – not "berg", I knew that much at least – although I hadn't yet made the short trip out to the place. As far as I could tell, very little happened there and what did was part of the domain of Ena Mackenzie, who published a little village quarterly magazine. Now Ena was pretty much the first person I'd met apart from Jim when I'd arrived in Stockford back in the spring. Nice old gal, showed me round all the town's watering holes and how to find the Cliff Edge nightclub which was a closely guarded secret apparently. They should let their guard down – I'd been there on three Saturday nights and there were never more than twenty punters in, and most of those were spotty youths. I'd written it up for the Spectacle *but Jim had been quite cross when he read it; said it's not the sort of place we want to be associated with.*

So I was staggered when, with Ena's name in my thoughts, the phone rang again just after I'd hung up on Pop and it was none other than her on the line.

'Hey, canny lass,' she started, obviously assuming that I knew what language she was speaking. 'I've got a story for you.'

'What sort of story?' I asked, as you would.

'Well, less of a story, more of a favour for me, if I'm truthful. I'll let you off all those drinks you owe me.' I understood that to be Scots humour. I'm not sad enough to count who buys the drinks when I'm out but my memory told me it was rarely Ena.

So, anyways, she starts on about some pub in Idleborough that was probably closing and being sold to money-grabbing developers for housing that the village didn't need and didn't want when all they truly wanted was a place where they could carry on drowning the sorrows that come of living in a place called Lazytown, as even I knew it was referred to hereabouts, and how this could be the beginning of the end of civilisation as we know it. And of course my mouth starts hitting the floor and rolling across the Spectacle's *grubby carpet. It sure wasn't the first time my old man had been described as money-grabbing and I wasn't going to be docking any friendship points off Ena for that observation, especially as she didn't know who the particular money-grabbers were in this case, and I wasn't going to bring her up to speed on that, not yet anyway.*

So, keeping my eggs firmly clutched to my girly chest, I agreed to check it out and bring the full weight of the mighty Stockford Spectacle to bear. I didn't mention the conflict of interest I had vis a vis Pop's earlier instructions, but figured one way or another, bearing in mind my father's a complete tool but that I also have no interest in the dreary lives of the drinking inhabitants of Lazytown and would in any case shortly be back whooping it up in west London and making a fortune out of my soon-to-be-flourishing fashion empire, I'd be able to kill both birds with the single cartridge, no problem.

Ena had called the pub The Farts and when I'd asked what the fuck, had corrected herself so when I'd acted all dumb to Sam the not completely unattractive so-called writer later on, I was, not to put too fine a point on it, lying through my pearly-whites. Not sure why I did that, to be honest, possibly just trying to squeeze stuff out of Sam that might not have come out otherwise. I also hadn't mentioned to him that I'd had a good old look-see around the pub before I'd pitched up at the completely macabre-sounding Slaughterhouse Cottages. And when I say good old look-see, I mean inside and out. Oh, yes, siree, proper reporter me, a bit of illegal breaking and entering means nothing to me, although there wasn't much breaking to be done, truth be told, a convenient bathroom window being left, in official parlance, unsecured, in other words, open.

Once I'd gotten used to the general air of squalor and filth that pervaded the place I'd done a bit of Sherlocking and it didn't take me too long to find some papers inexpertly hidden in an old suitcase under the saggy main bed. Most of them were the sort of thing that normal people would have long since consigned to the trash, a receipt for fifteen cases of pale ale that seemed to be in pounds, shillings and pence, for example. However, there was one sheet of paper that might prove very interesting to Pop, assuming that he or I could manage to decipher it. I tried taking a picture of it but either Apple's claims about the quality of its imaging systems were wildly overstated or they just bowed down in ungracious defeat to the gloom of the room, which even the meagre overhead bulb couldn't dissipate. Either way, the world's most eagle-eyed codebreaker couldn't have made anything of the best photo I could come up with, so I simply took the sheet of paper and stuffed it inside my bra for safe keeping. I wasn't wearing gloves (a grievous error, given the filth of the place) but, even if the theft was reported, I was pretty sure the dust would hide any fingerprints I might leave.

Spending half an hour in The Three Pigeons had left me in need of an urgent hose-down so I was quite proud of myself not to have resorted to full-body scratching during my visit to Sam. However, I made sure I stopped off at my temporary apartment for a long power shower before returning to the Spectacle.

5
MONDAY 15TH JULY
ANORAKS AND HEDGES

'How about FAGS?' said Banjo.

I'd asked the four other members of the newly formed Farts action group to come to the first meeting armed with suggestions for a name we could call ourselves.

'I'm not sure that's very appropriate,' said Daisy, doubtfully, with her fingers poised over the keyboard of her laptop. 'What does it stand for?'

'Well, it was Mucker's idea,' said Banjo, backtracking. 'I think it stands for Farts Action Group. You know, straight to the point and all that.'

'What about the S?' persisted Daisy. 'What does the S stand for?'

Banjo had to admit that he wasn't completely in tune with Mucker's thought processes and that the latter's other suggestion was even less suitable.

'Why? What was it?' I asked, whilst at the same time rather wishing I hadn't. I was beginning to be quite pleased that I'd managed not to invite Mucker to be part of the group.

'FARTS,' said Banjo. 'Even more to the point,'

'Is that one o' them anachronisms?' asked Daisy's Dad, Dick.

'No,' said Banjo. 'That would be an anorak.' Now I was thinking that both Dick and Banjo should have joined Mucker on the reject pile, but then I saw that Banjo was grinning, which hopefully indicated that anorak was a joke.

'They're acronyms, Dad,' said Daisy in the sort of exasperated voice that suggested that this was the kind of thing she often had to explain to Dick.

'Talking of acronyms,' I said, 'Big Brian also suggested SOFT, because, and I quote, "you lads're all southern softies, I say southern softies," but that again includes the word fart in its full unabbreviated glory: Save Our Farts Today. At least that makes some sort of sense, although I'm not sure that farts is the sort of word I'd feel comfortable spreading about.'

'You're not usually shy about spreading your farts about,' murmured Banjo, *sotto voce* but not so *sotto voce* that I couldn't hear him. My living room isn't very big, after all.

'Anyway,' I continued, ignoring Banjo, 'perhaps it would be better if we just removed the word farts from any other suggestions we may have. It's not the actual name of the pub, if you remember.' I felt it was time to get serious. 'As it happens, I have a couple of ideas of my own.' Daisy still had her fingers poised expectantly. 'First one: Idle Threats.' I looked around. Daisy's fingers hadn't moved.

'Sorry, boy, but I don' get it,' said Dick, shaking his head again. I wished he wouldn't do that, I found the wobbling jowls quite disturbing.

'It's a play on words, isn't it, Sam?' suggested Daisy, correctly but not sounding as if she understood why. 'Idle, yes, I see, but I'm not sure who we're threatening.'

'No,' I said, 'it's not us doing the threatening. Well, I hope it won't come to that at any rate. It's the threat to Idleborough as a community that it represents. If the green light is given to shoving up new houses on the site of the Farts it just opens the door to more expansion. Before you know it, every gap in the village will be filled with little boxes made of ticky-tacky. That field by the recreation ground, for example.'

'Not doing any good though, that field is it?' said Dick. 'Wouldn't mind a house there mysel'. Less of a walk to the Farts.'

I felt that the conversation was becoming a trifle unfocused. 'Leaving aside the fact that the Farts wouldn't be there any more,' I said, 'that field is a natural boundary to the village. Build there, next it's the rec itself. Any redevelopment of The Farts is the start of a slippery slope.' There was at least some nodding at this. I was aware that I may have been shouting and, given that various bottles of beer clutched in various hands were becoming dangerously empty, I expect they felt they needed to keep me onside if they wanted refills. Daisy, whose beer was sitting on the table beside her, started to type again.

I had another suggestion. 'Okay, if you don't like Idle Threats, and I agree that it could be clearer, how about InnKeeper, as in keeping the inn?'

Daisy stopped typing again. 'I quite like that,' she said, 'although strictly speaking, I believe being an inn means you have to be able to offer a bed for the night. I don't think Clem has ever offered that.' The thought of sleeping in one of Clem's bedrooms, if the state of the bar was any guide, made me feel slightly queasy.

'I've thought of another anorak,' said Dick, suddenly.

Daisy sighed again. 'Acronym, Dad.'

'Oh, yes, that too,' said Dick. 'How's about STOP. As in Save The Old Pigeons.' Several heads nodded thoughtfully. I had to admit, it wasn't that bad.

'Okay, minute that, please, Daisy,' I said. 'We can have a think about STOP or InnKeeper for the next meeting. More beer,' I added and went off to what I liked to refer to as my cellar but which was really just the cupboard under the sink: I'd been known to grab a bottle of washing-up liquid by mistake after a particularly heavy day, not a pleasant experience.

I returned and distributed four bottles of beer. The fifth member of the group, though, had a mug of tea in his hand and a thoughtful expression on his plain, smoothly-shaven face. Jeremy Jeavons, not unusually, had so far been very quiet, sitting in the corner on an upright dining chair I'd hauled across from the other room. In terms of soft furnishings I only possessed a two-seat sofa and a couple of armchairs so someone was always going to miss out on a comfortable seat if we were to carry on having the meetings at 1 Slaughterhouse Cottages. And that person was always going to be Jeremy unless I did something to prevent it. Jeremy seemed to make deferral to others a life mission but I was aware, as few others in the village were, that beneath an exterior so mild-mannered that he made Clark Kent look like the Hulk, Jeremy had hidden depths and a brain, if not quite the size of a planet, then certainly bigger than anyone else's I knew. Even bigger than Daisy's Dad, Dick, who as the proud possessor of the biggest head, with or without jowls, of anyone in Idleborough, should by rights have had a brain to match. The previous conversation about anachronisms and anoraks suggested that might be a forlorn hope.

Anyway, Jeremy, being Jeremy, had not volunteered to be part of the group but I'd managed to time a toilet visit to coincide with one of his in The Bull yesterday and had coerced him into joining us. Now you may think that coerced is too strong a word but only I knew that away from the village, Jeremy is the company secretary of a not inconsiderable national chain of hotels and, therefore, his knowledge of the hospitality sector together with an extensive string of contacts would in all probability be very useful to our cause. He did not want this to become common knowledge, as I knew, so I was able to threaten him, mildly, as I'm not normally that sort of bloke, with full disclosure if he refused to join us.

'Jeremy?' I asked encouragingly. 'Any thoughts?'

'Well, er, yes. Sorry,' he said, getting his apologies in early. 'I, er, hope you don't mind, but I've taken the liberty to jot down a few ideas I've had about what in practice we might be able to do to save The Three Pigeons. Sorry.' Jeremy, I have omitted to mention, was the one habitué of the pub who had never quite brought himself to calling it The Farts.

'Yes, Jeremy,' I said enthusiastically, mentally patting myself on the back for persuading him to join us. 'That's great. What have you come up with?'

Jeremy put down his mug, rummaged in the inside pocket of his blazer and pulled out several sheets of closely typed A4 paper which he straightened out and flattened with the palm of his hand on the small table next to him before looking up and peering at us all over the top of his rimless spectacles. I was interested to note that he had everyone's full attention. Jeremy didn't speak much and when he did he usually had something interesting to say.

'I think the main issue is the land attached to The Three Pigeons, which patently makes it attractive to developers.'

'What land?' asked Banjo. 'It's just the pub and the bit

out back, the so-called garden that people just use as a car park.'

'Ah, no, you're wrong. There is also approximately four acres of what is currently only scrubland behind the hedge to the rear of the, um, garden.'

'Hedge?' said Dick. 'I don't know about no hedge. D'you mean that mass o' thorns an' stuff behind Clem's old car?'

'Um, yes,' said Jeremy. 'I agree it's not terribly hedge-like.'

'I didn't know the land behind there was Clem's,' said Daisy, talking and typing at the same time in a multi-tasking sort of way. 'I thought it belonged to Squire Jonty.' It was a reasonable assumption; Jonty assuredly had possession of more of the village than is good for one man to have.

'No,' I said, 'Jeremy's right. In fact, I asked Clem about it once and he said it was for a rainy day. Looks like the weather's turned wet.'

Jeremy continued. 'Should Clem wish to sell that plot by itself, the problem for any builder would be access. It's surrounded on three sides and abuts the Idlebrook to the rear so the only way to reach it is through the pub car park. And the entrance is only just wide enough for one car, so it would be impossible to get planning permission without, er, demolishing the pub itself. Anyway, that is the principal consideration, and as for our options as an action group, whatever we call ourselves, we first need to gain support, both locally and from further afield. We will need to utilise the local press, which is why I am disappointed that Miss Fillery could not attend this meeting. But there is also social media, Facebook, Instagram, X and other conduits of that kind. I am not an expert but doubtless Sam, as a writer, will have more experience of such things.' I nodded. Jeremy hadn't finished, however. 'We will need in the first instance to approach both Parish and District Councils, the former to gauge the level of their support or otherwise, the latter because they, as you know, are the planning authority.' I suspected that only Jeremy, Daisy and I knew that, but let it pass. 'Finally,' Jeremy said, putting his papers back in his pocket, 'If Clem is determined to sell, can the village itself afford to buy?' He sat back and sipped his tea although it would have been cold by now. Astonishingly, everyone clapped.

6

TUESDAY 16TH JULY
INCEST AND LOCKS

I couldn't get my head around the fact that everyone else in the village seemed to be aware that the nondescript Maeve was Clem's wife, when I'd always thought she was just a terrible cleaner. Why hadn't I known that? I felt more than a little insulted. I considered that I kept an ear pretty close to the ground regarding all things Idleborough. I was after all on three important village committees. Not only had I been Chairman of the Cricket Club for the last five years and Treasurer of the Idle Players for six, but I was also a leading light in INCEST.

INCEST? Ah, yes, you may well ask. First of all, it's another reason why I'm not that keen on using acronyms (or even anoraks). Someone thought they possessed a sense of humour when it was formed way back in the allegedly swinging sixties. However, whilst the name is appalling, the group to which it is attached is nothing but wholly commendable. The Idleborough Neighbourhood Committee for Establishing Seniors' Trips organises several fundraising events through the year to pay for the village's Old Age Pensioners (not terribly PC but that's what they're called in the constitution) to go on various outings, usually to the seaside or the Cotswolds in the summer and to the theatre in London once every winter. The events they organise include such rural staples as beetle drives and bingo evenings. They also now operate the Duck Race referred to previously, and every August Bank Holiday they put on an afternoon of sheep racing with a fête worse than death attached.

For a while now I had also had a hankering to be on the Parish Council but that was a closed shop. Squire Jonty and his cronies from what the rest of us referred to as the Old Quarter of the village, where the three-car garages were worth more than most of the actual houses in the rest of Idleborough, had had that sewn up between them since time almost immemorial. None of us was too sure exactly what went on in the council meetings. They were supposed to be public but the dates, times and venues were closely guarded secrets. Maybe we should form an action group about that instead of The Farts but I suspected that I was the only one who cared that much about local politics. Not further than potholes and bin collections at any rate, and the Parish Council was responsible for neither of those nor for Idleborough's single remaining street light which stands, a lonely beacon in the Market Square, acting as an evening focal point for the village's teenagers.

So I decided to dig deeper. The obvious thing to do would be to buttonhole Clem and Maeve and have it out with them but the pair had disappeared off to sunny Benidorm at the crack of dawn. This information came from Postman Pat when he called round with the usual dispiriting collection of rejection slips from magazines ("not quite what we are looking for but please do not be discouraged") and brochures from estate agents convinced they could make 1 Slaughterhouse Cottages saleable despite its history. Oddly, Pat is his real name and he's been delivering the mail in Idleborough since I was a lad. Twenty-five years' experience hasn't made him particularly efficient. He hardly ever arrives before midday and doesn't bother at all on Mondays when he claims there's nothing worth delivering any more. That may well be true in these days of email and WhatsApp; it's just bad luck I suppose if you happen to be celebrating a birthday on a Monday.

Yesterday evening's action group meeting had voted unanimously in favour of everything Jeremy had suggested although I'm not sure if Dick, who seemed to be imbibing my ale twice as quickly as the rest of us, was too sure of the finer points of Jeremy's argument. Having decided that, yes, as a first step we should rapidly approach both councils and the local newspaper, as well as set up dedicated social media accounts for the action group, there was only one person who was going to be doing all these things. I'd known it all along of course, and on the basis of, if you want it done properly, do it yourself, had agreed to get on to things today. Daisy, in any case, was the secretary and would happily assist and Jeremy was the ideas man and was never going to be a success at marketing the ideas he came up with. I could see that the thought that he might have to made him even paler than he generally was. And Dick and Banjo? Well I knew exactly what they were good at. Gossip. Especially Dick, who lumbered around the village seven days a week, knew everybody and talked to everybody. He wasn't averse to visiting all four pubs in one lunchtime if the mood took him. He would get the word out whilst hardly being aware he was doing it. Daisy had suggested that her dad might also like to consider lying down in front of the bulldozer if the worst came to the worst. 'Gonna need a fucking big bulldozer if he does,' Banjo had muttered.

What first, then? I'd already been visited by the delightful if mysterious Mallory Fillery, so a second conversation could wait for a little while. And I could talk to Exhausted Ena again later to see if she had any more useful contacts in the press.

I usually try to take a morning constitutional before sitting at my desk, staring at my non-growing vegetables and starting what occasionally turns into something closely resembling work. So, with Clem and Maeve off enjoying the high life in Benidorm, I thought I'd take a wander up to The Farts to see if any inspiration struck me and in particular to have a closer look at the parcel of land to the rear. Whilst I had always been aware that it was there, I'd never paid it much attention. It wasn't noticeably connected to The Farts in any meaningful sense, cut off by the non-hedge from what Clem referred to as the garden, but which only really qualified as such by dint of being outdoors. The barrier of thorns and indeterminate bushes might have been a hedge once upon a few decades or so ago. These days, and for as far back as I could remember, it was more a deeply unwelcoming clump of green stuff that had never been introduced to a hedge trimmer.

I strolled down the side of the pub, through the broken farm gate. Jeremy had been absolutely correct when he said that the passage was not wide enough to allow proper access to a new housing estate. At its widest, it was barely more than eight feet, and it contained a curious dogleg halfway down that bent around a chimney stack that the original builder of the pub had presumably forgotten to place within the building itself. The chimney stack bore the scars from innumerable minor scrapes. I walked into the garden and surveyed it thoughtfully. Apart from a scrubby green bank, topped by a genuine, if untidy hedge, down the left-hand side and the Granny's Bobbins pitch down the other, the space was more car park than anything else, covered in a tired scattering of old gravel and ground up builders' rubble. Clem had thoughtfully placed a couple of rusting metal tables and some old white plastic garden chairs outside the rear door, so that the many smokers amongst his "clientelly" could puff away in a modicum of comfort. The metal tables had been purloined in the distant past from the Coach & Horses in Stockford in recompense following a controversial away Bobbins league defeat. There were a further two tables, made of some thoroughly weather-beaten wood, within which lived any number of tiny creatures, and whose provenance was not so firmly established, next to the Granny's Bobbins "Commencement Oche". One of these tables was for the scorers and one for spectators. It gave those of us who liked to support the Pigeon Fanciers when the temperature was sufficiently ambient a clear view of the often comedic carryings-on. There was one outbuilding, painted the same off-white as the pub itself, which leaned tiredly against the back wall of the snug. This was the Ladies' toilet. The Gents' was inside. If you were a woman and did not want to get soaked to the skin, you needed a strong bladder on rainy evenings in The Farts.

There was room for about five cars at a push, four if you discounted the permanent presence of Clem's old Land Rover Defender, which deserved to be in a museum if it could ever be persuaded to start. With all four wheels long-since replaced by bricks and with a mass of thorns, on a long-term visit from the "hedge" to the rear, trailing in and out of its moss-covered cab, it would be a major undertaking to get rid of it if the developers ever did move in. Clem's other car wasn't much less of an eyesore, a 1973 Morris 1800, which used to be blue but was now more grey than anything. It was, however and remarkably, still mobile and, as it wasn't in evidence this morning, I assumed that Clem and Maeve had used it to drive to the airport.

I wasn't seeing anything I hadn't seen a thousand times before so I thought it might be a good idea to take a look at something I **hadn't** seen a thousand times before; in other words, what lay beyond the barrier of thorns, brambles and nettles. However, not having properly thought through my expedition beforehand, I was, like most "workers from home", dressed in an elderly t-shirt, shorts and sandals, so that gaining access to the land in question without being scratched half to death was a problem. I am not entirely without ingenuity though, and I recalled Clem once showing me inside what he referred to as his man-cave, which had originally been intended as a meeting-room for hire but which had rapidly morphed into a kind of Aladdin's cave, assuming Aladdin's cave contained the sort of larger tat that Clem could find no space for in the snug, and not piles of diamonds and gold lamps, or was I mixing up my pantomimes? Perhaps that was Ali Baba.

There was a padlock on the door of the ex-meeting room but it wasn't a padlock that would have caused a five-year-old much concern as it was padlocking a door so rotten it might have spent the last three years under water. I pulled gently and the lock came away fully intact accompanied by a small shower of wood shavings and a couple of woodlice. I wasn't quite sure what I was looking for but almost immediately spotted a long, foot-wide plank that looked ideal for my needs, assuming it wasn't as rotten as the door of the man-cave. I tested its strength and durability by propping it against an old one-armed bandit and jumping up and down on it a few times. It bent slightly but held, so I hauled it out and dropped it over the nettles at the rear of the car park in a place where they were thinnest.

Treading as carefully as a man wearing no trousers and open-toed footwear can tread, I walked the plank up and over the thorns, nettles and other assorted weeds and jumped gently onto an unexpected patch of long but spike-free grass the other side. I started to look around, discovering that although the proposed development land was overgrown, and liberally festooned with bushes of an indeterminately aggressive nature and some surprisingly majestic trees, it was less difficult to move through than I'd expected. I wondered if we could we get a preservation order on the trees if push came to shove.

I found the hole in the ground by falling into it. Luckily, not completely, as I managed just in time to grab a branch of one of the aforesaid surprisingly majestic trees, an oak I think. There were some stone steps leading down into the hole but I hadn't noticed them in the shade of the majestic trees. I pulled myself back on to *terra firma* and made a more dignified descent via the steps. There were twelve of them. At the foot, hidden from above by an overhanging bank covered in more brambles, there was a door. I wasn't going to be able to pull the padlock off this one. For one thing there was no padlock. There was instead an intrinsic Yale lock. It may have been a mortis e lock, although I'm not an expert. Whatever it was though, it screamed security and the door itself was of studded steel or iron, which screamed security even louder. There were traces of rust, but not many and my considered opinion was that this was a door that had been used quite recently. It didn't make sense. There was a handle below the lock, so I gave it an experimental pull and then an experimental push, neither of which produced a millimetre of give. I gave up, took a few photos of the door and its lock, and climbed back up the steps.

A few yards away I came across a smallish tent. I stopped. This was something else I wasn't expecting. It looked of relatively recent vintage but was zipped up. I stood and listened but could hear nothing apart from summer birdsong, the lowing of Farmer Trickle's Red Herefords in the middle-distance and the breeze through the majestic trees. I stepped closer, shrugged and unzipped the flap of the tent. Inside, sheltered by the trees, it was pleasantly cool. Like the door a few yards away, the tent was being used, that was obvious. There was a camp bed with a *Toy Story* sleeping bag laid out on top, a half-full, plastic container of water and a metal table and chair. A kettle stood on the table with a camping stove open next to it, along with a tin mug and a couple of plastic plates. None bore much evidence of any washing up having been attempted.

Who the hell was living there? And what the hell was behind the iron door? And, if someone was living in the tent, how did they get in and out of the parcel of land? Four acres of it, Jeremy Jeavons had suggested. I hadn't covered the full four acres but there was definitely no easy access into Clem's garden. I mentally reviewed the other three sides, as best I could recall the adjacent geography. To the rear was the Idlebrook, that I did know because a footpath ran the other side of it right through Farmer Trickle's Big Field, something he was not happy about. He had indeed given full expression to his unhappiness on several occasions by brandishing an empty double-barrelled shotgun at innocent walkers. Us locals were aware it was always empty. Those from further afield, eyes gazing at laminated OS maps, less so. There was a six-foot bank down to the Idlebrook on this side, although the footpath on the far side was much lower, and local youngsters often paddled in the water on hot weekends. I supposed it was possible someone could run another plank across the stream to gain access to the door, but it would make a precarious forty-five degree bridge.

Round to the right, the west, by way of a *bona fide*, tractor-sized bridge over the Idlebrook, there was a gate from the Big Field into Farmer Trickle's farmyard. The farmyard itself was separated from Clem's back garden by a twenty-foot, red-brick wall. Outside drinkers had often been forced inside by the smell of manure. It was rumoured that the Pigeon Fanciers Granny's Bobbins team had nose plugs handy just in case. Home advantage they called it, as out-of-town opponents blanched at the smell drifting across the wall.

Finally, to the east, behind a hedge (a proper hedge this time, yew to my untutored eye) that was unkempt from this side but which I was betting would be rather tidier from the other, was a usually unoccupied second home, belonging to some out-of-towner, maybe a banker – and I use the word advisedly – who spent most of the year in London and only a couple of fortnights in Idleborough. The house, when glimpsed through the forbidding, rarely opened gates, was a monstrosity, some pseudo-Elizabethan, post-war, thatch-roofed hash-up that could have been designed by a telly-tubby on amphetamines. Even during his two fortnight-long annual visits, the wa... banker, whoever he may be, failed to spend any money in the village; not in any of the pubs, nor the hardware store nor Mrs Bee's Bazaar. It was a sore point. He was so up himself that when Squire Jonty had tried dropping in for a chat when the bloke first arrived, Jonty told us that he was treated to a shouted instruction through the solid oak of the front door to the effect that hawkers and tinkers were unwelcome. Unnecessarily choice language was used, apparently. I wondered if I'd ever heard anyone refer to the owner by name. I didn't believe I had. He was usually just called The Banker. And, as far as I knew, no one could swear with any certainty that they knew what he looked like. Or whether there was a she with him.

So it was true, there was no access, vehicular or pedestrian, from the parcel of land except through the narrow, dog-legged passage down the side of The Farts. Which only left one answer. Whoever was occupying the tent had to be coming and going via the studded-iron door.

That, I decided, was quite enough to be going on with for one morning, and I felt in need of a drink, which of course The Farts could not currently supply, so I retraced my steps to the plank, pulled the nearest end down and returned nimbly across the nettles and other assorted greenery before storing it back in Clem's man-cave. I noticed in passing that the window to the Gents' toilet was half open – unlike the Ladies', the Gents' is, as I've mentioned, intrinsically within the pub – which would afford relatively easy access to the bars and living quarters. I briefly considered continuing my investigations inside the building but I'd spent enough time on my little foray and I was extremely thirsty. And I had some serious thinking to do.

7
WEDNESDAY 17TH JULY
TOASTED TEACAKES AND FAMILY HISTORIES

I woke up exhausted on Wednesday morning. In fact I couldn't remember actually going to sleep. I'd spent the night turning over in my mind the discovery of the iron door and the tent in the overgrown four acres behind The Farts. Whilst it was clear that I hadn't lain awake all night, I undoubtedly didn't feel as refreshed as I should have after eight hours under a low tog summer duvet, and was in no mood to get my mind working on the three writing jobs sitting in my In Tray. Needless to say, it's not an actual In Tray, just an email Inbox. If I had a physical In Tray I would have to print off every work offer just to put something in it, which would not only be a waste of time but phenomenally expensive, given the exorbitant price of ink cartridges. Also, I would have nowhere to put my cup of coffee, without which I would fail to function on any level known to humanity.

So, talking of coffee, rather than go to the trouble of brewing some myself, I thought I'd try to clear my head of Farts stuff with a brisk walk around the Short Circular followed by a cup of Balthazar's coffee. There are two walks around Idleborough, both found in the local guidebook last published in 1967 and both circular, starting and finishing in the Market Square. The Long Circular wends its way for about five miles in a roundabout sort of way, passing close by the possibly ancient but more probably Victorian disputed site of the apparently Roman settlement of Asinusorum. The Short Circular cuts that out, along with the unexpected patch of quicksand in Farmer Trickle's top field and the not entirely unheard of chance of being chased by his herd of Red Herefords. The walk keeps within the village boundaries, taking in St Brendan's Church where they filmed several marriages, all doomed to failure, in the long-running religious soap opera, *Holy Trinity!*. It also passes through the field where the Sheep Racing and fête take place every August Bank Holiday, a field, now I come to think of it, that serves no useful purpose and which would be a much more accessible and acceptable site for new housing than Clem's back garden. Except of course that it has the distinct advantage of backing onto Squire Jonty's own back garden, so ensuring that any proposed development would get the shortest shrift imaginable.

The whole walk only takes about half an hour, so it was still quite early when I entered Mrs Bee's Bazaar, picked up a copy of *The Guardian* (failing to spot any *Stockford Spectacles*) and made my way through to the little café called Balthazar's at the rear of the shop. Beatrice Balthazar herself, the formidable proprietress of both the café and the store, was waiting on tables when I arrived. The shop, which she had purchased from Spar ten years ago to avoid the village being rendered grocer-less when Spar decided it was no longer economically viable, was originally to be called Beatrice Balthazar's Bazaar, which even Beatrice herself quickly decided was a mouthful much larger than a slice of her home-made lemon drizzle cake, so it was rapidly changed to Mrs Bee's. She could not, however, be persuaded to remove the word Bazaar from the shop's name even though most of the village had at one time or another suggested to her that, as it was neither a market in a Middle Eastern country nor a fundraising sale of goods, the name was completely inappropriate, although undoubtedly fun.

'Squire's in, young Sam,' said Beatrice in a stage whisper that carried to every corner of the smallish café, including the table occupied by Squire Jonty himself, who looked up from his *Telegraph* and his half-eaten toasted teacake and nodded at me, beckoning me over to join him.

'Who eats toasted teacakes at ten o'clock in the morning, Jonty?' I asked, sitting down.

'The doctor says I'm not to eat heavy food for twenty-four hours, and this is the lightest thing on Mrs Bee's menu.'

'Doctor?' I asked, trying my best to sound sympathetic.

'Yes, I've just come back from an Abdominal Aortic Aneurysm screening.'

'That's easy for you to say. What does it involve?'

'Well, in my case, it involved a large Sikh gentleman rubbing grease provocatively over my stomach and then pressing down with some implement or other in a series of frankly quite erotic gestures. All a trifle disconcerting.'

'Implement? Is that what they're calling it these days?' I murmured.

'Never mind all that, I saw worse in the war,' Jonty said. I wasn't sure which war he was referring to. Whilst I could picture Jonty, in khaki shorts, chasing Rommel across the Sahara alongside Monty in 1942, he wasn't anywhere near old enough. He would, after all, have to be past his century and I knew he was only in his sixties. However, Squire

Jonty's ongoing health was something in which I had an interest. His sudden incapacitation might open up a vacancy on the Parish Council for one thing, and for another it could affect the sale of The Farts. I wasn't entirely sure how, but Jonty had his nose in most things, so it was a reasonable guess.

'What was the result? Are you going to die?' No point beating about the bush.

'Possibly,' he said drily and with raised eyebrows. 'But not from that.'

We were interrupted by the not inconsiderable presence of Beatrice Balthazar arriving between us.

'Ready to order, Sam?' she asked, licking the end of her pencil like only people in bad sitcoms do. Living in Lazytown often had the feel of being in a bad sitcom.

'I'll have a skinny cap please, Beatrice.'

'The breadth of the cappuccino is for me to determine and you to put up with,' she replied in her best customer service voice.

'More tea please, Beatrice,' interrupted Jonty.

'Three extra bags in the pot?'

'Absolutely. Strong enough to stand a builder up in it.'

'I thought that was teaspoons,' I said.

'Now then, Samuel,' he continued, mouth full of the remnants of his toasted teacake. 'That email you sent me.'

'Email?' I said, trying to remember.

'Yes, some blithering idiocy about the blasted kebab van.'

I recalled the email in question. I had sent it a full three months earlier following the sudden disappearance of the ancient, hardly roadworthy kebab van that had taken to parking up three evenings a week outside the hardware shop in the Square. Its absence had prompted complaints from some locals, who had considered it an invaluable aid to their weekly menu planning. Daisy's Dad, Dick had been the loudest complainant, closely followed by Mucker and a few others. Dick would have happily consumed two giant mixed kebabs seven evenings a week if he could have but had suddenly found himself reduced to none. However, the complaints had been short-lived, as a week after the kebab van's last, black-smoked departure from the village, it had been replaced by a bright, shiny yellow camper-van of considerably more recent vintage with the words The Codmother emblazoned along the side and a scarily big-bosomed matriarch, the eponymous Codmother herself, glowering out from behind two deep-fat fryers. More out of curiosity than anything else, I had purchased a cod and chips on the van's first Friday in residence and found it so good that my Friday supper had consisted of little else ever since. The food was even tasty enough to overcome the Codmother's own warped sense of what makes for good customer service.

Daisy's Dad, Dick had taken a little while (two days) to be convinced, however. 'Where am I goin' to get my greens now?' he'd asked, referencing the kebab van's meagre scattering of lettuce and purple onion on each giant kebab.

'What about the mushy peas?' I'd asked.

'Peas!' Dick had replied with all the disdain in the world. 'Peas are pointless at the best o' times, rolling around, falling off yer fork, but mushy peas, have you seen the colour? Nah, they're full o' chemicals, them. Wouldn't catch me eating that muck.'

I dragged myself back to the present as Beatrice Balthazar hove into view with something akin to a skinny cappuccino in one hand and a near-black cup of tea in the other. 'Another teacake, Squire?' she asked. 'Anything for you, Sam? Got a nice carrot cake fresh out of the oven.'

We both shook our heads, the squire because there are only so many toasted teacake crumbs one mouth can take, and me because I'd inadvertently partaken of Beatrice's carrot cake before. Too much carrot, not enough cake had been my considered opinion.

'Don't worry about the email,' I said to Jonty. 'It was about the old kebab van but I think the furore' – well, that was one word for it, especially bringing to mind as it did Dick's regular post-kebab bowel movements – 'has died down now that we've got The Codmother in its place.'

'Yes, indeed,' said the squire. 'Splendid woman. Pays the going rate too, not like... what was his name?'

'Abdul?' I ventured, that being the name of the kebab van's proprietor.

'Yes, Albert,' agreed Jonty. 'Swarthy fella, not sure if he was familiar with a shower. Refused to pay his taxes too.' I should explain that "rates" and "taxes" were Jonty shorthand for the extra, unofficial tariffs he and the Parish Council slapped on street traders who had the temerity to show up in Idleborough. It sounded as though the Codmother was more amenable in that respect than Abdul had been.

'You think the Codmother's a splendid woman?' I said. It was only three days ago she had called me a snivelling, ungracious piece of piss after I'd queried the absence of a tomato ketchup bottle that delivered tomato ketchup when prompted.

'Yes, indeed,' said Jonty, a dreamy, or conceivably rheumy, look appearing in his eyes. 'Mind you,' he continued, the rheumy eyes switching to gimlet mode in a nanosecond, 'not a patch on the Fillery filly, eh? The legs on that one, eh? Eh?'

That threw me. Not the overt sexism, I mean, I took that for granted, along with the barely concealed racism, but the fact that (a) Jonty knew Mallory Fillery and (b) he knew she knew me. Anyway, I hadn't seen her legs, so couldn't really discuss their quality. I mean, I knew they were long but they had been encased in denim during our meeting two days ago, so their overall shape was an unknown. I felt myself sliding into the same sexist pit as Jonty.

'I didn't know you knew our local reporter,' I said.

'I know everything and everybody, young Sam,' he said, tapping his nose. 'I know something else you don't too, m'lad.' I waited. He definitely wouldn't be able to resist telling me. Eventually: 'Do you know who her father is?'

'No,' I said, suddenly interested. 'Who?'

Squire Jonty mopped his mouth with one of Beatrice's large pink napkins, looked around us furtively and leant forward. 'Harrison Makepeace Stamp,' he whispered. Why he whispered, I'm not sure; by now, we were the only people in the café, even Beatrice having disappeared off to do what Beatrices do when not serving customers.

'I've heard of him,' I said. 'Bit like Rupert Murdoch but ten times worse.'

'With knobs on,' said Jonty, who knew a thing or two about people who were ten times worse. 'Imagine some sort of bastard offspring of Trump and Murdoch and you'd be close to the mark.'

'Interesting,' I said. 'Also unsettling. So what's his daughter doing working on the *Stockford Spectacle*? And what about the name? Why Mallory Fillery, not Mallory Stamp.' A worrying thought occurred, although quite why it was worrying was beyond me. 'Is she married?'

'No, she's not married. Fully available, I understand.' He leered disconcertingly. 'Fillery's her mother's maiden name. His second wife. He's on number three now. First one died in the bath, so they say.'

'And Mallory's mum?' I said. 'What did she die of?'

'Oh, she's not dead. Divorced, living it up in Cannes with several millions of old Stamp's fortune. No love lost there, and the same goes for the filly. Word has it she can't stand the old bastard.' This from one old bastard about another. 'Anyway,' he added, 'if you look like that young lady, you're not going to moniker yourself with the name Mallory Stamp, are you?' And he laughed, a few rogue crumbs of toasted teacake making a hurried exit from his mouth. 'Anyway, Samuel, why are you making a play for the gal?' I hadn't been aware I was, although the prospect had its attractions, even if Harrison Makepeace Stamp wasn't one of them. 'Buttering up the local press, eh? Thinking of standing for the PC?'

'PC?' I ventured. PC was something Jonty would never be.

'Parish Council, young fella. After my job, are you?' The previously rheumy and more recently gimlet eyes were now twinkling.

'I thought that was dead men's shoes,' I said.

'That's slanderous. Free and fair elections every, er...'

'Four years?' I prompted.

'If you say so. Anyway, might be a vacancy soon, keep it to yourself. We might be able to squeeze you in.'

'You're very kind,' I said. Something about keeping your friends close and your enemies even closer sprung to mind.

Time was moving on, however, and I needed to move the conversation on as well, specifically to Clem's back plot. I had work to do and one more of Mrs Bee's version of a skinny cap would have me climbing the walls and then falling off them on to the sofa for three hours.

'Talking of The Farts,' I started. We hadn't been but it was occasionally useful to catch Jonty off his guard.

'Eh, what?' he said, brushing a lapful of crumbs onto Beatrice's fake, stone floor. 'Were we?'

'Have you ever been on to the parcel of land behind Clem's car park?' I asked.

'Don't be ridiculous. I've never even been into Clem's car park. Never get the Bentley past the dogleg for one thing and it's a breeding ground for dog shit too.'

This was patently untrue. If there was a breeding ground for dogshit, it was inside the pub, not in the garden. 'I was in there this morning,' I said. 'Found something interesting; two somethings in fact.'

Jonty had half-risen to his feet and stayed in that position for a few seconds, a remarkable display of core strength, given his age. 'Not like you to go trespassing, young Sam,' he said, finally, standing fully upright, the gimlet eyes now back in business. 'Don't want to hear any more.'

'But...' I started, quite thrown by the change in his demeanour.

'No, no.' He raised his palm. 'Nothing there of interest. I suggest you forget about it.' And he walked out without a backward glance.

I sat and thought. Although Jonty had "never been into" the likely development land, he clearly knew about the iron door and perhaps the tent. He just wasn't very good at lying. Which was decidedly interesting.

8
WEDNESDAY 17TH JULY
FUMIGATION AND MISSING LETTERS

When I returned to my rented flat at the top of Stockford High Street after visiting Sam Bryant on Monday, I'd thoroughly fumigated both myself and the letter I'd taken from the bedroom of the Farts, Sparrows, Pigeons, or whatever the heck the place was called. Jeez, it was confusing. I wasn't entirely sure if something subliminal from Slaughterhouse Cottages hadn't seeped into me either, although that may be a trifle unfair on Sam. His place seemed clean enough on the surface, or at least as clean as the house of a bachelor can be. Bachelor? Yes indeedy. I'd done my research in advance, for purely professional reasons you understand. And once I was in his cottage, the absence of cushions was a clear giveaway.

I hadn't had time to look too closely, either during what was left of Monday or through Tuesday, at what I'd borrowed – borrowed in the same way that Pop borrows companies that their present owners don't want to let go. Tuesday afternoons are reserved for Jim's weekly editorial meeting, which comprises the two of us sitting down in Jim's fusty, wood-panelled office with Jim giving me the full, unexpurgated life-stories of everybody in the town who'd snuffed it that week. Occasionally we're joined by the paper's photographer, Lugubrious Lenny, although Lenny's presence doesn't lift the overall mood any.

Tuesday mornings I'm supposed to write up or sub-edit the reports of the weekend's sports events. Events might be too grand a word. Stockford City's (think Dodge City but with more violence) interminable soccer season had finally reached its nadir with relegation (whatever that means) to the 4th Division of The Wessex County Intermediate League five Saturdays ago, but summer had brought with it some strange English version of standing around aimlessly in a field wearing white clothing, which Ena had assured me was the national pastime known as cricket. Stockford Cricket Club was keen to see reports of its victories (less so, its more usual defeats) written up in the Spectacle, *so I had to trim the two-thousand words they sent us down to about two hundred, a task that stretched my high school précising skills to the limit since it was all gibberish to me in the first place. I'd been to one of Stockford's matches to get a feel for the game, eaten more cheese and pickle sandwiches than a girl who covets a waist should eat, and listened to some old buffer in a stained, yellow and red striped tie explaining the rules. I'd zoned out, so I'm still not sure if victory is claimed by the team who can remain awake the longest or whether it's to do with something more intricate. In truth, I couldn't see a whole lot of difference between cricket and the brief description Sam had given me of Granny's Bobbins.*

So anyway, it wasn't until today – Spectacle *publication day, which equals my day off, yippee-doo – that I was able to take a look-see at the sheet of paper I'd (okay, let's be honest) purloined from the trunk in the malodorous bedroom of the pub. I was in little doubt that it was the sort of thing Pop had asked – told – me to look for but unfortunately I now discovered it was largely indecipherable. It's not that the words on the paper were written in some kinda Olde English legalese, more that they'd been typed on a keyboard which lacked an e. Even I know that e is used more than any other letter in the language so what I was reading looked like it had been redacted big time. They couldn't have broken the q instead?*

The ribbon used had seen better days also. Yes, ribbon. This was a genuine old type-written document. Typed on a typewriter. By somebody who'd definitely not won any spelling bees in their time. The machine on which the paper was typed had been sitting on the dressing table under the grubby window of the pub bedroom. It looked pre-war, but which war it was pre was anyone's guess. I'm not sure I could have lifted it even if I'd wanted to. I was a mean squash player in my teens but I'm not an Olympic weightlifter. Anyways, I didn't want to. Leaving my hand-sanitiser in the car had been a mistake I wouldn't be making should I ever return to The Farts.

Th Thr Pig ons

    High Str t

    Idl borough

    OX32 5TY

    D ar Sir aw Madam

Is thankm yous for yourn l tt r which youm s nt. Is hop s you lik md yourn

    Visit two th Pig ons and lik md th b r which youm drink d.

    Mys wif and m 'm hav giv ms yourn proposal grat thort and d w

    dilig nts. Ma v sh m say w m workins two hard and abowt timing w ms

    s llin up pub. Min ol da h m bort m for fiv hunn rd ginnis back in m day som s yourn off r o caught r million pound quit tookm by th priz . Ma v m

say two good m two t rn darn som's ims xc ptin it.

Ma v m's bookm an holiday to b nnidorm in to w ks so am happy to sin

yourn contrac b fors th n.

The first thing I realised was that my burglarising skills weren't up to snuff: I'd only gotten page one. There must be a page two somewhere which I'd missed. I sure as hell wasn't gonna be heading back to Clem's bedroom to look for it though.

I read that darn letter at least a dozen times. Slowly, a few words started to emerge from the mass of illiterate drivel. "Proposal" was obviously proposal. "Million" was clear enough. The "holiday" we knew about. So "caught" before million... quarter? Had whoever written this, the landlord, Clem presumably, been offered a quarter of a million pounds for the heap of shite masquerading as a drinking establishment? It certainly looked like it. If so, whoever was doing the offering was pulling a fast one. Heap of shite or not, and even way out here in Nowhereland, that building was worth way more than £250,000. Even I knew that: I'd seen the property prices in the Spectacle *and they were enough to make my eyes water.*

What I should have done at this point, what I'd been expressly instructed to do by Pop, was pick up the phone and call the old bastard and tell him what I'd got. But I paused. I mean, sure I wanted to keep my allowance – I have my pride but not that much, and I sure as fuck couldn't afford to live in my swish apartment on my own earnings – but if somebody had offered Clem £250,000 for the Three Pigeons, that person wasn't Pop. If the offer was the old man's, why would he need me to go snooping for it? Unless there was something else he wanted found? That wasn't an appetizing thought. It would mean going back into the place and I didn't have a full set of HazGear to hand.

So when I dialled, it wasn't Pop's number I rang but Sam Bryant's. I didn't need an excuse to ring Sam of course; I was supposed to be reporting on The Farts' demise in any case. But I can't deny I was starting to get a little lonesome out here in the sticks. There'd been no one in the Cliff Edge nightclub on any of my visits who could accurately be described as a catch, and the patrons of the local pubs were mostly past fifty. So I wasn't averse to getting to know Sam, all curly brown hair and pleasantly crumpled features, a bit better. And I thought I could see how our next conversation went before deciding whether or not to show him the letter. Or anything else.

9
THURSDAY 18TH JULY
PUPPETS AND VIEWS

The first person I saw when I entered the relatively plush saloon bar of The Trout was Puppet Pete. When I say plush, that's only compared to The Farts. Mind you, my garden shed is plush compared to The Farts and The Trout did boast a sort of faded grandeur. It also boasted a wall devoted to cartoons of fish, and not just trout. Stickleback rubbed shoulders with snapper and marlin with mackerel. Once upon a time, it had been the Railway Hotel and I remembered my parents telling me that it used to have a sort of *Brief Encounter* feel to it. Then Dr Beeching had his wicked way and now it was just fish and Puppet Pete.

Who was, as I say, in residence at the end of the bar as usual, with his permanent puppet, Pirate Pete attached to his right arm and a pint of lager attached to his left arm. Puppet Pete was the strong, silent type, only lacking the strong part, but Pirate Pete was never short of things to say, invariably obnoxious things. So obnoxious in fact that Clem had barred him from The Farts a year previously for excessive foul language and you had to be extremely excessive in that department to get under Clem's skin. Puppet Pete hadn't been barred but nevertheless informed Clem that if Pirate Pete was barred, he, Puppet Pete, could no longer in all conscience cross The Farts' sticky threshold himself. Surprisingly, Matt Handcock, the landlord of The Trout, was more forgiving of Pirate Pete's frequent outbursts, surprising that is until you found out that Matt is Puppet Pete's older brother.

'Hallo,' squawked Pirate Pete as I entered. 'Some poncey old fucker's decided to slum it in your hostelry, Matt.'

'Nice to see you too, Pete,' I said. 'Done any ravaging on the high seas lately?' It was a sore point with Pirate Pete that Idleborough and the sea were as far removed from each other as it's possible to be in England, and any ravaging days he may have had were long since consigned to history. Barbs like this were guaranteed to get under his varnish. He glared at me through his left eye, his right eye being obscured by the obligatory pirate's patch. Polly the parrot, perched precariously on his left shoulder, stared at the floor; one of her legs was inadequately reinforced by sticky tape and she lurched at an everlasting angle of forty-five degrees.

'Fuck off, you wire-haired twat,' Pirate Pete retorted.

'Now, now, Pete,' said Matt Handcock, hurrying across from the other end of the bar where he had been serving a group of customers who were wisely electing to stay as far away from Pirate Pete as possible. Matt was looking his usual harassed self. It was hardly surprising. He was father to five noisy offspring aged between three and ten and the number of customers in his pub, and thus his income, had dropped significantly since Pirate Pete had taken up residence. 'Sorry, Sam. What can I get you?'

'Nothing yet, Matt,' I said. 'I'm waiting for someone. I'll

come over when she gets here.' I strolled across to a secluded table as far away from the bar as possible.

'She?' shouted Pirate Pete. 'What piece of skirt you shagging now, dickface?'

I ignored him and at that moment, the door opened and Mallory Fillery entered. 'Whoor...' began Pirate Pete in his most lecherous rasp before Puppet Pete, who until now had been quietly supping his lager and not getting involved, placed his free hand over Pirate Pete's mouth. Pirate Pete tried to bite the hand but failed and fell silent. Mallory spotted me and wandered across.

'Sorry about that,' I said, standing. When Mallory had phoned yesterday evening and suggested a drink, my first thought was that I should drive into Stockford to meet her but she'd said she wanted to see more of Lazytown so I'd plumped for The Trout, Pirate Pete or no Pirate Pete. It was the pub with the widest selection of non-beer-related drinks in the village. I wasn't sure what Mallory's tastes might be but I was betting they might not include warm bitter. The menu was better than average too. Mind you, the bar was set quite low in that respect by The Fleece and The Bull, and the food in The Farts was, as previously mentioned, non-existent

'What can I get you, Miss Fillery?'

'Dry white wine, please,' she said. 'As dry as possible. And it's Mallory. I don't stand on formality.' I decided I'd have the same and fetched the drinks, running the gauntlet of Pirate Pete's now mercifully silent glare, and we took them into the garden. Unlike The Farts, The Trout's garden really **was** a garden, although it too contained a Granny's Bobbins pitch, tucked away on one side behind a carefully pruned hedge. Matt's wife, Sharon, when she wasn't running around after her brood or trying to persuade her husband that if they wanted to pay the bills next month he'd have to join The Farts and every other pub in the village in barring his brother's puppet, was a mean gardener and the secluded garden of The Trout, where once the single-track line to Stockford and, ultimately, Oxford once ran, was now an oasis of peace with colourful flower beds and a pond full of koi carp. We found a table next to the pond and I showed Mallory to a seat with a view between pretty Cotswold stone cottages and out across the open farmland that surrounded the village.

'Well, Sam, this is mighty pleasant,' she said, sipping her wine, sitting back and admiring the view. I too was admiring the view, but not of the pretty stone cottages or the wide green swathes of countryside beyond; I'd been looking at that view all my life. Today, Mallory had forsaken the double-denim and, in deference to the continuing hot weather, was wearing a white t-shirt that accentuated the figure I had previously only guessed at, and a short, but not indecently short, powder-blue wraparound skirt. I now had a more accurate idea of the quality as well as the length of her legs. The former unquestionably matched the latter.

'Enjoying the view?' she asked, archly. I looked up. The red hair, now tied back in a loose pony-tail, appeared rather more golden today. It sparkled in the sunlight every time she moved her head.

'I was going to ask you the same thing,' I said. I refused to be embarrassed. I was far too old for that sort of thing and she hadn't decided on her choice of clothes for a bet. Mind you, I hadn't made as much effort myself. My jeans were only my third smartest pair and the maroon polo shirt I was wearing was one of many I'd rescued from one of Stockford's plethora of charity shops.

'Okay,' she said. 'Tell me about the puppet. There's some weird shit going down in Idleborough, that's for sure.'

'You learn to ignore him most of the time,' I said, shrugging.

'Him? You do realise it's made of wood, don't you?' And as if she thought she hadn't made her point sufficiently: 'It's a puppet. What's with the vent? Is he simple or what?'

I had to give that some thought. 'No,' I said eventually. 'Pete's not simple but he had a condition that prevented him speaking until he was twelve. Not a word. His parents despaired. Finally, he was given a puppet for his birthday by an uncle or somebody and something just sort of clicked overnight. I mean, he still didn't say anything himself but the puppet did. Everyone was delighted. Until he got given a second puppet that is.'

'Uh huh? How so?'

'Well, the first puppet was a sort of schoolboy doll, you know, blazer, peaked cap and so forth. Pete called it Prep School Pete and butter wouldn't melt in its mouth. Polite Pete would have been a better name. That all changed though when a friend of the family presented Pete with the pirate puppet, to ring the changes as it were. Pirate Pete started off by being just piratey, you know, all "ooh-aah, me hearty" and "walk the plank" and suchlike, but gradually he – it – just got ruder and ruder.'

'So why do you all put up with it. Couldn't someone just take it away and give him back the schoolkid puppet, the nice one? What about his parents?'

'Ah, well, that's an issue. His parents were killed in a car crash a few years back, so really Pete is Matt's responsibility now, and Matt thinks that psychologically, taking Pirate Pete away might tip him over the edge.'

'Matt?'

'The landlord here. He's Pete's older brother. He doesn't know what to do.'

'He needs help, wouldn't you say?'

'Well, we've offered, made suggestions, but...' I shrugged.

'Not Matt, dummy – Pete. He needs "help", professional help.'

I knew she was right but before I could think of a suitable reply, Billy walked into the garden, pint in hand. This was unusual; in fact I didn't think I'd ever seen Billy in The Trout, although, with The Farts closed, I suppose he had to drink somewhere. He dragged a chair over from a neighbouring table and sat down uninvited.

'That buggerin' parrot's just bitten me,' he said by way of introduction. Now, Billy, nineteen years old and, thereby, the youngest Farts regular, was by nature one of life's moaners. He was also one of life's followers and the people he followed most often were Banjo and me. As Banjo was not in evidence, it appeared that I was his preferred option for today. Mallory's presence wasn't putting him off; indeed it may well have been an unexpected bonus. The fact that he was now unashamedly copying me in enjoying the view afforded by the t-shirt and legs suggested that this was indeed the case.

'I doubt if it did,' I said, replying to the comment about Pirate Pete's parrot. 'It's made of fake fur and foam.' Mind you, there could have been any number of tiny creepy-crawlies lurking within the fake fur and foam that might be capable of giving you a nip if you brushed past it. However, it seemed that that had been merely an introductory moan.

'Dump this, aint it?' he said, tearing his eyes away from Mallory's breasts and scanning the glorious technicolour splendour of Sharon Handcock's garden.

'Aren't you going to introduce us, Sam?' said Mallory. She seemed to be taking Billy's arrival and appraisal in good part. She was doubtless used to it.

'This is Billy,' I said. 'Billy's just leaving.' Billy made no move to leave but merely sank a third of his pint. 'Aren't you, Billy?'

'Who are you then?' he said. As he knew who I was, I assumed he was asking Mallory although he still hadn't managed to raise his gaze to her eye level. In fairness, my introduction had been a little one-sided.

'My name's Mallory,' said Mallory. 'Good to meet you, Billy.' I imagined she'd been the recipient of an expensive Canadian education that had devoted a large part of its curriculum to the cultivation of good manners. Either that or she'd been an actress in an earlier life.

'Where's Banjo?' I asked Billy.

'Eh?' he said, finally tearing his eyes away from Mallory's t-shirt. 'Dunno. It's you I come ter see, aint it?' My lucky day, I thought. Once Billy had attached himself to you, his leechlike tendencies were famous. I tried one last throw of the dice. My pleasant lunchtime trying to get to know Mallory Fillery a little better – or a lot better if her afternoon plans were as flimsy as mine – looked like being ruined. Any gooseberry would be bad enough but a gooseberry of Billy's persuasion doubly so.

'I think Daisy's Dad, Dick was asking after you,' I lied. Interestingly, people rarely referred to Daisy's Dad, Dick as just Dick. I mean, they may have done before Daisy was born but that was twenty-two years ago. 'I think I saw him going into The Bull earlier.' Damn, that was two "I thinks". Even Billy would see through that.

'Nah,' he said confirming my suspicions. 'He's gone on

the NOBS outing to Weston, aint he? Coach left two hours since.'

I'd forgotten about the NOBS outing. Every third Thursday of the month from May to September, the money that INCEST raised from events like the Duck Race paid for the village pensioners to go on a coach-trip to Weston-super-Mare, Bourton-on-the-Water or Bath. Today it was Weston. Lovely weather for it, I thought but unfortunately it meant that my untruth about Daisy's Dad, Dick could be quickly discounted even by someone with Billy's limited wattage between the ears. No one knew quite how old Daisy's Dad, Dick was, although it had been suggested that if you cut him in half and counted the rings, his girth was so great that he'd come in at about two hundred. However, in reality he could have been anything from fifty to seventy. Whatever the truth, he claimed he was a pensioner and as he usually led the singing on the coach (harmless old standards such as *Tipperary* or *My Old Man's a Dustman* on the way there, ditties of a more vaudevillian nature on the way home after several pints), no one argued that he didn't qualify. Daisy herself had been unable to confirm his age. He'd never possessed a driving licence or passport and all she could remember from her toddler days was that he'd always looked pretty old.

NOBS? Oh, yes, another village acronym or anachronism. Stands for the Nasty Old Buggers' Society. Not its official name, you understand, although frankly most of them are. Officially they call themselves the Houdini Club on the basis that once a month, they meet up to escape the village. The club is one of INCEST's worthy causes. As well as being one of the leading lights in INCEST, I was also on the rota to take charge of the NOBS excursions. Counting them all off the bus on arrival at Weston or wherever was an easier job than counting them all back on again later. The numbers rarely tallied. Us organisers had a longish list of favourite watering holes and seafront toilets where we might expect to find any waifs and strays at the end of the day, but it was always half an hour of your life lost rounding them up.

Back to the present and Billy was looking at his empty glass in an expectant sort of way, and as Mallory's was also in the same state, I drained the rest of my wine and stood up. 'I'll get refills,' I said. Mallory looked slightly alarmed. I could understand her thought processes. She was caught between the deep blue sea that was Billy and the devil that was Pirate Pete inside the pub. She clearly came to the conclusion that Billy was the lesser of the two evils and relaxed back into her chair. 'Won't be long,' I said.

When I returned with the drinks (having got away with just one "tosser" from Pirate Pete), I was surprised to see Mallory and Billy deep in conversation. 'Billy tells me he saw you the other day,' said Mallory.

'Billy sees me nearly every day,' I replied. Whilst it wasn't a small village, in some respects it was much too small.

'Ah, but he says you were doing something you shouldn't.' I couldn't think what that could be. Or, wait a minute...

'Oh yes?' I said to Billy. 'What was I doing then?'

'You was dahn the back o' The Farts,' he said. 'Yest'day mornin'.' It wasn't ridiculous to suppose that Billy had spotted me walking down the side of the pub – he was, after all, a habitual follower, of me in particular – but he hadn't followed me into the garden and couldn't, therefore, have seen me performing my minor feat of acrobatics to gain access to the extra land at the rear.

'I don't think going into The Farts garden is something I

shouldn't be doing,' I said. 'I was just checking that Clem had taken his car with him,' I added, extemporising rapidly.

'What, you thought his old motor would be over back in the woods, did yer?' Billy was enjoying this, grinning slyly. He didn't often get one over anybody.

'OK,' I said, holding up my hands in mock surrender. 'I come clean. I was having a nose around. We **are** trying to save the pub, you know. I wanted to take a look. But how did you know I was there?'

'Cos you went in my tent, dint yer? Trespassin', that is.' He sounded proud that he knew the word. 'You shoulda looked up. I was up a tree watchin' yer.'

'**Your** tent?' That wasn't a possibility that had crossed my mind. 'What the hell are you doing in a tent out the back of The Farts?' Billy lived with his hardly-ever-seen mother in a rundown cottage down an alley behind the hardware shop.

'I'm lookin' aht for people like you, aint I? Trespassers.' There it was again. He rolled the word around his tongue lovingly. He was going to get as much mileage out of it as he could. I took a moment to think. He wasn't doing this off his own bat. Someone was paying him. But who?

'Did the squire put you up to this?' I asked. It was a reasonable assumption, especially bearing in mind Jonty's evasiveness during our conversation in Balthazar's.

Billy suddenly looked shifty, or at least more shifty than usual. 'I can't tell yer that,' he said, but he already had. 'I thought you was goin' to open the door.' He sounded disappointed that I hadn't.

'How long have you been there?' I said. 'And have you seen anyone else?'

But Billy had evidently come to the conclusion that he'd said too much. I hadn't noticed him drain his second pint but the empty glass was evidence that he had. He stood up. 'Gotta go,' he said and scuttled off through the garden into the pub.

He nearly collided with Matt, coming into the garden collecting empties, including the one vacated by Billy. 'Are you having lunch, Sam?' he asked, plucking two menus out of his apron. 'And, er...' he looked at Mallory.

'Mallory,' she said. 'Sure, why not? I'm a hungry girl. And Sam and I have stuff to talk about.' She paused and looked at me. 'You may not be the only one who's been poking around in The Farts.'

10
THURSDAY 18TH JULY
RED HEREFORDS AND THATCHED ROOFS

L*unch in the beautiful garden of The Trout (something called Steak and Ale Pie for Sam, which sounded genuinely disgusting, and, deliciously unexpected, salmon and salad for yours truly; well, a girl's got to look after her figure and the white t-shirt I had on couldn't have taken much more strain, if you know what I'm saying) was followed by a walk around the village. We entered the cool of the beautiful 15th century church, named after some saint or other I've never heard of – Pop's educational proclivities hadn't included much by way of religious teaching apart from the religious necessity of making as much dough as possible – and Sam spent several minutes telling me about how it had been used for filming some TV show called Holy Trinity Exclamation Point (odd title but who am I to judge?). I'd not heard of that either but Sam suggested it was one of the more interesting things about Idleborough, so I made a mental note in case it developed a future importance vis-à-vis the Spectacle, unlikely as that seemed.*

Eventually, after a further meander down some back lanes, we hopped over something Sam referred to as a stile, which gave him an opportunity to see even more of my legs, so it might have been a deliberate choice of direction. Don't get me wrong, I'm not moaning; I'm usually more the blue-jeans type, so the skirt I had on wasn't a random choice. It hadn't rained for quite a while (I'd suggested to Jim back at the Spectacle *that this was surely headline material, given England is usually so rain-soaked, but he'd dismissed the idea) so the footpath we took across the fields was dry and dusty. Just as well; I was only wearing thongs. Even so, I couldn't help being aware that my head was an inch or so north of Sam's. It didn't seem to concern him, unlike the guys I'd so far met in London, where no fella under six-three ever gave me a second glance, and it sure as hell didn't bother me any.*

We crossed a bridge, a narrow structure made of loose wooden planks (you'd have thought they coulda run to a few nails) and with a rickety handrail down just one side. Still I wasn't too bothered; I'm not a health and safety nut and, in any case, Sam went across first and it took his weight okay (bit of a paunch threatening there, but nothing too serious if I could get him to stop eating the Steak and Ale Pies) so it sure as hell wasn't going to tip skinny me into the stream beneath. Sam tried to alarm me by suggesting there was a troll lurking under the bridge but the only trolls I know stalk your social media, so I guess the reference was lost on me and when he started trying to explain about three billy goats gruff I told him to shut up.

The stream was apparently called the Idlebrook, although if it was a brook it was disappointingly failing to babble. Sam referred to it as the local river but I grew up on the banks of the St Lawrence, so it hardly qualified as a stream to me. I've seen wider gutters, frankly.

We continued walking alongside it for about a quarter of a mile. Idleborough lay to our right, northwards, and to our left were fields, mostly empty although the largest contained a herd of reddish-brown cattle grazing peacefully and gazing disinter-

estedly at us as we wandered past. Sam called the field Farmer Trickle's Big Field. He emphasised the Big bit but I guess he was being ironic. It wouldn't even have passed muster as a field at all back in my part of Canada. Even some of our smaller fields could have swallowed up the whole of Oxfordshire.

At first, the arrival at The Trout of Billy the Kid had thrown a wrench in my plans as regards the letter I'd found in the bedroom of The Three Pigeons – or Farts as I'd found myself calling it, much against my conscious desire not to do so. I hadn't been sure whether it was information I should share with Sam at all, before, or instead of passing it on to Pop as instructed, and on which my continuing receipt of my allowance might depend. But Billy's revelation that he was being paid to camp out behind the pub and engage in a bit of snooping had made my mind up. As soon as I'd opened my mouth, however, Sam had put his metaphorical hand up (I was beginning to wonder whether there might be a spot of unmetaphorical hand-upping as the afternoon drew on) and glanced around at the rapidly-filling pub garden.

'Walls have ears,' he'd said, unoriginally. Hence the walk, and it was only when we'd found a part of the bank of the stream not used as a watering hole by the cows in Farmer Trickle's Little Field, and dangled our feet in the water, that I felt able to bring the subject up. Sam listened attentively, squinting a little bit when I got to the part about shimmying through the half-open bathroom window, but maybe he was just trying to work out how a six-foot girl could get herself through a window that small.

'Can I see the letter?' he asked when I'd finished.

'Sure thing,' I replied. 'It's in the car. I can show you later over another cup of your famously caffy coffee.' He didn't flinch at the implied suggestion there, but why would he?

He tore his brown eyes away from my green ones and

pointed across the stream. 'That there,' he said, 'behind that nightmare of brambles, triffidy things and surprisingly majestic trees, is the back of The Farts.' I stared but could see no building of any description in the direction Sam was pointing. Which wasn't to say it wasn't there, just that it would be a major excavation job to clear the land for housing or any other purpose. Over to the right, however, I spotted the largest expanse of thatched roof I'd ever laid eyes on.

'What's that place?' I said.

'Empty, usually,' he replied mysteriously. 'It's owned by someone who we locals like to call a blow-in. Some over-rich bastard who deigns to motor up from town a couple of times a year.' I knew all about over-rich bastards, of course. 'He never mixes and never, as far as we know, comes out of his house. I'm not sure I've ever seen him.'

'Or her?'

'Could be, although Jonty insists it was a bloke shouted at him through the door when he tried being neighbourly.'

'What's his name?' I asked. He sounded just the kind of man who Pop would have as a friend.

'No one knows. We call him The Banker.' I laughed. That was an expression I was well aware of. I was a city girl after all. I knew a lot of Bankers. Several of them had looked up my powder-blue skirt at one time or another.

'I'll find out for you,' I said confidently. 'I am a journalist, after all.' Sort of, anyway. 'Do you think he might have something to do with the offer for the pub? Does he want to expand his kingdom? Let's be honest, if he's as much of a blow-off as you say, he can't find it much fun living next to The Farts. I hear tell closing time's about cock-crow at weekends.'

Sam laughed. 'I said blow-in not blow-off. Mind you, there's often some blowing off going on at closing time, which, yes, you're right, can be a moveable feast in Clem's eyes. It can get quite noisy when he finally does throw us out the back door and down the side passage next to The Banker's fence, so you might have a point.' He paused. 'You didn't by any chance find a Yale key during your bit of cat-burgling? There's a door I need some help with.'

II

THURSDAY 18TH JULY
SHOWERS AND WARM ROLLS

It was almost time for the second meeting of the Action Group, which I had concluded should be called InnKeeper. Somebody had to make a decision and it was my action group after all. Otherwise, I could see us going round in circles names-wise until Farmer Trickle's cows came home or until The Farts was demolished and replaced with however many houses they could fit in the space. On that score, Jeremy Jeavons had promised to find out if any planning application was in place or expected and if so, for how many houses. I'd suggested that at six houses to an acre, at least twenty 3- or 4-bed detached properties could be constructed, especially with the pub itself demolished, something which would in any case have to occur for access reasons.

I'd sent an email round yesterday with an agenda for this evening's meeting. When I say I'd sent it round, I mean, I'd sent it to Jeremy and to Daisy. Daisy would show it to Dick, who didn't own a phone, being convinced they caused brain damage. Judging by how many people were slaves to their devices, he may have had a point. Banjo had a phone but it was incapable of receiving emails so I'd printed a copy of the agenda off and slipped it under the door of his tiny flat, which basically comprised a small part of the roof space of Mrs Bee's Bazaar. Beatrice appeared to consider Banjo the son she'd never had and allowed him to stay there free of charge, although in actual fact, he was hardly ever there. God knows where he went but days on end often went by without a sight of him. Beatrice paid him a sum currently about half the minimum wage to clean the store and café occasionally, help with the deliveries and act as some sort of night-time security. This last was wasted money given the "security guard's" frequent absences. Luckily, crime levels in the village were low, possibly because everybody knew everybody else and clips round the ear as a deterrent to juvenile misbehaviour had always been deemed an effective punishment.

Mallory had decided to stay on for the meeting, which pleased me no end and not just because her discovery of the letter under Clem's bed (presumably Maeve's too, something which wasn't easy to imagine) would give us something else to discuss. If truth be told, she hadn't had to stay on very long. A number of things had delayed her departure.

Firstly, we had been held up by bumping into Mucker, literally in Mallory's case. The Short Circular walk we had taken conveniently re-enters the bounds of the village proper via the lane past my cottage. The lane fords the Idlebrook alongside a more solid pedestrian bridge (one which has a rail on both sides) which leads to a second pair of cottages, one of which is owned by Farmer Trickle, and which he uses to house a constantly changing selection of seasonal farmworkers; friendly, multilingual ones from Poland and Romania and unsociable, barely monolingual

Brits. The other cottage is owned by Mucker, who inherited it from his parents, who inherited it from their parents before them. From the outside there doesn't appear to have been any money spent on upkeep since the days of Mucker's grandparents and nobody I know has volunteered to go inside, so we can only assume a similar state of neglect exists within.

Mallory and I had just stepped onto the bridge when Mucker hove into view at the other end, staggering slightly, presumably after an extended lunchtime session in The Bull. It was by now about three-thirty and at a guess, Mucker had been in the pub for about four hours, so I stepped back to let him pass. Mallory didn't. Her sense of spatial awareness, at least when it came to avoiding unsteady drunks on narrow bridges, might be less finely honed than mine. Now, Mucker isn't a violent drunk, indeed he doesn't possess a violent bone in his body. He is, however, an extremely wobbly drunk, his disordered progress not helped by the Wellington boots he habitually wore.

'Wash 'appenin' t'Farts, then, Sham?' he said as he tottered towards us, spotting me but apparently not Mallory, despite her flaming, golden hair gleaming in the sunlight. 'Gorrit shorted yet, then? Beer'sh pish at t'Bull.' At which point, despite Mallory suddenly realising her predicament and backing up against the rail of the bridge to allow him past, he lurched into her, skidded slightly in his boots, put his hand out to grab the opposite rail, missed and slowly toppled over it into the ford five feet below.

Now, as Mallory had already pointed out to me, the Idlebrook is not a big stream, and at no point is it more than about three feet deep so Mucker was in no danger of drowning. However, he didn't look capable of exiting the water without assistance, which he was unlikely to receive from Farmer Trickle's Red Herefords, a group of whom were edging closer with an interested look in their eyes.

'Oh, my gosh,' said Mallory as we rushed off the bridge and scrambled down the bank to attempt to haul him out of the stream. 'Does he often do that?'

'What, drink until mid-afternoon or fall into the Idlebrook?' I said. 'Yes to the first and, well, maybe to the second. I don't have a camera trained on the bridge.' At this point, Mucker seemed to notice Mallory for the first time. 'Who'sh thish then?' he said and attempted a bow which was unexpected as well as inadvisable, and resulted in his sliding back into the stream whilst, miraculously, remaining on his feet

'Blimey,' I said. 'I've never seen him try to bow before. You must be very special.' Anyway, partly under his own steam and partly with our help, Mucker managed to exit the stream at the second attempt and swayed off towards his cottage, waving vaguely. 'Nishe to meet you,' he said to Mallory, tipping a non-existent cap at her as he left.

'He was wearing galoshes,' said Mallory wonderingly. 'It's what? 75 in the shade, dry as Arizona, and he's wearing galoshes.' I explained that, as far as we knew, they were the only footwear Mucker owned. 'Why?' she asked.

'That might be the answer to your earlier question,' I said. 'If he's in the habit of falling into the stream on his way back from the pub, waterproof boots are a sensible choice of footwear.'

We were both left rather wet and slightly grimy, either from the Idlebrook or Mucker himself, so when we'd collected the letter Mallory had found in The Farts from her car, which turned out to be a red convertible Jag – not bad for a cub reporter on a local rag, I thought but didn't say –

parked outside The Trout, and finally reached 1 Slaughterhouse Cottages, Mallory suggested a shower. I'd got to work firing up the percolator. 'I'm feeling a bit... dirty after our inadvertent encounter with Mucker and the mighty Idlebrook,' she said from the kitchen doorway.

'Sure,' I said. 'Don't blame you. Top of the stairs on the left, towels in the cupboard on the landing.'

She looked at me steadily, green eyes wide and innocent. 'So what are you doing fiddling about with that kettle?' she said.

So anyway, it wasn't far short of six o'clock by the time she showed me the letter. I looked at it whilst rustling up some soup and warm rolls for a light dinner. The letter could only have been written by Clem, I decided, but I had no clue about its likely recipient. I ticked off a list on my fingers but didn't require very many, especially as I had not yet told Mallory that Squire Jonty had informed me who her father was. Jonty himself was first on the list.

'Why him?' asked Mallory, who, distractingly, was wearing my dressing gown with nothing on underneath.

'Because if there's anything shady going on in the village, then Jonty either knows about it or created the shade himself.'

'Okay, who else? What about the mysterious Banker with the acreage of thatch?'

'Yep, definitely,' I said, raising a second digit. 'Also, Downwycherley Brewery. Big Brian said that Clem had gone there to sign papers. But what papers? Clem owns the pub, we know that, so does that mean he's selling it to them?'

'But that's good, surely? If a brewery buys it, it'll still be a pub.'

'I guess, but it won't be The Farts,' I said. I raised a third finger, although I seriously doubted if the brewery was going to buy it. It didn't own any other pubs for one thing and spending £250,000 seemed way out of its league, even if it was seriously underpriced at that amount..

'Okay, Boy Scout, next item. This door you want the key for?'

But the soup was ready. 'Let's talk about that at the meeting later,' I said. 'If we don't eat this soon, everyone'll be banging on the front door.'

'Eat?' she said. 'Where I come from, you drink soup.' And that discussion lasted until a hardly audible ring of my doorbell, now miraculously in full working order again, signalled the arrival of Jeremy Jeavons.

12

THURSDAY 18TH JULY
AGENDAS AND BACKHANDERS

'Hang about, we're a couple missing, aren't we?' I said. My living room looked emptier than it had on Monday evening despite the addition of Mallory to our ranks.

'Not a couple,' said Banjo. 'Just Daisy's Dad, Dick.' Dick was a sizeable bloke and had taken up most of my two-seater sofa three evenings ago, squashing Daisy and her laptop into a corner. Even so, I apologised.

'Sorry Daisy,' I said. 'I didn't mean to imply...'

'What, that my Dad's fat?' she said. 'Of course he's fat. Nice to have a bit more room, if I'm honest.' She turned to Mallory, sitting next to her and taking up rather less space on the sofa than Dick had done. 'Hi, I'm Daisy. I'm the secretary of the Action Group.' She indicated her laptop as if to emphasise her secretaryness.

'Important job,' said Mallory. 'Mallory Fillery,' and they shook hands as awkwardly as you might expect two people sitting alongside each other on a sofa to shake hands.

'Yes, sorry, everybody,' I said, raising my voice over the hum of conversation. 'This is Mallory Fillery from the *Spec-*

tacle.' Jeremy glanced up from a notebook he was consulting and nodded. Banjo, looking as though not managing to secure a seat next to Mallory was an error of judgement he'd live to regret, said, 'Banjo.'

'Pardon?' said Mallory, looking at me for support.

'It's his name,' I explained. 'Well, it is these days.' Judging by the blank expression on Mallory's face, I'm not sure if I was helping much. 'He's not inviting you to start strumming or anything.'

'Thank goodness for that,' she said, looking at me with wide-eyed innocence. 'I think I've had as much strumming as I can take for one day.'

'Moving swiftly on,' I said, hoping that wasn't a blush I could feel creeping up my neck. 'Daisy. Do we know where your dad is?'

'On the NOBS trip,' she replied.

'I thought they'd be back by now.' Even allowing for rounding up the usual lost souls at the end of the afternoon, the Weston-super-Mare return coach usually arrived back in the village before seven.

'I heard there was an incident involving Daisy's Dad, Dick and the pier,' said Banjo, mysteriously. 'Aint that right, Daise?'

'Yes, I believe he fell off,' said Daisy in the sort of voice that suggested that Dick falling off a pier was an everyday event. 'Something to do with the wind catching his Ninety-nine and tripping over a chihuahua in trying to stop the ice-cream blowing into the sea. He's all right. They threw lifebelts to him. He had to put one on each arm like water wings. The lifeboatmen laughed a bit but they managed to tow him to shore. He lost his flake though; that's what upset him the most. Anyway, the last I heard, the coach was still just north of Bristol.'

'Never mind,' I said. 'We can get on without him. Have you all seen the Agenda I sent round?'

I looked at the one in my hand. It wasn't very long.

SECOND MEETING OF INNKEEPER

Thursday 18 July
1 Apologies for Absence
2 Chairman's Report
3 Jeremy Jeavons' Report
4 Any Other Business

'Well, we've done one,' said Daisy.

'One what?' asked Banjo, draining his first beer. I could see I'd have to go to the Bazaar tomorrow to top up my stocks.

'Number one. Apologies for absence. My dad's apologised.'

'Well, er, no, strictly speaking, he hasn't,' said Jeremy Jeavons.

'Well, he's not here, is he? He's stuck on the coach.'

'Are we sure he's not still stuck in his water wings too?' said Banjo, edging past me towards the kitchen, looking for more refreshment.

Mallory looked at me and waggled her eyebrows attractively. Like her hair, they were red, and I'd ascertained during the afternoon that the colour was entirely genuine. I'd never had much of a thing for redheads previously, but a man can change. Anyway, I knew what the eyebrow-waggling signified. We weren't making much progress.

'I think we can assume that Daisy's Dad, Dick would have apologised if he'd been here to do so,' I said. That didn't sound quite right, now that I'd said it, but nobody picked me up on it. Banjo was still in the kitchen anyway. 'So, item two, my report.'

'Just one thing, Mr Chair.' Banjo was back in the room.

'Yes?' I said, trying to keep my voice level.

'It says here,' Banjo continued, waving the agenda, 'and I quote: "Second Meeting of InnKeeper".' I could guess what was coming. 'We haven't confirmed a name for the action group yet. So who decided on InnKeeper? I quite like FARTS myself.'

'And I don't think any of us is surprised by that, Banjo. However, given that this is supposed to be an **action** group, I felt we should try and move things along, so I made an executive decision.'

'Are you allowed to do that, Sam?' asked Daisy. 'I don't think it's in the constitution.' She peered closely at something on the screen in front of her, her glasses sliding forward on her nose. 'No, there's nothing here.'

'Nothing where?' I said. I was beginning to feel control of the meeting slipping from my grasp.

'Where did you get this, Daisy?' asked Mallory, leaning across and peering over her shoulder.

'Off the internet. It's a pro forma constitution for action groups. I thought it might be useful.'

'It appears to be all about badger culling, though,' said Mallory, doubtfully.' Still, it's a good idea. Perhaps we could put "Constitution" on the agenda for the next meeting, Sam?'

I looked at her gratefully. 'Absolutely,' I said. 'Make a note please, Daisy.' I glanced at Banjo, who had his nose buried deep in his second glass of my beer and appeared to have temporarily lost interest in what the action group should call itself. 'Item two: my report.'

I fished out the notes I'd scribbled down following my visit to the rear of The Farts and which I'd added to before the meeting, taking into account Mallory's discovery of the carbon-copy letter. I ran through what we'd both been doing, together with any conclusions – or lack of – we'd reached whilst dangling our feet in the Idlebrook and, later, dangling other things in the low-ceilinged bedroom upstairs. ('Ow,' and then, **'ow!'** Mallory had exclaimed, banging her head on the door frame and then again on the first ceiling beam inside the room. 'Sorry,' I'd said, having forgotten to warn her, 'but you're quite a tall girl.' 'You normally have your wicked way with dwarfs up here, do you?' she'd responded, throwing a pillow at me.)

Banjo looked up from his pint. 'You mean, Clem's left a window open?' Not for the first time, he sounded aghast. 'We could've helped stop the beer go off, if we'd known.' Everyone looked at him. 'I mean, we'd have started an honesty box.' This from someone whose bar tab at The Farts never dropped below forty quid. We all looked at him a bit more. He changed the subject. 'You don't look like a burglar, Miss Fillery. Why'd you do it? Did someone ask you to?'

It was a pertinent question, a question I realised I should have asked earlier in the day. Unfortunately, I'd been distracted by all the red hair. However, if Mallory was at all embarrassed by being called a burglar by a perfect stranger – not that anyone would describe Banjo as perfect – she didn't show it. 'I guess I'm guilty as charged. I can't deny I gained illegal access to a building and came away with something that isn't mine. Hey, "burglar" sounds good. I can add it to my résumé.' She smiled at Banjo, which seemed to have the same effect as brainwashing, or he could still be thinking about the gallons of undrunk beer in

Clem's cellar and how quickly he could gain access to it via the open toilet window. 'But, truly, I was just doing what any red-blooded reporter would do. If you want the power of the press behind you, then the press has gotta get some facts. I'm sure you'll agree there's no harm done by me climbing into the pub –'

'– only to your health,' said Daisy.

'– only if you left the beer alone,' said Banjo at the same time.

'– and finding the letter was just what any good newshound would do.'

This seemed to satisfy everyone, but I was still waiting for Mallory to reveal who her father was. I'd thought all afternoon about confronting her with the fact that I knew about Harrison Makepeace Stamp but hadn't wanted to spoil a good thing – more than one good thing. I'd done a bit of judicious Googling to confirm what Squire Jonty had told me yesterday and Stamp boasted quite a sizeable Wikipedia entry, including the fact that he had a daughter named Mallory. It also referred to another daughter, from wife number one, called Eve-May. If so, Mallory had got much the better of things when names were being handed out. In fact, unless Eve-May turned out to be a Miss World contender, then Mallory may have got first dibs on everything.

I'd made proper copies of the carbon-copy letter and handed them round but it didn't mean much to anybody beyond the fact that Clem typed as he spoke and had a broken typewriter. However, my discovery of the door and Billy's tent caused much more of a stir. Nobody had been aware of the existence of a hidden door to who knows where, but then nobody in the room had ever been beyond The Farts' garden.

'Not really hidden though, was it?' said Banjo. 'Not if you found it so easily, Sam.'

'It wasn't that easy. I nearly fell into the hole. If I'd noticed the hole before I fell into it, I'd have walked round it and never seen the steps or the door. So yes, it was hidden, either by design or nature.'

It was Jeremy who summed it up. 'So, Sam, you think Squire Jonty is paying Billy to keep an eye out for someone who might turn up and open this door? Although Billy hasn't confirmed it **was** the squire.'

'He didn't have to,' I said. 'His face was an open book when I made the suggestion.'

'Indeed, but it wouldn't hold up in a court of law.'

'Does it need to?' I asked. 'Let's just assume I'm right and that Jonty knows about the door. It follows that he doesn't have the key for it and wants to know who does.'

'Which may mean that he knows where the door leads,' said Mallory.

'There's only one way to find out,' I said.

'What, string Billy up by his bootlaces and waterboard him?' said Banjo, unhelpfully.

'I don't think we need bother ourselves with the monkey when the organ grinder himself is available. I'll have a word with his squireship in the morning.'

'Can I come?' asked Mallory.

'Don't you have a story to write?' I asked.

'Not before Tuesday, and it's not much of a story yet. Bit more juice wouldn't go amiss. Now, the missing key. Would another visit to The Farts be in order to see if the key is anywhere on the premises, while Sam is having a word with the squire? Whatever the heck a squire is. Tell you what, if you grill Jonty, I can undertake another spot of burgling, if you like.'

We all liked, especially Banjo. 'I could come too,' he said enthusiastically bordering on over-enthusiastically.

'Down, boy,' I said.

'Sure, why not,' said Mallory. 'Two pairs of eyes and all that. You can help me over the sill, Banjo.' Banjo looked like all his birthdays had come at once.

'Don't let him in the cellar, then,' I warned. 'We might never see him again. Anyway, next item. Jeremy: what have you got for us?'

Jeremy coughed gently into his fist, took a sip of tea – which must surely have been cold by now – and said: 'I have been onto the Stockford District Council website and studied the planning applications relating to Idleborough.' He paused.

'And?' I prompted.

'There is only one.'

'And?' Me again. I knew Jeremy wasn't being deliberately annoying. Outside the boardroom of the Great Mercian Hotels Group, he rarely enjoyed moments in the sun. The last one I could remember was when he'd supplied the correct answer to a football-related question ("Hamilton Academical") in The Farts Christmas Quiz ahead of self-professed football expert, Scooby, thus securing the grand prize (three bottles of Bud Lite, otherwise known as toilet water) for our table. Scooby and Banjo had glowered until New Year.

'It does not pertain to The Three Pigeons.'

'What **does** it contain?' that was Banjo.

'Pertain, not contain, Timothy: appropriate to, related to or applicable to, especially in this instance, the last of those. The only planning application for Idleborough in the last month is for the Hon. Jonathan Hardy-Hewitt for a dovecote.'

'Who the heck is Timothy?' whispered Mallory to me. 'And who's the On Jonathan guy?'

'Timothy is Banjo's real name,' I said. 'Jeremy's not one for nicknames; sometimes we don't know who he's talking about. And the Hon – Honourable – Jonathan is Squire Jonty.' To Jeremy I added: 'Must be a sizeable dovecote to need PP.'

'I believe we're talking House of Commons dimensions.'

'What makes him Honourable?' asked Mallory. It was a reasonable question, Jonty being one of the least honourable people I'd ever met.

'He's the second son of an earl. By about two minutes; he and his brother are twins. So Jonty's just a lost fight in a birth canal away from being Viscount Uppingshott and in a few short years, the Earl of Northavon. It never stops rankling with him.' I looked at Jeremy. 'To clarify then: no planning application. Does that mean we're barking up the wrong tree about The Farts being sold for housing?' **Was** just the brewery buying the pub? Could mean new carpets and a landlord who didn't tell you to "fuckem off" at closing time. Still, if it was the wildest of geese we'd been chasing, at least they'd flown towards Mallory so it wasn't by any means a complete waste of four days. However, my newly inflated balloon was soon punctured.

'Oh, no, not at all,' said Jeremy. 'Firstly, the fact that no planning application has yet appeared on the Council's website does not mean there is no planning application **not** on the website. If the planning officer does not consider it to be in the public interest, there are all sorts of delays that can be implemented, some of them legal. For example, the Council has to validate the application and whilst a decision on an application must be made within eight weeks, or more likely for a site of this size with the complexity of the access arrangements, thirteen weeks, that timeframe need not commence until validation has taken place.'

'Can you let me have that in writing?' asked Daisy. 'I need to make sure I minute it correctly, and I'm afraid I got a bit lost.'

'Looks like the application may have got a bit lost too,' said Banjo.

'Of course, Daisy,' said Jeremy. 'Here you are,' and he carefully tore a page from his notebook and handed it over.

Whilst quite complicated, I thought I understood the nub of what Jeremy had said. I turned to Mallory. 'What's the *Spectacle's* take on this? Have you known planning applications being hidden from view before?'

'Honestly,' she said, hands raised in mock surrender, 'I don't know. That's Jim's department; he's my editor. Far too complicated for a simple girl like me, I guess. Anyway, I haven't been there very long. I can find out. I think I've got some thumbscrews in my desk drawer.'

'Thanks,' I said. 'And if Jim knows of any other reason for not bringing applications to light, that would be helpful too.'

'Like what?'

'Well, sleepy little town or not, I don't suppose backhanders are entirely unknown. Can we get something on the planning officer? Don't minute that Daisy.' She looked up and I saw her delete a few words on her laptop. 'Do we know what his name is?' I asked Jeremy.

'Not a he, as it happens,' he said, and then, as if he thought I might be aware of a third gender, which I suppose in these sexually blurred times was possible, 'It's a she.'

'It's a she? That's confusing,' said Banjo, scratching his head and edging back to the kitchen for a further refill.

'Her name,' continued Jeremy, before pausing in the

manner of a particularly dull game-show host, 'is Felicity Hardy-Hewitt, or should I say Lady Felicity.' There was an even longer pause whilst that sank in.

'Whoa, hang on a goshdarn second,' said Mallory eventually, sounding like a bad actor in a cowboy movie. 'Hardy-Hewitt? You've just said that's the Hon Jonty's name. Are we talking even more crowded birth canal here?'

Jeremy pursed his lips slightly, the discussion taking a more risqué turn than he was comfortable with. 'Indeed, you're correct up to a point, Miss Fillery. Lady Felicity is indeed the squire's sister. His younger sister.' She would have had to be younger, I thought. If she was Jonty's older sister she'd be so far past retirement age that even Stockford Council wouldn't employ her. Still, it seemed a mundane sort of job for the daughter of an earl.

'Something else for me to lay before Jonty,' I said. 'I think we're beginning to see a pattern here.'

'Don't go in with all guns blazing, Sam,' said Jeremy. 'If you start throwing wild accusations about in front of witnesses, even if it's only Beatrice Balthazar, you could find yourself in trouble.'

'As if,' I said. 'Anything else, Jeremy?'

'One other thing. I have an appointment to see our Member of Parliament on Monday.'

'What? Old Digby? You never have? Didn't know he still did surgeries.' In truth, Stockford's MP for the past quarter-century, Sir Bartholomew Digby, was so rarely seen in public that there was a school of opinion that suggested he had expired sometime during the three years since the last election but that no one had noticed. In this neck of the woods, an ostrich wearing a blue rosette would be elected almost unopposed. And to considerably more effect than Digby.

'He doesn't. His agent conducts the surgeries on his behalf these days on account of Sir Bartholomew's gout. He doesn't leave home much now. I believe he has a proxy vote in the House. No, I'm visiting Stockford Castle itself. I have an invitation to elevenses.' Jeremy had genuinely used the word "elevenses" there; I hadn't misheard. 'Sir Bartholomew is on the board of my, er, company, so we are acquainted professionally.'

I wasn't sure exactly what help a gout-ridden, seventy-something-year-old nonentity like Sir Bartholomew Digby would be in the fight to save The Farts, but it couldn't do any harm. 'So,' I said, hoping we could bring the meeting to a close before Banjo had drunk all my beer stocks, 'Jeremy will talk to old Digby, I'll talk – politely – to Jonty, and Mallory will get something in next Wednesday's *Spectacle*. Meanwhile, I've started an InnKeeper Facebook page and Instagram and X-stroke-Twitter accounts, so we need as many likes and followers as possible.' We currently had two of each, me and Daisy, but it was a start. 'Mallory and Banjo are going to have a rootle around in The Farts for the key to the door. Just one other thing. The Banker's house, next to the pub. We think there's a possibility he might be involved but as far as I'm aware he's not there at the moment.'

'Surprise, surprise,' said Banjo. 'Hey. Miss Fillery and I can do his gaff when we've done The Farts.' Mallory looked alarmed, as the Banker's thatched mansion would also be.

'I don't think that's necessary,' I said. 'But it would be helpful to know who he is. Jeremy? Any thoughts?' Mallory had already promised to see what she could discover but two pairs of eyes were better than one.

'Oh, yes, Sam,' he said. 'I think I can find that out. May I suggest we all get on with what we have to do and arrange another meeting for, say, Sunday morning? In case there's anything we come up with that I can put before Sir Bartholomew on Monday.'

'As long as we're finished by opening time,' said Banjo. 'There's the big Fleece v Trout grudge Bobbins match startin' at twelve.'

13
FRIDAY 19TH JULY
LIME TREES AND BROWN BROGUES

Squire Jonty lived in The Manor. Well, of course he did. I'd tried Balthazar's first, eleven o'clock Friday morning, when Jonty was in the habit of sitting at his usual table drinking his usual builder's tea and reading the inevitable *Telegraph*, a newspaper so old-fashioned it had yet to reduce its tablecloth-sized pages to manageable proportions. Heaven help you if happened to be walking past his table with a hot drink in your hand when he was turning a page.

Anyway, Jonty wasn't there today. Mrs Bee hadn't seen him. 'He doesn't come in **every** day, Sam,' she said.

'Yes he does. Never misses,' I replied. 'He single-handedly keeps the toasted teacake industry alive.'

'Costs me a fortune in teabags though,' she complained. 'I have to put six in every pot or he moans. Anyway, you're right, he does come in every day, not weekends though.'

'It's only Friday,' I said. 'Not quite the weekend, although I've found more and more supposedly working people seem to treat it as such. Doubt if there's a solicitor in the country who doesn't play golf on a Friday.'

'Are **you** working today, Sam?' she asked disingenuously. 'Cappuccino was it?'

'*Touché*. And no, no coffee today, thanks. I do have to get on with some work as it happens but I also have to talk to Jonty. I'll toddle up to The Manor. I can get a cup of something there.'

'Don't hold your breath,' she said. 'There's a reason why he always comes here. Since Mrs Jonty passed away, I'm not sure if he's worked out how to boil a kettle.'

So The Manor it was, after I'd collected a twelve pack of local ale from Balthazar's to replenish my Banjo-attacked supplies and dropped them at the cottage. I'd sort of hoped that Mallory might still be with me this morning but she'd scooted off back to Stockford after last night's meeting. I guess she too had work to do and, in any case, there were things we were keeping from each other. In particular, her father. Sooner or later, I'd have to bring up the subject of Harrison Makepeace Stamp, even if she didn't, and as yet I wasn't sure how. Maybe I'd come up with something by the next InnKeeper meeting on Sunday morning.

The Manor was the biggest property in the village and, apart from the arguably non-existent Roman settlement, Asinusorum, the oldest. It also had the longest drive, a good hundred yards of it, flanked by two avenues of lime trees. Looking at the beautifully tended gardens, replete with colourful flower beds, luxuriant rhododendron bushes and immaculate lawns, it was clear that Jonty employed not just one, but a whole team of gardeners, even if he didn't have anybody who could boil a kettle for him. I wondered how he ate. Man cannot live on toasted teacakes alone.

Anyway, there were no gardeners in evidence this morning. No cheerful whistling of the honest working man, no gentle whooshing of sprinklers keeping the parched grass as green as possible. Just the birdsong from the lime trees and the copse of mature oaks and beeches lurking in the middle distance. The Manor was situated in the exact centre of the village, its lion-rampant-topped, pillared gates opening onto the Stockford Road just north of the Market Square. From without, it was impossible to see how its mass, surrounded by five acres of gardens and woodland, could be squeezed into the available space. It was like a stone-built Tardis.

Idleborough had a number of houses like that, smaller than The Manor admittedly, but whose grounds, hidden behind high stone walls, were often unfeasibly substantial. Once a year, on the May Bank Holiday, a Traditional Morris Dancing Festival descended on the village, including groups from all over the country, not to mention one from Norway, who were only traditional in a Morris Dancing way if traditional included the wearing of horned helmets. During the festival, many of the larger gardens of Hidden Idleborough were opened up as performance areas for the dozen or so troupes as they wended their way around the village; it was an opportunity for the great unwashed masses to have a good nose around as they followed the dancers from house to house. (And, it must be said, pub to pub, so that by the end of the afternoon, most of the village, including the Morris Dancers themselves, were rather the worse for wear. There had been one memorable performance when a twelve-strong troupe from Little Spliffing ten miles over the border in Gloucestershire had fallen en masse over a wall and into the Stockford Road eight feet below as they reached the climax of their dance. Six broken bones and two concussions had resulted.)

I reached the magnificent, solid oak, double door of The Manor eventually, and rang the bell. This wasn't as straightforward as you might imagine, involving as it did grasping the thick iron hoop at the foot of a weighty chain which disappeared into the stonework above the door, and tugging hard. The bell pull had been known to hoist small children off their feet and, on one occasion a female, temporary postal worker, but today, as I'd used it before and was aware of its power, I remained earthbound and heard the distant, muffled tolling of a bell deep within the interior of the house.

However, nobody came to the door. I decided my shoulder wasn't up to another pull of the bell-chain and tried peering through the window to one side but as it was constructed of tiny, multicoloured glass triangles, this was wholly unsuccessful. I took out my phone and tried ringing Jonty's number but there was no reply and eventually his patrician-sounding voicemail kicked in. So I wandered off round the side of the massive house in search of life. It seemed unlikely that Jonty was out. As he wasn't in the village itself, and as his car, a maroon Bentley that bore a remarkable resemblance to the one owned by the King, was parked to one side of the sweep of gravel behind me, it was hard to see where else he could be.

There were some French windows towards the rear of the southward-facing side of the building. I peered through them, shielding my eyes against the glare of sunlight, but the chintzy drawing room inside was empty. All remained still apart from the chirruping of the birds. Not being on a main road, or indeed any road that led anywhere much apart from Stockford, Idleborough was usually blessed with a blanketing silence. It was one of the main attractions of the place. I continued round to the rear, through a gate in a wall that turned out to surround a flourishing kitchen garden. More evidence of the employment of a gardener or two. There was a rear door into the house from the kitchen garden, green, in need of a lick of paint and evidently servants for the use of. I didn't consider myself to be a servant although Squire Jonty always gave the impression that he believed everybody in the village fell into that category. I tried the handle and it turned. Servant or not, I went through the door, which opened into a dim room containing sinks and cupboards; a scullery or garden room I supposed. There were gardening implements hung on hooks along one roughly painted wall. I thought about calling out for Jonty but it didn't feel like I was in a part of the building he would frequent very often, so I crossed the room and through a door on the far side into a passageway that looked like it led in a more Upstairserly direction away from the servants' quarters.

I found a kitchen proper, all shiny metal and spick and span surfaces, either hardly ever used or used by the tidiest culinary professional in the county. Then a dining room, dark red walls above a dado-rail (or "dildo-rail" as Banjo insisted on calling it). Like the kitchen, it too was empty. I called out now: 'Jonty!' as I didn't want to risk being shot as an intruder, which seemed a very Jonty-like thing to do. My voice echoed down the passage, which had now widened into a hall hung with pictures of extremely ugly people who could have been Hardy-Hewitts through the ages, although I presumed that both the Earl of Northavon and Viscount Uppingshott would have the most expensive and attractive of the family collection in their own country seats.

The next door I tried led into the largest study I had ever seen. Walls lined with leather-bound books that appeared untouched, unloved and unread for tens of years, and a huge dark-wood desk backing onto a window looking out on a stretch of water too big to be called a pond, although I had not been aware that there was a lake at The Manor. Maybe a fishing lake; maybe a fishing lake dug without planning permission, which sort of brought me back to the matter in hand.

Something else that brought me back to the matter in hand was that the room was not empty. Squire Jonty was there, not sitting at his billiard-table-sized desk but lying behind it. I could see a pair of brown brogues topped by some garish Paisley-patterned socks poking out from where one might expect a chair to be. As I doubted that this was where Jonty took naps at eleven thirty on a Friday morning, it could only be bad news. 'Shit,' I muttered and hurried round the desk.

It was indeed bad news, the worst. I momentarily thought what a shame it was that Mallory was not with me. Reporters might kill to come across a murder victim. Bad choice of words, but that Jonty was indeed the victim of a murder seemed in little doubt. I hadn't been able to see a chair because it was on its side behind the desk, resting on what was left of the squire's head. It was a big, heavy chair, much bigger and heavier than the head it had been used to pummel. Whoever had done this had to possess some serious strength. I felt for a pulse but knew from the amount of blood and the stone-cold skin that I was wasting my time. I stood up, feeling slightly dizzy and struggling to keep my breakfast down, and dialled 999.

14
FRIDAY 19TH JULY
WIVES AND KEYS

'Cat got your tongue, Princess?' It was the call I'd been dreading. God knows what time it was back in Toronto; the old man never did keep what you might call regular hours. If my phone was to be believed, it was coming up to five in the morning here; even the local bird population was only just beginning to clear its collective throat. I tried to work out the time difference whilst willing myself to get my brain in gear for the awkward conversation that was only a wheezy pause from continuing. Jeez, it must be about midnight back home: Pop'd be on his second brandy, I guessed, or more likely, second to last brandy.

'Good to hear from you, father dear,' I managed eventually, hoping that the wheezing I could still hear down the line might signal something terminal and not just a normal midweek surfeit of alcohol and cigar smoke. 'How's little Maddy? Getting a bit close to her sell-by date, I'd've thought.' I always tried to get something like that in early in a conversation. Nothing was guaranteed to rile the old bastard more, not that he sounded as if he could get much more riled than he already was. Madeline, a sweet, blushing bride of nineteen when she became the third Mrs

Stamp, was now a less than sweet thirty-nine, and beginning to show the first symptoms of wanting away with half the remaining billions. My own dear mama, Mary-Lou, now living it up in Cannes, was a previous beneficiary and certainly hadn't been too upset to be thrown over in favour of the pubescent Maddy. Before Mary-Lou, there was of course the first, the original, the wife who'd married Pop for love, not money, hard as that was to believe from this far distant. Her name had been Elizabeth but she was no longer living it up anywhere, unfortunately. The circumstances of her death were still unclear. Suicide, accident, nobody knew for certain, but a bath, a hairdryer and a wet bathroom floor had all borne witness to her demise.

Pop brushed off the barb. 'She's in bed, getting her beauty sleep.'

'I'm jealous. That's exactly what I was doing until your unwelcome call.'

'Shoulda thought o' that before not phoning me first,' he said. *Convoluted language like that kept his employees on their toes, or at least, those he deigned to talk to. Most of his 10,000 strong team of cursed minions were lucky that they never got to meet the old goat at all.* 'I seem to recall I gave you a job to do, young lady, a job that should've been within even your limited capabilities. You not managed to tear yourself out of some dingy, local bar long enough to get yourself to Idleberg yet?'

That was rich, coming from him. Lucky for Pop that he owned a distillery, or maybe it was just foresight. 'Been, gone, come back, nothing to see, less to report,' I said in as withering a voice as I could muster at 5.05 in the morning. 'You may need to be more specific.'

'Thought you were a reporter,' he said. 'Oh, no, my mistake, you're not, you're the up-and-coming fashion queen, aren't you? Oh, no, second mistake, you're not that either. I **was** specific. How much more specific do you want? Not simple enough for *you? Words don't come in less than one syllable. This bar or whatever they call it over there, The Three Pigeons. Did you go?'*

'Yes, I went.'

'And?'

'And nothing. It's closed. I met some people who don't want it closed. That's all.'

'So you just got your pretty little ass in your pretty little automobile and went and looked at its pretty little outside, did you, Princess?' "Pretty little outside?" He'd obviously never seen a picture of The Farts. 'You need to get back over there, today – not tomorrow, not next week: today – shift your ass inside,' (apparently the prettiness of my ass was no longer of any consideration) 'and find what I need.'

'And that is? I don't recall anything in particular from our last friendly chat, less-than-one-syllable or not.'

'A Key.' He pronounced it with a capital K.

'Well, if you'd said, I'd have rounded up every key in the place. Anything special about this particular one?'

So he told me. And that was going to be very helpful indeed. Whether to him or to Sam and his pals, I hadn't yet decided. Money talks but so does the heart. It was interesting that the old bugger hadn't mentioned anything about a letter though.

'NICE MOTOR,' said Banjo, extinguishing a cigarette against the mottled, off-white wall of The Farts as I drew up. 'Goes with your hair.'

'Only in the same way your face goes with the wall of this building,' I replied, deadpan, hopping out and considering whether to put the roof of the Jaguar up. On the face of it, Idleborough was a safe enough place but I'd met too many of the locals to be entirely confident that the car would still be there, with or without wheels, on our return from our little burgling *jaunt.* However, Banjo was already leading the way down the side passage of The Farts, past the strange dogleg and into the garden.

'Where's this window, then?' he said, standing about four feet from it.

'Eyesight not so good, Timothy?' I said. 'You're not going to be a fat lot of use inside if you can't see anything.'

'Hey, less of the Timothys, lady,' he said, sounding genuinely upset. 'Banjo, if you don't mind, Tim at a push. Only my ma calls me Timothy and she's dead.'

I realised I was still letting off some residual steam following my conversation with Pop earlier. 'I'm sorry, Banjo,' I said. 'That was uncalled for. Here's the window. Can you give me a shimmy up?' I thought the offer might make up for my rudeness and I was right, although he'd have got a kick in the face if his hand had remained on my right buttock during the shimmying two seconds longer.

Anyway, once we were both inside, I searched for and found a light-switch. It may have been bright, midsummer sunlight outside but it hardly penetrated the interior through the dingy windows. 'What you doing?' asked Banjo, pushing past me to flick the switch off again. 'We don't want the world to know we're here. I've got a torch.' He held it up; it was very small and, switched on, hardly made any difference to the gloom.

'I doubt if the world is going to be interested if they see a light on,' I said, 'and we're in for a long haul if we have to rely on that feeble thing. Especially if we're forced to stay together, what with only having the one flashlight. No, sorry, Banjo, we need illumination. Remember, we're looking for a small key, a what-do-you-call it? Yale?' Why the Brits named their keys after US universities I had no idea, but that was what Sam had said. I turned the light on again. 'Let's split up. I'll take down here, you do upstairs.' I thought the keys were more likely to be on the *ground floor, in the kitchen or one of the bars, and I reckoned that, being a woman, I'd be more likely to spot them than Banjo. I knew all about man-looking, the sort of looking that doesn't involve opening things or moving stuff.*

'OK, makes sense,' said Banjo. 'I'll start in the cellar, then.'

'In what possible universe is the cellar going to be upstairs? No, we'll do the cellar last. If we've found the keys, I'll allow you one drink from whatever stock's left down there. If we haven't, we keep searching.'

In the event, it was Banjo who found the key. Well, between us we found about a dozen keys of one kind or another but only one that looked likely to match the lock in the photo of the door that Sam had taken and which I had in my jeans pocket. No wraparound skirt today; foresight had told me that climbing through the window in a skirt with Banjo in close attendance might be more than he could bear. The key, inscribed with the word Yale, was hung on an Oxford United Football Club keyring.

'Where did you find it?' I asked as Banjo, following my earlier invitation, headed towards the cellar steps.

'There was some old trunk under Clem's bed,' he said. 'Seemed an obvious sort of place to look, if you ask me.'

I wasn't embarrassed by the fact that Banjo and not me had found the key, but I was that he'd found it in the same trunk in which I'd discovered the letter. I hadn't been looking for keys at the time of course. Mind you, I hadn't been looking for letters either but having come across Clem's carbon-copy, I'd not delved any deeper. I guess I needed a bit more reporter training.

'So, are we planning to see if it fits?' asked Banjo, closely examining one of a half-dozen metal barrels laid horizontally on a wall-length rack at the back of the cellar. A pint glass had appeared as if by magic in his hand and he started to fill it from the barrel.

'Not now,' I said. 'Sam needs to be involved, and in any case neither of us knows exactly where the damn door is. If it's past all the prickles at the back of the car park as he says, we're going to need something to clear a path first.' In any case, Banjo had by now settled himself on a rickety old wooden chair, was already halfway through his pint of beer and didn't look as if he'd welcome any interruption to go door-hunting. 'I think I'll go find him. Are you coming?'

'Laters,' he said, finishing his beer. I couldn't see the attraction myself. It was a warm-looking, dark, syrupy brown. As far as I'm concerned, beer is pale and cold, the paler and colder the better. 'I'll lock up,' he added, grinning and refilling his glass.

LEAVING Banjo to complete his one-man attempt at preventing The Farts' beer supplies from going off, I let myself back out of the window and into the sunshine of the pub's unattractive garden. I wandered across to the impenetrable tangle of vicious-looking bushes and nettles that marked the rear boundary. What lay behind was as impossible to determine as it had been yesterday from the other side of the Idlebrook. I couldn't work out how Sam had managed to gain access to the land but no doubt he'd be happy to show me now that we'd obtained the key. I was sure he'd want to test it out as soon as possible, so tried calling him. He didn't pick up and after a while his voicemail kicked in, so I left a message. Presumably, he was still giving the squire the third degree. I'd never been too certain which degree was the third, although I was fairly sure Diana Ross was the first.

Out front, I was relieved to see the Jaguar still in possession of all its wheels. It had taken a goodly chunk of Pop's allowance to buy the thing and I loved it, although it had been of limited use back in Notting Hill. Out here though, driving it around the neighbouring Cotswolds on my days off had been an unadulter-

ated pleasure. I could try and convince myself that giving it up in the event that the allowance ran dry would be no great hardship, but heck, who was I kidding?

As no harm had come to it, I decided to risk leaving it where it was and walk the couple of hundred yards to the Market Square and the café which Sam had told me about at the rear of the oddly-named village shop. I thought I might find Sam and Squire Jonty engaged in less than idle chitchat, but in any case, it was coming up for lunchtime and I was getting peckish. Another salmon salad at The Trout held its attractions but two in two days might be overdoing it, and I didn't want to run the gauntlet of Pirate Pete, nor eat alone in the pub garden in case Billy the Kid should wander back in for another gander.

I'd hardly taken two steps when I heard the wailing of emergency sirens approaching at speed from my rear. A few seconds later, two police cars roared past and disappeared around the Square heading towards Stockford. From the fact that I could still hear the sirens ten seconds later, albeit muffled, I deduced that wherever they were going it was somewhere within the village. I wasn't the only person taking an interest. The previously deserted stretch of High Street was suddenly awash with curious locals. As the district reporter for the Spectacle, *I felt I should take a professional interest and so, suppressing my need for lunch, I cut across the Square and headed off in pursuit of the still audible sirens. As I reached the Stockford Road at the point it left the Square on its northern side, the noise abruptly stopped and, turning the corner, I could see no sign of the police cars. However, help was at hand. I recognised the scruffy bulk of Mucker, plainly no worse for his unintended dip in the stream yesterday, standing on the pavement outside yet another pub, The Bull, with someone else, pints of dark brown beer in hand.*

'Hey, Mucker,' I called across. He looked up. 'It's me, Mallory,' I continued. 'We, ah, met yesterday?'

'Ah, yes, me booty, I remembers. How couldem forget? Lovely to see youm.' He sounded quite sober if a little over-chivalrous. I guessed it was early into the current drinking session.

'Did you see where the cop cars went?' I asked.

'Yes'm,' he said. *'Just up there on the right. They'ms in Manor.'* He paused. *'Squire's house.'* Another pause. *'They'm an ambulance too.'*

15
FRIDAY 19TH JULY
POLICE AND TWINS

After calling in the discovery of Jonty's body and waiting around for the police and ambulance, I'd had to go to Stockford nick to make a statement and, all in all, it had taken quite a while, especially as halfway through my interview, none other than Viscount Uppingshott had bounced in alongside his sister, Lady Felicity Hardy-Hewitt, Chief Planning Officer for Stockford District Council. I'd recognised the viscount at once as he was Jonty's twin and the likeness was remarkable. And the woman with him could only have been Lady Felicity who, although a few years younger than her brothers, possessed a similar set of features. They didn't sit as well on her as on them.

I was left alone in the interview room for nearly half-an-hour whilst the requisite amount of bowing and scraping was carried out in an undoubtedly plusher part of the station. Then, the door was thrust open and Viscount Uppingshott marched in with a harassed-looking police-woman in close attendance.

'You're Bryant,' he said belligerently. It wasn't a question. 'You found my brother's body.' Another non-question, but I answered it anyway.

'Yes, er, your Grace, sir,' I said. I wasn't sure what the correct form of address to a viscount might be so was trying to cover all the bases.

'I'm not a bloody bishop, you fool,' he responded. Too many bases then. 'You knew him, I understand.'

'Everyone in the village knew him. He was the squire.'

'Harrumph. Squire indeed. Poppycock.' The viscount was beginning to sound like an extra in a Wodehouse story. 'Did you notice anything odd?'

'What, apart from the fact that he'd been bashed on the head with a chair?' Not the most diplomatic answer, but Uppingshott's rudeness was beginning to piss me off.

'No, young man, I meant his appearance. Clothes for example. Was there anything unusual about his clothes? What about his face? Or his hair?'

What the hell was he talking about? Jonty's hair had only looked odd because it was covered in blood. And I'd hardly noticed his clothes, my attention being more taken up by the blood, together with the overall deadness of the squire. I'm not sure whether I'd have noticed if he'd been wearing pyjamas. However, before I could come up with a suitable, non-rude reply, Lady Felicity walked in.

'There you are, Rupert,' she said. 'We must go. Father's just called.' She hadn't given any indication that she was aware of my presence but then she turned to me and said, 'Mr Bryant, I wonder if you would be good enough to call upon me at my office in the Town Hall on Monday morning? Shall we say nine o'clock? Excellent.' She turned and walked out, followed closely by the viscount, still harrumphing. I'd never actually heard anybody harrumph before, not even Squire Jonty. I guessed there was a level in Debrett's you had to reach before you were permitted to give it a go.

Leaving the police station, I noticed that Mallory had left several messages on my phone. The first was to say that she and Banjo had found what looked like the key to the door in the woods. Somehow that didn't seem so important any more. By the time I'd listened to the last message, it was clear that news of Jonty's sad demise had spread. I called her back and told her that I was the one who'd found the body.

'I guess it'll push the closure of The Farts off the front page of Wednesday's *Spectacle*,' I said. It turned out she'd already rung her editor, an old bloke called Jim Simkins, but not even the likely murder of a local dignitary had been enough to get him out of his back garden on a sunny Friday afternoon.

'He said we could write something up together on Monday,' she said. 'I can see where this is going. I'll do the work and Jim'll stick his name on the piece.'

It sounded like she needed cheering up and, as we were both in Stockford, I volunteered to be cheerleader. However, she turned me down. 'Thanks, Sam,' she said, 'but I'm gonna write a preliminary draft for Jim and then catch an early night. Perhaps I could come over tomorrow and we could try the key.'

'Tomorrow's a bit difficult,' I said. Tomorrow, Saturday, was the day of Idleborough's annual cricket match with Stockford, our biggest game of the season. At this point, following Jonty's murder, I wasn't sure if it would be going ahead but whether or not it did, there was no harm waiting another twenty-four hours where the door was concerned.

I suggested we could see if the key fitted before the next meeting of InnKeeper on Sunday morning.

'OK,' she said and suggested that, as she was responsible for sub-editing the cricket reports in the Spectacle, she might turn up and watch if the match did take place. I promised to let her know.

16

SATURDAY 20TH JULY
SAUSAGES AND BLACK ARMBANDS

Saturday dawned bright and sunny with a light haze over the fields beyond the ford at the end of my lane. No surprise there with the present warm, dry spell into its fourth week. Under normal circumstances I'd have been cheering from the rooftops. Because today was Saturday, and not just any Saturday but the day of the village's annual cricketing grudgefest with our old sparring partners, Stockford.

As Chairman of Idleborough Cricket Club, it was down to me to decide whether the game should go ahead following the death of Squire Jonty, who held the purely honorary position of Club President. This basically involved him putting a hundred quid behind the bar at the club's annual dinner and then drinking most of it himself. I couldn't remember when he'd last been seen attending an actual match. I also couldn't remember exactly when he'd been made President; in fact, there was a widespread suspicion that he'd proposed and seconded himself for the then non-existent post about a quarter of a century ago. It could not be put off much longer. People had lives to get on with, particularly those players with families. One of those was my next-door neighbour, Bob Baker the butcher, who knocked on my kitchen window and pushed open my back door as I was debating whether or not to pick up the phone and call Stewart Stewart.

'Do we still need the sausages, Sam?' Bob asked. Bob's sausages, made to a secret recipe handed down over the generations from Baker to Baker, were renowned as far afield as Gloucestershire and Wiltshire and, frankly, were the main reason why so many clubs were still happy to visit Idleborough; it manifestly wasn't for the quality of the cricket or the state of the outfield. No, a combination of Baker's sausages and Beatrice Balthazar's home-made cakes made the Idleborough cricket teas the talk of the league. Even Stewart Stewart, the previous evening, had cited them as an important reason not to cancel the match.

'I don't know, Bob,' I said, pouring him a coffee. 'What do you think?' He hadn't been in The Bull last night so his opinion was unknown.

'I think they need eating,' he said, 'and I know Beatrice was halfway through baking the cakes before the news of Jonty's death.' He paused. 'All in all, I think we should play the match. The food's got to be eaten and you could always say a few words about the squire at tea-time. You know, a sort of tribute.' That might be difficult, I thought, unsure how many complimentary remarks I could come up with. 'Anyway, practically speaking, we need the points.' That was undoubtedly true, however unlikely it was that we would get them against Stockford and their new Jamaican fast bowler. We were currently bottom of the league and would be staring relegation in the face if such a thing existed. As the West Oxonian Village League comprised only one division of fourteen teams, there was, luckily for us, nowhere to be relegated to, although Sharon Handcock's all-girl Granny's Bobbins team, the Trout Treacles, had offered to give us a good going over if the worst came to the worst and we were thrown out of the league. As their star player was the Codmother, it wasn't a going over that many of us relished.

But Bob was right. We should play the match. We couldn't let the glorious weather and even more glorious sausages and cakes go to waste. And you never knew, miracles might happen. Everyone remembered the famous victory over Little Spliffing twenty years ago, when an unlikely last wicket pairing of Clem and Percy Pocock had knocked off fifty runs between them in four overs. It could happen again, although Clem was in Benidorm (although that had yet to be confirmed) and the match in question had been Percy's last; he had after all been several years past his non-existent prime even then.

When Bob had gone, I went out and pinned a notice on the board in the square announcing that the match was on and that there would be a Memorial Tea for Squire Jonty with a minute's silence between innings. I'd first phoned Stewart Stewart, who sounded surprised but pleased. 'Excellent news, Sam,' he drawled. 'My boys are champing at the bit, particularly Curtley.'

'Curtley?' I asked.

'Curtley Hendrix, lovely lad, built like a brick shithouse. Been dying to have a bowl on your wicket.' This would be the Jamaican fast bowler, I guessed. 'Took a six-fer last week against Mudhampton and broke their skipper's nose. Wicket was a shirt-front too.' The implication being that the pitch at the Rec is anything but a shirt-front. Strangely, I couldn't remember reading about Curtley's wickets in this week's *Spectacle*, but I let it go. Mallory may have had to cut chunks of the match report.

I called in at the hardware shop where its proprietor, Mavis Tingle, seventy-plus, iron-grey hair, shiny-faced and wearing a razzle-dazzle ensemble that Helena Bonham-Carter would have rejected, was as ever sitting behind the counter, knitting. 'Have you by any chance got some black material of any kind, Mavis, silk perhaps?' I asked. 'I need enough to make some armbands for the cricketers this afternoon.'

Mavis looked up. 'I don't think so, Sam,' she said. This was her standard response to all requests, even if the items asked for were clearly visible on the shelves. I knew that hardware shops don't as a rule sell silk or indeed any sort of material, except dishcloths and tea towels, but Mavis's was a hardware shop like no other. So I had a quick look around and, whilst I didn't find anything an actual haberdashers might stock, I did discover two old academic gowns hanging up at the rear in her "clothing department", which apart from the gowns contained nothing but various items of apparel knitted by Mavis herself. I took the gowns to Mavis who, as well as being a knitter of extraordinary output, was also a dab hand with a sewing machine.

'Do you think you could run up twenty-four armbands from these by one o'clock, please Mavis?'

She put down her knitting and took the gowns from me. 'Of course, Sam,' she said. 'Happy to help. I wasn't sure if you'd be playing this afternoon in the circumstances. Give me a fiver for the gowns and I'll do the bands for free. Squire and I went back a long way, if you know what I mean.' And, extraordinarily, she winked. 'You give those toffee-nosed buggers from Stockford a good seeing-to for both of us, won't you? Pick them up on your way to the game.'

I thanked her and left, trying not to think too hard about Mavis and Jonty having enjoyed a shared history. You learn something new and faintly disquieting every day, I reflected, my insides squirming slightly.

17

SATURDAY 20TH JULY
ABSENTEES AND ACCIDENTS

'Anyone seen Banjo?' I asked, counting heads, of which there were ten, including mine.

Under normal circumstances, Banjo's absence wouldn't have been a disaster as he was arguably the worst cricketer ever to pull on whites. He would in fact have been more effective if he used his banjo rather than an actual cricket bat. But against Stockford, today in particular, we needed eleven men and what Banjo lacked in cricketing ability, he more than made up for with his expertise in getting under the skin of the opposition. He was, not to put too fine a point on it, renowned throughout the West Oxonian League as the king of the sledgers.

He wasn't answering his phone. I looked for and found Billy who, although not a player, was as usual lurking around. I sent him off to find Banjo and turned my attention to the rest of the team. 'Right, guys,' I said, handing out the black armbands. 'This one's for the squire.'

Adrian Featherstone looked doubtful. 'I'm not sure we should be playing, Sam,' he said. 'It doesn't seem right.' Rarely a week went by that Adrian didn't express doubts about the wisdom of playing, or at least the wisdom of him playing. These were doubts we knew had been sown rather more forcefully a little earlier by his wife, Sally, aka The Shrew, in their picture-postcard cottage at the far end of the village. Either one of the children had a cough, or Adrian's mother-in-law was staying, or the nursery needed painting, or the weekly shop was overdue. Doubts like that. The rest of us ran a sweepstake on which excuse Adrian would come up with each week. Unfortunately, the squire's death had come too late to make it into this week's sweepstake so nobody would be going home with the weekly tenner. We were lucky to get six games a summer out of Adrian and, as he was comfortably our best batsman, I was only glad that he'd turned up for this match.

'It's what he would have wanted,' I said.

'I wouldn't have thought so,' said Postman Pat. 'The squire never knew if there was a game on at all.'

Several of us wandered out to inspect the wicket, a ritual undertaken by every village team since the dawn of time, although none of us had the slightest idea what we were inspecting. The wicket at the Rec was mainly green despite the hot weather. Where it wasn't green, it was brown, in random patches that suggested the local bird population had made off with beakfuls of grass seed soon after it was laid. The grass could have benefitted from an extra cut or five. I bent down to get a closer look and squinted up the pitch, hoping that, by some miracle, it had suddenly become flat. It hadn't. We possessed a roller but as it could be lifted comfortably by two men it wasn't especially effective when put to work doing the job for which it had presumably been designed. Pat squatted down alongside me and asked the same question he asked every week.

'What do you reckon then, Sam? Have a bowl?' It was a

no-brainer. Whilst virtually every other team in the country would be praying for their skippers to win the toss so they could put their feet up in the pavilion in the heat, Idleborough's only real chance of winning cricket matches was to suffer potential sunstroke by inviting the opposition to take first use of the uneven wicket. Ten years ago, the Rec had been one of Farmer Trickle's fields and Red Herefords had roamed freely over what was now our pitch.

At this point, half a dozen cars, mostly high-end Range Rovers and Beamers, pulled into the car park and Stockford's players emerged, stretching and pulling out kit bags. Not so much kit bags as unnecessarily huge, foursquare, black "coffins", which the rest of the West Oxonian league clubs considered way over the top and more than a little pretentious. At Idleborough, the coffins would have to be left outside as there was no room for them in our tiny pavilion. Stewart Stewart, wearing burgundy cords despite the heat, strolled over to our little group clustered on the square. He was accompanied by one of the biggest, darkest, most athletic looking men I had ever seen, at least in this part of Oxfordshire. This would be Curtley Hendrix, I surmised. If he was as fast as he looked, it could be a short afternoon, which would at least improve Big Brian's bar takings in The Bull later.

'Afternoon, Sam, Pat,' said Stewart, extending his hand. 'Sad times indeed.' He almost looked as if he meant it.

'Stewart,' I said, shaking his hand and holding out eleven black armbands. 'We had these made up.'

'Of course,' said Stewart. 'Excellent idea. Only right.' He turned to Pat, whose usual cheery countenance had turned dark red at the sight of his old adversary. 'Ready to toss up, Patrick?' Pat hated being called Patrick, which Stewart knew full-well. Showing a remarkable level of self-restraint, Pat grunted and they moved a few steps away to conduct the ritual of the toss. It **was** purely a ritual as well. If Pat won it, Stockford would bat first and if Stewart won it Stockford would also bat first on a lovely day like this, dodgy pitch or not.

I turned to the giant next to me and held out my hand. 'Hi,' I said. 'I'm Sam. Welcome to Idleborough. I guess you're Curtley.'

Curtley grasped my hand so tightly I was immediately grateful that I wouldn't have to grip a bat handle for at least a couple of hours. 'Yo, man,' he said. Now I won't lie. I was expecting the voice that emerged from the gigantic Jamaican to be deep. I mean, you know, **really** deep. What I heard instead sounded more like Joe Pasquale. I nearly laughed. I expect I would have done if my hand hadn't been hurting so much. It was a voice that Banjo could have a great deal of fun with, sledging-wise, that is if he ever decided to turn up.

I was distracted by the sound of Stewart drawling the word, 'Heads,' as Pat's "unlucky half-crown" spiralled up into the clear blue sky. It landed silently somewhere in the overlong grass and both Stewart and Pat bent down to peer at it as if expecting it to impart some piece of infinite wisdom. 'Heads it is,' said Stewart, straightening. He glanced across at the rest of us players, nodded in Curtley Hendrix's direction, and smiled wolfishly. 'You know,' he added, before pausing slightly, 'I think we might have a bowl.'

Suddenly my half-crushed hand hurt even more. Luckily it was my right hand, which for a right-handed batter, is far less important than the left. Or at least it should have been, except that like many village cricketers, my go-to shot was the hoick over mid-wicket which requires quite strenuous use of the right hand. No classic cover driver me, unlike Adrian, our leading run scorer, who would have scored a lot more runs had the outfield grass been cut to suit his turf-caressing drives in front of the wicket. I didn't think that Adrian had ever wilfully hit the ball in the air. Most of the rest of us had never wilfully hit the ball along the ground.

I saw a miserable-looking Adrian beginning to strap on his pads inside the pavilion, which we liked to call picturesque, and it may well have been, once – say around the time of the second world war. It had, let's be honest, seen better days. It basically comprised one large room, wooden-floored as well as wooden-everything-elsed, containing benches and clothes hooks for both teams, a giant tea urn on a rickety counter to the rear and a notice directing people towards a less scenic toilet block (no showers) hidden in a small copse a few yards away. The front wall of the pavilion was made up of two floor-to-roof shutters which could be raised with immense difficulty to form a roof over a balcony stretching the length of the structure and on which the batting team and scorers could sit. Alongside Adrian, looking equally unhappy, was his regular opening partner, Morris Clunes. If Adrian had genuine pretensions to being a batter, Morris had none. In nine years of turning out for Idleborough, he had a career-best score of 14 to his name, made in his very first appearance. The fact that he had held down the opening position for over eighty matches since then without once threatening to go past 14 said more about the twin truths that (a) nobody else wanted to open and (b) it was, truthfully, the only position in the order he could be placed, especially as he couldn't bowl. And he had to play somewhere as he was the Club Secretary, another position no one else wanted.

I moved inside to join them and started rummaging in my bag for my pads and gloves. I hadn't needed to check with Pat that I would be at number three; it was yet another position nobody else wanted. And I needed to be ready to go, as Morris had only once survived the first three overs of a match this season.

Whilst I was getting ready, Mallory poked her head inside the pavilion. A little behind her stood Billy, busy staring at her rear, which was encased in a pair of jeans today, despite the ongoing heat. The jeans were pretty tight though, which seemed to be giving Billy at least some satisfaction.

Before I could ask Billy if his hunt for Banjo had been successful, Mallory spoke. 'Billy tells me you sent him off to find Banjo. He says he's not in his apartment and Mrs Balthazar – Balthazar, yes?' I nodded, '– has told him Banjo hasn't been home all night.'

'That's not unusual,' I said.

'Well, OK, if you say so, but I left him in the cellar of The Farts just before lunchtime yesterday and he was already making serious inroads into the beer stocks. I'm guessing he may still be there, sleeping it off.' This wasn't good news but would have been worse had we been fielding. Banjo was due to bat at number eleven. When he headed for the wicket, the rest of us headed for the tea table. 'Billy and I'll go and find him, shall we?' she continued.

'Thanks, Mallory,' I said, smiling. 'You're a star. Be as quick as you can or you might miss seeing me bat.' Suddenly, there was a loud shout from the field of play and Morris Clunes started walking disconsolately back towards the pavilion while the Stockford players began high-fiving each other in the sort of way you might expect if they'd dismissed Joe Root and not the worst opening batter in west Oxfordshire. Adrian had taken a single off the first ball of the match and Morris had been castled by the second; and it hadn't even been a ball bowled by Curtley Hendrix, who was prowling the boundary at fine leg just in front of us. 'Too late,' I said to Mallory, standing up and pulling on my batting gloves. 'You might as well hang around to watch me. I shouldn't be too long and then we can go and find Banjo together.' I smiled ruefully, picked up my bat and headed out into the sunshine.

Stockford's regular opening bowler, Old John Wynne, had taken the first over and it was he who had bowled Morris. He was called Old John as his son, Young John, also played. Old John used to be a decent cricketer – a bowler who was once quite fast but now relied on experience and a slower ball that was hardly any different from his faster ball – whilst Young John would never make a cricketer of any hue, although he was admittedly a step up in quality from Banjo. I was surprised that Stewart had not given the ball to Curtley Hendrix first up, but he could be indulging in mind games. I didn't mind one bit. At least I'd have the chance to face four balls before Curtley could get at me. I usually reckoned four balls were enough to get my eye in.

However, I may have been more distracted by Jonty's death than I'd thought and had hardly moved before Old John's first ball skipped past the edge of my bat and into the wicketkeeper's gloves. 'Too fast for you, Sam?' Old John enquired, advancing down the pitch. Everyone in earshot laughed. Old John hadn't bowled a fast ball for ten years. I smiled at him and said nothing. His next ball pitched a little short and I threw my bat at it, aiming for the skateboard park, where a couple of little oiks were busy adding to the already impressive display of graffiti. However, I hadn't allowed for the fact that it was John's even-slower ball. It caught the inside edge of my bat and shot just past my leg stump and down towards fine leg. I managed a simultaneous silent curse and a sigh of relief and set off for the easy single as Adrian called, 'One.' But then a strange thing happened. Curtley Hendrix, down on the fine leg boundary, bent to pick the ball up as it rolled quite gently towards him, the long grass having slowed its initial progress. He did indeed pick the ball up but instead of hurling it back to the 'keeper, he somehow contrived to throw it over his own shoulder and it hit the wall of the pavilion inches from where Pat was sitting. Pat collected the ball and lobbed it back to Hendrix with all the Idleborough players laughing their socks off. Hendrix put his hands out but missed the ball completely and it thudded into his, shall we say, nether region. It was hardly travelling fast but these things still hurt. The laughter of the Idleborough players was now added to by guffaws from his Stockford teammates. As everybody who has ever played village cricket knows, it is compulsory to laugh when a player gets struck in the balls. Standing open-mouthed in the centre of the pitch, the streakiest of fours to my name, I turned to Stewart Stewart, who, unlike the rest of his team, was scowling. 'Hope he's a better bowler than fielder, Stewart,' I said cheerily. He didn't answer.

I defended Old John's next ball and pushed the last ball of an eventful first over to deepish cover for a leisurely single, leaving me to face the wrath of an embarrassed Curtley Hendrix, who would presumably be steaming in from the pavilion end imminently. 'Just watch every ball, Sam,' said Adrian quietly as we met in the middle. 'No random swinging.' That was like telling a dog not to bark at a cat.

I took a centre guard from Percy Pocock, who was our regular umpire these days, despite having only a cursory understanding of the laws of the game, and looked up. Curtley Hendrix did not appear to have moved from the fine leg boundary (now deep long off), but that nevertheless he did indeed have the ball in his hand and a menacing scowl on his face. Then he set off with a peculiar high-stepping run towards the opposite wicket. It was the longest run up I'd ever seen. Finally, he charged past Percy, his right arm came over and I stared at the little red ball of death as it left his hand. And immediately lost sight of it. The next thing I heard was a sharp cry of pain from somewhere behind me. I turned to see Young John Wynne, who had been fielding at second slip, lying on the ground, while the ball shot away to the third man boundary behind him. Curtley Hendrix was standing in the middle of the pitch looking confused as five Stockford players rushed to help Young John, and the ball rolled over the boundary. Percy signalled four wides to the scorer, Doc Duckett, who, as our local GP, was by now, however, trotting on to the field of play to see if he could assist the injured man.

It turned out that the ball had only struck Young John a glancing blow and the game continued after a few minutes with John sitting in the pavilion holding a bag of ice to his head. Anyway, long story short or, rather, short over long, Curtley Hendrix's first – and as it turned out, only – over lasted a record seventeen minutes. His first five balls went straight to the slip cordon and were called as the widest of wides, and his next two were high full tosses that passed way over my head, which Percy, trying hard not to laugh, called as no balls. Eventually, Hendrix managed to send down six legal, very slow full tosses from a standing start, all of which I hit for four. At the end of the over I yelled across to a crimson-faced Stewart, 'How many wickets did you say he took last week, Stew?'

The 'keeper, a generally friendly bloke called Dave something, muttered, 'Last week? We never seen 'im before. Turned up Monday an' said he was a fast bowler.'

'Well, he's certainly fast,' I said. 'Needs to work on the accuracy a bit though, I'd say.' I looked up to see Pat putting a score of 53 for 1 off two overs onto our elderly scoreboard. I already had 29 to my name.

The innings settled down after that. Young John came back on to patrol the deep midwicket boundary in a slightly concussed sort of way and Curtley Hendrix was moved as far away from the laughter at his expense coming from the pavilion as possible. Inevitably, this being Idleborough playing Stockford, wickets began to fall at distressingly short intervals, starting with Adrian, out for a classy ten, caught behind. Our next three batters, Evans the Brick, Bob Baker and Pat, made about half a dozen between them; Big Brian, in mainly for his bowling, hit two giant sixes before holing out to cow corner and I was joined at number eight by Doc Duckett, who could usually be called on to defend stoutly for a while. 53 for 1 had become 92 for 6 but amazingly I was still there. My excellent start, handed to me on a plate by Curtley Hendrix or not, had given me extra confidence and I'd been defending the good balls and hitting the bad ones more effectively than at any time for about three years. I'd only been dropped twice, which was pretty good going for me.

'You're on 48, Sam,' said Doc as he arrived. 'I'll stay here and you just carry on.' Next ball, I advanced down the wicket to Stockford's fifteen-year-old slow left armer and hit him high and true over the pavilion to reach fifty. This was not something that happened very often, about once every three years in fact, and with Doc as watchful as he'd promised to be at the other end, the score crept up. I'd reached a career-best 75 in the last over of the scheduled forty before my luck ran out and I skied one straight up in the air. Dave, the friendly wicketkeeper took three steps, steadied himself and called 'Mine!' but just as the ball was about to land securely in his gloves, Stewart Stewart, running at the maximum speed his fifteen stone could manage from the direction of cover, arrived at the same spot and also shouted 'Mine!' Both players had their eyes fixed firmly on the ball and the inevitable collision was terrible to behold. There was a collective wince as the two players came together with a noise like thunder. The ball plopped gently to earth.

It appeared I was reprieved, but with Doc Duckett confirming both Stewart and Dave unconscious, an ambulance was called and the remaining players agreed to shake hands on a draw. We had reached 136 for 7, our highest total of the season. It would doubtless still not have been enough for victory, though, what with our best two bowlers being in Spain, so we were more than happy to call it a day.

After the ambulance had departed and I'd managed a few complimentary untruths about Squire Jonty, we took tea on two tables set up under a temporarily erected gazebo next to the pavilion. Despite the two injured fielders, three if you include Young John Wynne, most of the chatter over the sausages and cakes was about Curtley Hendrix. He too had disappeared and the general consensus was that he'd played his first and last match for Stockford.

'What made you think he was a fast bowler?' Pat asked Old John.

'Well, look at the size of him. If he came to you and said he could bowl, you're not going to disagree, are you?'

'Didn't you give him a net to see if he was any good?' Everyone laughed. Whilst Stockford, unlike Idleborough, possessed a proper, practice net, it was considered unsporting in the West Oxonian Village Cricket League to use it once the season was underway. In any case, the holes in Stockford's net were so big that quite large dogs could run unhindered through them.

I was halfway through my second slice of Mrs Bee's Victoria sponge cake before I realised that both Mallory and Banjo were still absent. Banjo hadn't been required as things had turned out, but where was Mallory? Abandoned match or not, she'd missed the knock of my life and, whilst that shouldn't have been important as I'd only known her five days, somehow it was.

'Have you seen Mallory?' I asked Bob Baker, sitting next to me.

'Who's Mallory?' he asked, understandably as he'd never met her.

'Hot redhead,' said Big Brian, sitting opposite, who had somehow managed to acquire four of Bob's sausages and was currently engaged in devouring two of them at once. 'I said, lovely girl, young Sam's latest squeeze, am I right, Sam, or am I right?'

I wasn't quite sure what had given Brian that idea but nothing much got past him. 'Sort of,' I said. 'She was here earlier but went to look for Banjo.'

Anyway, none of the players could remember seeing her leave and Billy, who could have been relied upon to keep his eyes on her, was for once also nowhere to be seen. I got up and fished my phone out of my bag. There was a message from Mallory on it, or at least, part of a message. 'Sam,' it started. Her voice sounded odd. 'You need to get down here fast.' There was a pause and I could hear a second voice, male, in the background, but too indistinct to make out what it was saying. Then, 'Sam,' again from Mallory, followed by, 'No, wait, stop, what the hell...?' Then there was a thump and a muffled bang and the phone cut out.

18

SATURDAY 20TH JULY
ROLLING PINS AND GUNS

I'd been planning to watch Sam's inning, or innings as he called it, even though as far as I could tell, he would only have one; and I had stayed and watched for a little while. He'd been lying when he said he wouldn't be long, though, and after half an hour that felt like three, despite the rest of the Idleborough team walking back and forth to the diamond, or whatever they call it, at increasingly short intervals, Sam stayed resolutely out there. The longer he stayed, the more excited his teammates became, although I didn't know what was getting them so worked up. Frankly, I was bored. Give me baseball any day. Throw ball, hit ball, run. Now **that's** a ball game. This was more throw ball, watch ball, stand still. I just didn't get it. Anyhow, I thought I'd be more useful going back to The Farts to see if Banjo was still there and if not, well, I still had the key and was itching to see if it worked. I reckoned that a resourceful girl like me could find a way past the prickles to get to the door in the woods.

The window of the Gents' was still ajar so I leant in and called out. 'Banjo?' Nothing. I tried again. Still nothing. I was beginning to feel a little foolish, truth be told, shouting through a *toilet window, so I hoisted myself up on to the ledge and pulled myself into the pub, stepping gingerly down from the dirty bathroom basin inside and out into the corridor leading to the bars to my right. The door into the living accommodation in front of me was also open so I called again. Still no reply. Either Banjo had left or he was still sleeping the alcohol off. Was that likely though? It was well over twenty-four hours since I'd left him to it.*

I reached the door leading down to the cellar. It was shut. I distinctly remembered leaving it open when I'd left yesterday, which implied that Banjo was no longer down there. I thought I'd better check though, but the door wouldn't open. After a few seconds of fruitless pushing and pulling, the inescapable conclusion hit me that it was, in fact, locked. And there was no key visible. Not another fucking locked door, I thought, getting seriously pissed now. I stood and thought, and the more I thought, the more nonsensical it became. Banjo wouldn't have locked the door. Even if he'd found a key, why would he? It hadn't been locked yesterday. We'd found a few surplus keys in the hunt for the Yale and I remembered leaving them on a counter in the kitchen. Finding them still there, I collected them and went back to the cellar door to see if any of them fitted. I sort of knew none of them would though. I banged on the door with a rolling pin I'd also found in the kitchen and yelled, 'Banjo!' one last time but there was no reply and no noise apart from a lot of floorboard creaking from under my feet. I wasn't completely convinced I wouldn't fall through the rotten floorboards into the cellar without having need of the door.

I decided to take a look upstairs in the vague possibility of finding Banjo asleep on the bed, but he wasn't there so I concluded that that was me done. I'd go back to the Wreck – strange name for a sports field but entirely in keeping, particularly with the rickety old clubhouse – and see if Sam had finished his game yet. It had been going nearly two hours by now so I reckoned he must have done; no game on earth lasts more than two hours, does it?

I'd started back down the stairs when I heard a noise coming from below. I held my breath. There was movement for sure and it sounded like it was coming from the bar area. I heard a thump which could have been a door slamming, and then the sound of heavy breathing. I took out my phone and dialled Sam, squatting and peering through the banisters halfway down the staircase. After a few seconds Sam's voicemail kicked in and at the same moment an old guy wearing a flat cap and tweed suit despite the weather, walked out of the bar, wiping his hands on a towel, and saw me. Suddenly and with an impressive sleight of hand, the towel was replaced by a small revolver.

'Sam,' I said urgently into the phone, scrabbling to my feet. 'You need to get down here fast.'

'Who the devil are you?' said the old boy, reaching the foot of the stairs. Neither he nor the gun looked especially friendly.

'Sam,' I said again, even more urgently, although I knew it was only his voicemail, goddammit. I turned to get back up the stairs away from the man, although what I was going to do once up there I had no idea. I didn't make it. I slipped on a loose bit of stair carpet and immediately the man was on me, gun raised. 'No, wait, stop, what the hell...?' I managed, before realising I was still holding the rolling pin in my left hand. I threw it awkwardly at the man and somehow managed to hit him straight between the eyes. Don't ask me how. As the rolling pin struck him, he must have involuntarily pulled the trigger of his little gun. I was vaguely aware of a flash and then I felt a sharp pain over my left ear and nothing further.

. . .

THE FIRST THING I heard when I came to was Sam's voice, followed immediately by the sound of sirens in the distance. My head hurt like hell. I reached up above my ear and touched cloth. A bandage of some kind, I assumed. I looked around through hazy eyes. I was lying on a bed, and disturbingly it appeared to be Clem's bed, the one with the box under it, where both the letter and key had been hidden. I wasn't too thrilled about being on Clem's bed: I could catch any number of things. Still, I guessed one of the sirens I could hear might be an ambulance and I supposed I could be hosed down thoroughly if they were planning to take me to hospital. Sam wasn't in the room but I could still hear his voice.

'That'll be the cops, your lordship,' he was saying in a tight-sounding voice. 'You going to tell me what the fuck this is all about before they get here and arrest you for attempted murder?' That'd be the attempted murder of me, I guessed. And lordship? Who the hell was the old guy?

'Don't be absurd. The gun went off accidentally. The girl was trespassing on my property. And she was armed. I was merely protecting myself.'

'Armed? Is that the rolling pin you're referring to?'

'She hurled it at me with absolutely no provocation.'

'I'm not an expert, but I'd have said this gun was ample provocation.' Go, Sam. I tried to smile but it made my head swim, so I stopped. 'Your property, you say. Since when?'

'None of your business, Mr Bryant.'

'And what's with the gloves? It's the middle of summer. Only people who are up to no good wear gloves in the middle of summer.'

If there was a reply to that I didn't hear it because it was drowned out by the sound of a number of vehicles, sirens still blaring, pulling up outside the pub. There was a brief silence as the sirens were switched off, and then there was a banging from downstairs and somebody shouted, 'Open up! Police!' like we were in a movie or something.

Sam said, 'Down we go, your majesty. You first,' and I heard footsteps heading downstairs. I tried to hoist myself off the bed to hear better, but that turned out to be a bad decision. I blacked out again.

19

SATURDAY 20TH JULY
ANDERSON AND ROSE

Mallory was whisked off to the John Radcliffe Hospital and I was "invited" to make a return visit to Stockford Police Station along with Viscount Uppingshott, but in separate cop cars. Once inside, we were taken to different rooms. I was left alone for some time with a cup of tea and a bored-looking constable.

There had been a certain amount of questioning at The Farts but, despite the presence of the gun and the wound on Mallory's head, my assertion that the viscount had tried to kill her didn't seem to be gaining much favour with the sergeant in charge. Disappointingly but predictably, Uppingshott's title seemed to hold much greater sway. So, all in all, I was quite relieved when it was decided we'd all drive back to Stockford for the local inspector to take up the questioning.

An hour had passed, and the constable had fetched me a second cup of tea and allowed me to take a visit to the lavatory. I was still in my cricket whites and feeling a bit smelly if I'm honest. The lavatory didn't run to any deodorant but at least I felt a little less unappealing after a wash. On my return, the constable gestured to my cricket gear and said, 'What was the result? I should have been playing, you know.'

'How come?' I said. 'I thought you looked familiar.'

'I should do. I bowled you for a duck at our place last year.'

I remembered suddenly. The young copper had pretty much cleaned us up at Stockford in last summer's game. 'You did, didn't you? You took three or four wickets. Shame you're on duty this year.'

'Duty's got nothing to do with it,' he said. 'I was dropped for some big, West Indian bastard who turned up out of nowhere this week.'

So I told him all about the match and Curtley Hendrix's less-than-auspicious part in it and that cheered him up no end. I'd just finished when the door opened and a man and a woman walked in. They were in plain clothes but the clothes still shrieked "policeman". Well, "policeman" and "policewoman" I suppose. Both were on the short and wide side and neither looked particularly happy, although they possessed the sort of faces to which happiness would be a relative stranger at the best of times. It seemed these weren't the best of times. The man nodded at the young constable, who left, making a faintly disturbing throat-slitting gesture behind their backs as he did so.

'Detective Inspector Anderson,' said the woman, sitting opposite me. 'This is my colleague, DS Rose.' She paused. 'You got something against the Uppingshott family, Mr Bryant?'

This was an uncomfortable opening gambit. 'Do I need a lawyer?' I asked.

'Up to you. But we're not going to waste time while you decide. Let's recap, shall we? Yesterday, you "find" Jonathan

Hardy-Hewitt with his head stove in inside a house you had no right to be in. Today, you "find" his brother and your girlfriend, both injured, inside another building you shouldn't be in. And then you accuse Viscount Uppingshott of trying to kill your aforesaid girlfriend.'

Had she really just used the word "aforesaid"? Perhaps it was taught at police training college. 'She's not my girlfriend,' I started, weakly.

'Shut up. Uppingshott wants us to arrest you for murdering his brother.'

What the fuck? 'On what grounds?' I said, seriously alarmed.

Anderson leant back in her chair which struggled to survive the manoeuvre. 'None whatsoever,' she said. 'He's obviously barking mad.'

'Are you allowed to say that?' I said.

'Shouldn't think so but then this interview isn't being recorded and if you start putting it about that I'd called a peer of the realm barking mad, I'd deny it.' I suddenly realised she was right. The interview wasn't being recorded. Why was that? She continued. 'There are things about this that don't add up.' She held up a pudgy hand and raised a finger. 'One: Uppingshott and his sister were in here yesterday and something about their body language was all wrong.'

This was getting more and more intriguing. 'What?' I asked.

'Their brother had just been murdered.'

'Murdered,' contributed Rose, speaking for the first time.

'You'd have thought they'd be upset. But it was more that they were worried about it. We both felt it, didn't we Sergeant?'

'Worried,' agreed Rose. Clearly a man who chose his words carefully.

'Now why would that be?' Anderson held up a second finger. 'Two: he claims to be the owner of The Three Pigeons.'

Momentarily, I forgot what The Three Pigeons was. Stress, I imagine. 'Yes, that surprised me,' I said. 'Clem still owns it as far as I'm aware.'

'Clem?'

'The landlord.'

Anderson seemed to consult a mental notebook. As well as the lack of recording equipment, neither detective had brought pen or paper into the room with them. 'Ah, yes, Mr Clement Spaggott. Whereabouts at present unknown.'

'He's in Benidorm,' I offered. 'With his wife, Maeve.'

'Not so,' said Anderson. 'Checks are ongoing, but Mr and Mrs Spaggott have definitely not left the country. Also, we're still checking if Mr Spaggott was in fact the previous owner of the pub or just the tenant.'

I was astonished. 'That's not what he told us. If Clem doesn't own it, who does?'

'Well, as I say, Uppingshott says he does.'

'And does he?' We were going round in circles.

'Sorry, Mr Bryant, but that's something I can't tell you.'

'Can't or won't?'

'Can't. The ownership situation looks to be a little complicated.' She paused. 'I can tell you this though. Mrs Spaggott's name is not Maeve. She was born Eve-May.' I looked at Anderson and Rose. I could feel my mouth hanging open in shock. There surely weren't two Eve-Mays in the world. 'That appears to mean something to you, Mr Bryant. I thought it might. I'm guessing your girlfriend hasn't told you that her half-sister's been running The Three Pigeons.'

I couldn't get my head round this. 'You're telling me that Maeve Spaggott is really Eve-May Stamp?'

'I am. How long has she been around, Mr Bryant?'

I thought back. I reflected that I was probably the wrong person to ask as I couldn't even remember the wedding back in February. I reckoned Maeve had turned up a couple of years ago, a shadowy, insignificant figure who occasionally flitted in and out of the bar. 'I always thought she was just a terrible cleaner Clem had employed,' I said.

'One more thing,' said Anderson, holding up a third finger. 'You have a meeting with Lady Felicity Hardy-Hewitt on Monday morning, I believe.' I'd forgotten all about it, to be honest. 'What's that about?'

'I don't know but I assume it's about the non-existent planning application to buy The Farts. Why?'

'Farts?' said Anderson.

'Farts,' echoed Rose.

'Sorry, I mean The Three Pigeons. It's a sort of nickname.'

'All right. We don't nick people on account of names.' She paused. I understood a joke had been cracked and smiled weakly in acknowledgement. 'I'd appreciate it if you could drop in here after your meeting and tell us all about it,' she continued. 'There's something going on here I can't get my head around. Your help would be appreciated, that's all.' And then, amazingly, she smiled for the first time. It made all the difference to her face, which grew dimples in unexpected places. 'Now, I imagine you'll be wanting to get yourself over to the JR to see how Miss Fillery is.' At least she hadn't called her my girlfriend this time. I wasn't sure if she was or not but yes, I did want to find out if she was all right. And now I needed to discover what she knew about her elder sister.

'I do, thanks,' I said. 'And yes, OK, I'll let you know what dear Felicity has to say.'

'If you think of anything else,' Anderson said, standing and reaching across to shake my hand, 'let us know, yes?'

I promised I would but just at the moment I was still in a state of shock. I couldn't think of anything. A police car was summoned to take me home. It was past eight o'clock by now, too late to clean myself up and get across to Oxford to see Mallory but I could at least make a call. Which I did. Mallory was asleep and not in any danger, thank goodness. It wasn't until I was back at 1 Slaughterhouse Cottages that something came to me. Something Uppingshott had said yesterday. He'd asked me about Jonty's face, hair and clothes when I'd found him. I couldn't think why at the time but now, suddenly, I thought I knew. And if I was right, I knew who'd killed Jonty.

Except that would mean it wasn't Jonty who was dead.

20

SUNDAY 21ST JULY
RAIN AND BANDAGES

The weather had broken at last, the rain slanting against my living room window as I stood drinking my coffee. There had been thunder in the night too, great crashing waves of it. It matched my mood, at once sombre and angry. This was all supposed to be about a pub closing and finding out why. And whilst it was still about that it was now also about the murder of a man and the shooting, accidental or not, of a girl I'd only known a few days but of whom I'd become very fond. Fond? What the hell kind of a word was that? You were fond of an elderly aunt or Rich Tea biscuits.

There was supposed to be another meeting of InnKeeper this morning but there wouldn't be. Banjo was still missing and Detective Inspector Anderson, with all her roly-poly thoroughness, was investigating his disappearance. I was beginning to suspect that Banjo, who had arrived in the village in such a sudden and surreal way two years previously, had just decided to make his exit in a similarly unfathomable and abrupt manner. Also, The Farts was now completely out of bounds. The police had even strung up some "Do Not Cross" tape along the front wall and across the narrow access to the car park. I picked up my phone. There were only two calls to make. What with Banjo's absence and Mallory occupying a bed at the John Radcliffe Hospital, that only left Jeremy Jeavons and Daisy. The former was his normal quiet, restrained self when I broke the news and if he asked more questions than I was expecting, then that was understandable. Daisy was horrified, particularly about Mallory's injury; I hadn't realised the two women had bonded so quickly. Again, the call went on longer than it should have but that was because she insisted on relaying everything I said to Dick, and at a volume that suggested her dad was still in bed upstairs.

I'd already phoned the hospital again, but it had been very early and Mallory was still sleeping. She'd been given something to help but, other than that, was more or less OK. The bullet had merely grazed the skin above her ear. Who had fired it, Uppingshott or Jonty, I was still trying to work out. I'd asked if I could come and visit and was told, of course, and if I could take her away with me at the end of the visit, then that would be extremely helpful. Assuming that's what she wanted when she woke up. It sounded very much as though they'd quite like to fill the bed with another, more seriously shot, patient. Mallory had been incredibly lucky but then, she probably shouldn't have started lobbing rolling pins at elderly blokes wielding guns.

I'd asked Anderson about the gun as I was leaving Stockford Police Station last night. Why would Viscount Uppingshott have had a gun on him in the first place and why was he wearing gloves when I'd found him? She couldn't – or, again, wouldn't – answer, but to me, the gloves were another dead giveaway about the true identity of the man. Gloves equal no fingerprints. Fingerprints, I was sure, that would have revealed that the person now walking around in Uppingshott's expensive Oxford brogues was in fact the less than Honourable Jonathan Hardy-Hewitt.

MALLORY WAS NOT in bed when I arrived at the hospital. She was sitting up in a chair, wearing the same clothes she'd had on yesterday; white vest – now ruined by a significant smear of dried blood – above blue jeans. She had a blanket round her shoulders but was still shivering. Her face, pale at the best of times, now looked almost transparent. There was a large white bandage wrapped tightly around her head above her eyes and her shock of red hair was piled loosely above it. She looked dreadful, or at least as dreadful as a stunningly attractive woman can look.

She rose when she saw me, swaying very slightly and holding the chairback for support. 'Hi,' I said. 'Are you sure you're fit enough to be discharged?'

She seemed to answer without moving her lips but then I realised the voice I'd heard had come from behind me. And was, in any case, Irish, not Canadian. A pretty, dark-haired nurse had followed me to Mallory's bedside. 'She's not for staying,' the nurse said. 'I t'ink she should be getting herself back into bed, but she's havin' none of it. Stubborn wee lass.' I wasn't too sure about the "wee" bit: Mallory must have been six inches taller than the nurse.

'I'm fine, Sam. I need to get home. I'll rest up, I promise, Siobhain.' This last to the Irish nurse.

'OK, then,' said the nurse. She turned to me. 'Make sure she does.' I refrained from saying it was none of my business how much resting up or otherwise Mallory did. 'Keep the bandage on for four days and then get it looked at by your GP,' continued Nurse Siobhain. 'He'll decide whether ye need a new one.'

'I'm not sure I want to take it off at all,' said Mallory. 'They've shaved my head. I must look a fright under there.'

'Yes, ye'll be scaring the horses, so ye will. Now, get out of my sight, ye gorgeous creature you.'

Back in my car, I spent the thirty minute journey back to Mallory's flat in Stockford updating her about what had gone on at the police station and my as yet unvoiced suspicions that Jonty had murdered his twin brother and taken his place and that, therefore, it had been Jonty, not Uppingshott, who had shot her.

'You're kidding me, right?' she said. 'But that's crazy. Are you sure?' I admitted I was far from sure. 'Why would he do that? What's his motive?'

'It's always rankled him that he's the second twin. No viscountcy, no earldom. The English aristocracy can be an unforgiving place to inhabit.'

'Hmm, yes,' she said. 'Presumably there's no *droit du seigneur* either if you're only the second son.' I glanced across. She was trying not to laugh. 'Have you told the cops?'

'No, not yet. I think I need a bit more proof first. I don't want to be done for slander.'

'But you say your conversation with the detectives was off the record.'

'Records can suddenly be rediscovered. Anyway, out of bounds or not, I'm going back to The Farts. You say Uppingshott – or Jonty – appeared out of the bar and I think I know which part of it he appeared from. I haven't given up on the locked door in the woods and I haven't forgotten that you found the cellar door locked too. And I need to make sure Banjo's not still there somewhere.'

'Leave it to the cops, Sam,' she said, looking worried. 'They'll be swarming all over the place, won't they?'

'Not tonight they won't,' I said. 'Not after dark.'

'Well,' she said after a long pause. 'I guess that gives me a few hours to freshen up and catch up on my beauty sleep before we leave.'

'Whoa, lady,' I said, taking my eyes off the road for longer than was sensible and staring at her drawn, pale face. 'You're in no state to go sneaking around the pub again.'

'Just try and stop me.' I thought a reasonably active kitten could have stopped her in her present state but wisely didn't say so. Still, if she was determined to go with me, I'd be glad of the company – her company especially – and there was, in any case, still one thing I hadn't mentioned.

I drew a deep breath. 'Do you happen to know what your sister, Eve-May is doing these days?' I said.

21

SUNDAY 21ST JULY
WET CARS AND CLOSING TIMES

Back in Stockford, Mallory went to bed and I returned to Idleborough. The relentless downpour stopped at last just as I reached the village. The rain was particularly unfortunate for Mallory's Jaguar, still sitting where she'd left it yesterday outside The Farts and still with its roof down. I'd come equipped with a small bucket and some cloths as well as her car keys. I put the roof up and set to work bailing out the car. I'd only just started when a middle-aged female police officer, whose grey face displayed her displeasure at having to stand outside The Farts in the wet, approached.

'Is this your vehicle, sir?'

'No, officer,' I said looking up and accidentally sloshing some water over her police-issue boots. This seemed to make her even more displeased, although frankly, she wasn't the only one getting wet and at least she was being paid to do so. 'It belongs to a friend of mine. Miss Fillery?' It looked like the name meant nothing to her. Presumably standing guard outside a crime scene was on a strictly need-to-know basis. 'She was shot in there yesterday,' I added, gesturing to the pub. I couldn't see any other coppers but there were two police cars behind the Jag so presumably some of her colleagues were inside in the dry (unless they were in the snug, which had had a leak in the roof for at least five years) sifting the evidence. I only hoped they were wearing full PPE. Scrabbling about in Clem's private quarters was not something I'd want to be doing.

'Can I see your driving licence, please, sir?' asked the policewoman.

I stood up slowly and emptied a half-full bucket of water into the gutter next to her. This was ridiculous. 'No, you can't, I'm afraid,' I said truthfully, my licence being back at the cottage. I was trying not to get angry. I didn't want to risk being hauled back to Stockford nick for the third day running. 'As you can see, I'm not driving the car, just drying it.' Mind you, it was certainly my intention to drive it back to my place once I'd got the footwells water-free and the driving seat as dry as possible. To that end, I had the engine running so as to get the heated seats warming up, and they were beginning to steam. As was I, although that wasn't as good a sign. Anyway, I didn't want the Jag to still be sitting outside The Farts when Mallory and I returned at dead of night.

'Are you trying to be funny, sir?' I'd rarely felt less funny in my life and was about to tell her so and damn the consequences when there was a scrunch of gravel from the side of the pub, a scrunch that could only have been produced by Boots-Police-For-The-Use-Of. The young, fast bowling constable from yesterday appeared around the corner. I'd remembered his name: Joe.

'Hiya, there, Sam,' he said, cheerily. 'Thought I recognised your voice. How are you and how's the reporter girl?'

The sour-faced policewoman turned to him. 'Do you know this man, Joe?'

'Yes, Mum, stand down. This is Sam Bryant, the chap who found Uppingshott and the shot woman here yesterday.'

All I could think was: Mum? That must be awkward. I wondered what sort of conversations they had if they ever went on duty together in the same Panda car. Did they still have Panda cars? Car, anyway. "Keep your eyes on the road." "Yes, Mum." "Indicate, signal, manoeuvre." "Yes, Mum." "Have you washed behind your ears?" I realised I was getting carried away.

Joe looked at the Jag and tutted. 'What a shame,' he said. 'Lovely motor. Ruined, I expect. Does it still go?'

As the engine was running smoothly, I hoped the answer to that question would be yes. 'I was just going to take it home,' I said, contradicting what I'd just told his mother. 'Miss Fillery will be able to collect it later. She's OK, thanks for asking. It was just a graze. She's sleeping it off at the moment.' I got into the driver's seat before Joe's mum could stick her oar in again. 'Anything going on in there?' I asked Joe, in as innocent a voice as I could muster.

'Nah,' he said. 'Nearly wrapped up, I reckon. Dusted everything. Well, dusted the dust anyway. Not sure how useful that'll be.' I was about to ask if they'd found anything but stopped myself just in time. After all, what would they be looking for? I didn't want to put ideas in their heads. I put the Jag in gear, executed a neat three-pointer and drove back towards the centre of the village, leaving PC Joe and PC Mum together on the pavement.

. . .

MALLORY HAD BEEN STAGGERED to hear that Maeve Spaggott was really her half-sister, Eve-May. In fact she refused to believe it at first. I'd had to come clean at the same time that I knew that Harrison Makepeace Stamp was her father. 'Of course you knew,' she said. 'You wouldn't be the man I think you are, Sam, if you hadn't found out by now who my Pop is.' I hoped that was a thinly disguised compliment.

I asked her if she had a photo of Eve-May and she hadn't; and I'd never felt the need to take a picture of Maeve either. In any case, she was such a shadowy figure, it might not have come out even if I had. It would have been like one of those nineteenth-century fake photos of fairies.

'I wouldn't recognise her if I bumped into her,' Mallory said. 'I wasn't born when Elizabeth died.'

'Elizabeth?' I said.

'The old bastard's first wife,' and Mallory went through the Stamp family tree as far as she could. In actual fact, I knew almost as much as she did. Wikipedia's a wonderful thing, if not necessarily to be relied on. However, in this case what I'd read stacked up pretty much against what Mallory could tell me.

'Elizabeth died in the bath. It was tragic. She was only forty. Still, I wouldn't be here if she hadn't.'

I sensed a bit of self-denial there. It was public knowledge that Elizabeth's death had been the subject of a very full enquiry and although no charges were brought, the theory that Harrison Makepeace Stamp had already met Mallory's mother, Mary-Lou, and would have found a way to rid himself of Elizabeth one way or another, held a lot of water in a lot of circles. Mary-Lou was twenty at the time, an "actress" so the story went and, well, twenty versus forty: do the math, as they say in North America. I didn't say any of this to Mallory. Slightly concussed or not, it had already been established she was a mean shot with a rolling pin. I'd very much enjoyed Thursday afternoon and was hoping it was an enjoyment to be repeated frequently. Not a good idea then to accuse her father of uxoricide. She'd called him "the old bastard" but that could be a term of endearment in Canada, for all I knew.

'I think I did meet Eve-May once more later on,' continued Mallory. 'Some wrangling over an allowance. Hey, I know all about that, trust me. Anyways, she came out to the ranch on Lake Huron. I'd have been about six or seven, I guess. I can't seem to get a picture in my head though. I think she was pretty small, thinnish, but I wasn't taking much notice, I'm afraid.'

'Well, Maeve's smallish and thinnish.' It wasn't a lot to go on but Inspector Anderson had been pretty sure they were the same person. 'Could you go and ask the police what they know? I mean, you're the local reporter investigating a murder and a shooting, as well as being a family member. That should give you leverage.'

'You don't think there's a conflict of interests there?' she said smiling.

I grinned back. 'Just a teensy one.'

IT TOOK a long time to grow dark at this time of year, although the lowering clouds, still dispensing the occasional burst of heavy rain, helped. Just after eleven, we set off for The Farts, dressed in black or as close to black as we could. I didn't have any black tops of my own. Mallory had offered to lend me the sort of Little Black Dress all self-respecting women keep in their wardrobes for sartorial emergencies. She had a rackful herself. 'Don't you need this?' I'd asked, not entirely unsarcastically. 'It was cheap,' she said. 'Less than a hundred bucks. I can manage.' That would be Daddy's allowance again, I guessed. In the end, I'd found a navy blue sweatshirt I'd forgotten about but the LBD would have done in a pinch – although it looked like it would have pinched in all the wrong places – and it was short enough to pass as a shirt. I looked forward to seeing her wear it herself in the not too distant future. Mallory had jammed a black, woolly ski hat over her bright red curls and the gleaming white bandage, both of which were probably visible from space.

'Isn't this pub-closing time?' she asked as we set off up the potholed lane towards the Market Square. I was impressed by her knowledge of UK licensing laws but reminded her that we were in Idleborough, where licensing laws were considered merely an initial bargaining point, as she had mentioned herself only a couple of days ago.

'Not for another hour or so,' I said. 'Most of the pubs like to observe the Sabbath by bringing chucking out time forward to about midnight. You know, as a mark of respect.' The empty roads and sounds of laughter and music from The Bull as we passed backed me up.

It only took five minutes to reach The Farts and we met nobody *en route*. Neither PC Joe nor his mum were in evidence and the pub had an unmistakable air of desertion and dereliction about it. The dereliction was normal, the desertion less so. 'Are you sure you want to come in?' I asked Mallory. She nodded, so we bent under the police tape and made our way through the side access. The first problem was that the Gents' window was now firmly closed. I tried the rear door but it was locked. I supposed that police training manuals must include a few pages on the securing of premises.

'What now?' Mallory whispered.

'Well, we have two options,' I said. 'We could go back to the cottage and open that very nice Pinot Noir I've got sitting in the kitchen. Or we could try a bit of breaking and entering. This is The Farts after all. I bet Clem's back door is riddled with woodworm. One good shoulder charge should do the trick.'

She looked across the dark car park to the thicket of thorns and trees to the rear. They were a serious obstacle even in daylight, but in the dark and with flurries of raindrops still trying it on for size, the prospect of fighting our way through them looked unappealing to say the least. A repeat bout of athletics would be dangerous, particularly for Mallory, who had after all been shot yesterday and was far from fully recovered. Adding a broken ankle or worse to that injury seemed uncalled-for. However, I wasn't prepared to go back home, Pinot Noir or no Pinot Noir, without at least making an attempt to gain entry. I stuck my head inside Clem's man-cave, the door with the padlock I'd broken on Tuesday still hanging open, and shone my torch around. I was aware that there was no access from the room into the pub proper, but the plank I'd used on Tuesday was still there, leaning up against the broken one-armed bandit where I'd left it.

I was quite prepared to utilise it again if we couldn't get into the pub, although I'd prefer not to in the dark and rain, and it would mean doing it alone. I wondered if Billy was still occupying his tent. I guessed it unlikely, what with Jonty now dead, or at least dead as far as the world was concerned.

'OK,' I said to Mallory. 'Plan A is attractive but Plan B is my favoured option.'

'And Plan B is what?'

'This,' I said, handing her the torch and charging, shoulder-first at the rear door of the pub. Now I've never been a rugby player, mainly because I quite like my ears the shape they are, so it's possible I didn't execute the charge in the approved manner. Or could be the door was just stronger than it looked. Whatever the case, when Sam met door, Sam came off worse. Much worse. Something in my shoulder scrunched painfully and it was all I could do not to scream. It was the same shoulder I'd strained slightly pulling Jonty's doorbell on Friday.

'Fucking hell, that hurt,' I said, grasping my injured shoulder with my left hand and trying experimentally to see if I could move my right arm. I could, after a fashion, so I presumed I hadn't broken anything.

'That was exciting,' said Mallory, sounding remarkably unsympathetic. 'It's just wall-to-wall entertainment in this village, isn't it? Here, allow me,' and she handed me back my torch and dragged a key-ring loaded with half a dozen keys out of her jeans pocket. 'Shine that torch over here.'

'What the hell are they?' I said.

'What do they look like?' She grinned. 'I found these in the kitchen before my encounter with Jonty yesterday. None of them fitted the cellar door but, you know, second time lucky and all that. Ah, this looks likely.' She selected a key, inserted it into the lock and turned it. It worked and she opened the door with a flourish. '*Voila!*' she said, still grinning.

'You could have told me you had those keys before I broke my shoulder,' I complained.

'Where's the fun in that? Anyway, I didn't know you were about to do your He-man thing.'

The door opened directly into The Farts' main bar which was distinguishable from the snug by dint of being bigger and, frankly, snugger. Neither room could be described as comfortable as per the dictionary definition of snug.

'Are we going to try the cellar?' asked Mallory. 'The door's locked, remember, and I'm not sure you could get much of a run-up if you were thinking of repeating your human battering-ram impression.'

'We are,' I said. 'But there's another way in and my thinking is that when you saw Jonty or Uppingshott yesterday, that's where he'd emerged from. Ah ha, here we are.' I bent down and shone the torch at a large wooden trapdoor set into the floor behind the bar.

'Where does that lead? I was down in the cellar with Banjo and I sure as heck don't recall any trapdoor.'

'No, you wouldn't. You were in the beer cellar. This leads down to the soft-drinks cellar. It's much smaller but I believe there's a way to get through to the beer cellar if you know what you're looking for.' It was smaller because Clem didn't hold much store by soft drinks. True, he usually kept a crate of Coke and one of lemonade down here "for the ladies" and he also had some cider, which in Clem's world qualified as a soft drink.

Handing my torch to Mallory, I grabbed hold of the old bit of rope that was used to open the trapdoor and hauled. This caused an agonising spasm to shoot down my right arm from my injured shoulder and I promptly let go of the rope. The trapdoor had only opened about a foot but it crashed shut again with a noise loud enough to waken the dead. I only hoped one of those dead would not turn out to be Banjo.

'Thank goodness we're trying to keep quiet,' said Mallory. She's lucky that I like sarcasm in a woman. She handed me back the torches. 'Are you sure you can carry both of those with your poorly arm?' she asked solicitously.

OK, I may like sarcasm in a woman but there's a limit. She spat on her hands like a true woodsman, bent and grabbed the rope and hoisted the trapdoor to a vertical position as if she'd been doing that sort of thing all her life. Perhaps she had; she was Canadian after all and I understand it's quite a physical life over there. I shone both torches down into the dark but it was hard to make much out apart from a ladder leading downwards until, that is, the cellar was suddenly flooded with light.

'Who the fuck did that?' I said, taking an involuntary step back. I had a momentary premonition of a bullet whistling past my head, but it turned out to be Mallory, tapping me on the shoulder. Her other hand was still holding the light switch on the wall next to her.

'I wonder,' she said, eyes wide. 'Must be magic, hey?' OK, now the sarcasm was tipping over towards the unacceptable.

22

SUNDAY 21ST JULY
CELLARS AND PASSAGES

We made an unpromising pair of burglars, Sam and I, as we inched our way down the rickety old ladder into the cellar. Sam effectively had just one usable arm, which meant he momentarily had to let go of the ladder every step he took. And I had a ferocious headache. I hadn't let on about that to Sam but I was surely still suffering from concussion. The British NHS is undoubtedly a wonderful institution but it didn't believe in keeping people in its beds a second longer than possible. OK, I'm aware it had been my decision to discharge myself, and Nurse Siobhain had been quite concerned about allowing me back out into the big bad world, but she was pretty much the only one. The doc had shone a light into my eyes and pronounced me fit – or fit enough, anyway – to leave, especially as I'd gotten a lift home. Or maybe because I'm Canadian and he didn't want to be seen spending too much of the British tax-payer's money on me.

Anyway, any faint dizziness I was feeling was not enough to prevent me successfully reaching the cellar floor. It was, as Sam had suggested, a much smaller room than the cellar I'd been in *with Banjo yesterday. I shone my flashlight around and spotted Sam trying one-handedly to heave an empty wall-rack aside. There was no sign of Banjo, not that I'd expected there to be. I wasn't overly concerned about him, to be honest; I still reckoned he was most likely to be sleeping off the beer in the next cellar. Sam was obviously trying to find a door to that cellar but the rack he was attempting to shift, empty or not of whatever it was supposed to store, was not playing ball. Especially as he was only using his left hand. I guessed I may have been a little unkind about his injured shoulder so moved across to help. Just as well I did as the rack, more cumbersome than weighty, started to topple on to him. I managed to reach up and catch it and between us we succeeded in lowering it to the floor.*

A wooden door was revealed in the wall behind it. Not a big door, only about four feet high, which seemed a bit crazy. The pub presumably hadn't been designed for dwarfs. Perhaps we were in Wonderland and we'd discover Alice the other side taking tea with the Mad Hatter. Nothing about my experience of Idleborough so far suggested that was particularly unlikely. I hadn't noticed too much normality hereabouts for sure. Anyways, leaving aside its size, why was the door hidden behind the racking? Sam was by now trying the handle but I wasn't surprised when he couldn't open it. I waved the key ring at him again. And again, one of the keys worked its magic. Pulling open the door and bending to peer through it, we were confronted by what looked and smelled like an old blanket, an old blanket that hadn't been introduced to a washing machine since the millennium. It was a streaky grey but could have been any colour originally. More importantly, however, I recognised it. I'd seen it or its twin yesterday hanging innocently on one wall of the beer cellar. I was reluctant to touch it; I'd already had to take more showers in the week I'd been visiting Idleborough than my water bill could stand.

Sam had no such concerns. He gave the blanket a yank and it collapsed onto the floor in a cloud of dust and other things that might have been alive. The beer cellar was in front of us. Sam ducked through the doorway and I followed on hands and knees; I'm a tall girl and I didn't fancy cracking my already injured and aching head on the lintel. We shone our flashlights around. The smell of beer was intense but if Banjo was still there, he was well hidden.

'Where's the light switch?' I said.

'Either in the bar or the corridor at the top of those stairs,' Sam replied, nodding to the steps which Banjo and I had used yesterday. 'Should have thought about that.' He paused, looking worried. 'No Banjo then. What the hell's happened to him?'

I thought a bit. 'This may not be particularly encouraging,' I said finally, 'but if he left of his own accord, it wasn't through either of the doors we know about, the one up the steps or the Oompa-Loompa's portal we've just crawled through.'

'I guess he could have been taken out through there,' Sam said, sounding doubtful, and shining his flashlight upwards and away from the steps leading to the locked door into the corridor. 'But I don't see how.'

'What the fuck!' I said as the torch-beam revealed another hatch in the ceiling. 'You said there was no trapdoor into this cellar.'

'Not from the bar,' he said. 'That leads straight into the High Street. How do you think the draymen get the barrels down here?'

I had no idea what a drayman was but that wasn't the most important question. 'So why couldn't we use that to get in here?' I hissed.

'Two reasons. Only the brewery and Clem have the means to open it. And we'd have attracted quite a lot of unwanted attention standing in the street trying to force it open in the middle of

the night.' It made sense, so I shut up. 'For the same reasons, Banjo's not gone out that way, either forcibly or under his own steam. Which means there must be another way out.'

We shone our flashlights around the cellar again but could see no other doors. 'I guess we've got a bit more furniture shifting to do to find out for sure,' I said.

Unlike the racking in the first cellar, the ones in here were mostly full of beer barrels. They looked pretty darn heavy although if Banjo had done as good a job as he'd promised, at least some of them should be empty. Sam, however, didn't appear to be in the mood for taking the barrels off their racks in a methodical way. 'Stand back,' he commanded, tugging one-handedly at the end of one of the racks. His intention seemed to be to bring the whole section crashing to the ground, beer barrels and all, which would suggest he'd given up on the whole keeping quiet thing. The rack though had other ideas. Instead of falling, it swung smoothly and noiselessly towards us. I had to take a couple of rapid steps back to avoid it. It came to gentle halt at a ninety-degree angle to the wall.

And behind it, a door was indeed revealed. I was beginning to think there were far too many doors in this lousy pub. Mind you, when I say a door was revealed, it was only revealed if you possessed keen eyesight or a powerful flashlight. Luckily, I possessed both. This door was disguised, papered over with a reddish-brown brickwork pattern that blended almost, but not completely, with the real bricks on either side.

'Faux,' said Sam, feeling it.

'Foe?' I said. 'As in fee, fie, foe, fum? If you're suggesting there's a giant the other side he sure as hell didn't get in here through the four-foot door we've just crawled through.'

'No, faux, *as in* faux *books usually. In this case, wallpaper printed to look like bricks.*

He started picking at the wallpaper and soon managed to tear off a long, ragged strip. The door itself appeared to be pretty new, although the glue from the wallpaper made it hard to be sure. The only un-doorlike thing about it was that it had no handle and no noticeable lock.

'How do we get through it?' I asked.

'Well, there's nothing to pull it with, so I guess we just try this,' and he pushed gently. The door moved. 'Open sesame.' I shone my flashlight through the opening and Sam stepped through, holding his flashlight aloft. If there was a giant or, more realistically, another old bastard with a gun the other side, I doubted if the flash would be much use, especially wielded left-handed. I needn't have worried, though; there was no one there.

*What **was** there was an empty passage, walled in brick and stretching about thirty yards to what was either a dead-end or a right-angled bend. It was dark and the torchlight created shadows where there should have been none. There was a pervasive air of damp, no, not damp, clamminess, and a tingle ran up my spine. The wall beside me was dry to the touch but I still felt the need to wipe my hand on my jeans afterwards.*

'Shall we?' said Sam.

'Wait a sec. There are lights down here, look,' and I shone my flashlight along the ceiling, which was arched and rudimentarily plastered in a pleasing taupe colour. More usefully though, the light revealed half a dozen bare bulbs strung out along its length to the corner up ahead. 'Where there are lights, there must be a switch.'

'Unless that's upstairs too.'

That seemed unlikely though and sure enough, tucked in a corner behind the open door was a surprisingly new-looking light switch. I flicked it on and the corridor was suddenly brightly illuminated. Doubtless, whoever was in the habit of using it didn't want to risk tripping on what the light showed to be an uneven, concrete floor. The person who'd laid the concrete was probably the same person who'd plastered the ceiling.

We made our way down the passage, Sam in the lead. This was his thing after all; I was just the girl he'd asked along to report on the closure of the pub. Since then, my non-existent reporter's notebook had gotten a bit fuller than anticipated, what with the murder of whoever it turned out to be, not to mention being shot myself.

We reached the right-angled bend, which confusingly was to the left. I found myself momentarily wondering what a left-angled bend would be, but Sam came to a halt and I had to stop wondering to avoid crashing into him. There was a time and a place for that. We peered cautiously around the corner. Sam had bent slightly so I poked my head above his. We must have looked like a couple of stooges out of a pre-war comedy film. And wouldn't you just know it? There was another fucking door.

I presumed we were staring at the door in the woods. Steel, solid and shut, the door stared back at us. I looked up, half expecting to see tree roots poking through the ceiling. I plucked the Yale key out of my pocket and handed it to Sam. It was extremely uncomfortable keeping all these keys in a pocket that, given the skin-tight nature of my jeans, wasn't designed to have hard, pointy bits of metal in it. I'd be glad when I was rid of them. 'I don't think we're going to need that,' he said, and annoyingly he handed it back to me even though his own pockets were proper manly ones capable of engulfing not just a few keys but an entire workbench-worth of tools. He was pointing to a prominent handle, less shiny and brassy than the one on the door at the other end of the passage. 'This must be the door I found. But what's it for?'

'Smuggling?' I suggested.

He laughed. 'Doubt it. Yo-ho-ho and a bottle of rum? Clem doesn't keep rum, not even for the ladies.'

'Smuggling?' The voice – the oh, so familiar voice – came from behind us. 'What sort of a bone-headed suggestion is that, Princess?'

23

SUNDAY 21ST JULY
FATHERS AND SISTERS

I spun round. There was an old bloke standing a few yards in front of us. Grizzled, grey hair and a nearly-beard, all a bit Alan Sugar for my liking. He was about as tall as Sugar too. In other words, not very. An open-necked, check shirt in a garish combination of primary colours, pale blue chinos and brown loafers took order below the half-hearted beard. He looked like the sort of man who would normally be used to getting his own way. Tonight wasn't normal though because behind and to one side of him stood Banjo. And Banjo had a gun in his hand.

I wondered momentarily where they'd come from, but that question was immediately answered. The passage we'd walked along hadn't just led to the door. There was a small room here too, a sort of entrance lobby complete with table and chairs. A laptop sat on the table.

I noticed all this in the half-second it took Mallory, turning also, to say, 'Pop?'

I said, 'Banjo?' at the same time. Then I said, 'What? Pop? As in father? What the fuck?'

Mallory said, 'How can you be here? You're in Toronto. You phoned me.'

I felt the more important question would be: **Why** was he here? I'd heard of aeroplanes, after all. It appeared their existence may have slipped Mallory's mind. And topping even that for importance was the question of why Banjo was there holding a gun. The gun wasn't pointing at anybody in particular but Banjo, who couldn't work out how mobile phones work or which parts of a banjo produced music, now had a cold look in his eyes that screamed competence. Before I could think of anything helpful to say, however, Stamp spoke in answer to Mallory.

'That was over two days ago, Princess. I could have gotten here three times over since then. **If** I'd been in Toronto when I called you, that is.' The words were more belligerent than the expression on his face. His eyes were red and puffy, his skin drawn and grey and his shoulders sloped. He looked a defeated man but whatever war he'd been fighting was a mystery to me.

Meanwhile, Mallory's mouth was working but nothing was coming out of it. She looked as completely dumbfounded as a person can look. Stamp continued: 'Great look, kiddo. Beanie hat and bandage. No wonder you're doing so crap at the fashion thing.' It sounded like he was speaking from memory though.

Mallory looked at me helplessly and as I'm a sucker for helpless females, particularly ones I'm already trying to get to know a bit better, I thought I ought to help out. However, I was more interested in Banjo and his gun than Harrison Makepeace Stamp.

'How was the beer, Banjo?' I asked. 'Left any for the rest of us?'

Banjo spoke. 'Oh, there's plenty left, Sam. You won't be drinking any of it, though. Sorry about that.' He didn't look sorry. 'Now, turn around, both of you.'

'Why? So's you can shoot us in the back? I don't think so, mate.' I was surprised at how fearless I sounded. I wasn't fooling myself but Mallory seemed to take heart. She edged closer and gripped my hand.

'Touching,' said Banjo, which was literally correct. 'I'm not going to shoot you in the back. That's not what I do. There's somebody wants a word first.' I wasn't sure I liked the sound of that "first". 'Now turn round and open the door behind you.'

'Going for a walk in the woods, are we?' I said. 'You want to be careful you don't lose us in the dark.'

'You probably shouldn't be telling the man with the gun your escape plans,' said the man with the gun. 'And in any case, it'd be hard to lose Mallory, however dark it is. I've never seen a face that white. However, all that's irrelevant. You appear to believe this is the door in the woods that you unfortunately discovered.' It wasn't? That took me by surprise. What else could it be? 'No, Sam, I think your sense of spatial awareness is playing you up, or your judgement of distance. One of the two. Open it, please.' Hearing the words spatial awareness coming out of Banjo's mouth was almost as big a surprise as the gun, which he now waved vaguely in the direction of the door. It wasn't a particularly menacing wave, but the important bit was that it was a gun being waved. I turned and grasped the handle.

The door opened inwards. Until ten seconds ago, I'd expected it to reveal the hole I'd nearly fallen down a few days before, with the set of steep steps leading up to the majestic trees and so forth. But it didn't. The door opened on to yet another cellar, although calling it a cellar was doing it a disservice. This room, underground and windowless or not, was plush. I mean the sort of plush of which royalty might approve. An expanse of thick pearl-grey carpet led to a set of oak-banistered stairs at the far end. Armchairs and sofas were clustered around a stone fireplace to our right with a drinks table, not noticeably short of bottles, to one side. The pictures on the walls looked expensive, although I'm not an expert. I was really just going on the depth of gilt on the frames.

Two questions occurred to me. I was sure there'd be many others in due course. Firstly, if this wasn't the door in the woods, which it wasn't, where was that door? We definitely hadn't passed another one. Secondly, where were we now? The answer to that question could only be that we were beneath The Thatched House. Banjo was right; my judgement of the distance we'd walked along the passage was indeed awry. So, did that make Stamp the owner? Was he in fact The Banker?

Banjo spoke again. 'Show your daughter and Mr Bryant to an armchair and pour them a drink, Stamp. They look like they could do with one.' Stamp wasn't used to being told what to do and he didn't look enamoured at being referred to as Stamp either but there wasn't much he could do about it. There wasn't much Mallory and I could do either, so we crossed the expanse of thick grey carpet and sat down on a sofa. It was a sofa so deep that leaping out of it in a hurry, should an opportunity to relieve Banjo of his weapon present itself, wouldn't be easy. Mind you, Banjo's new air of quiet competence suggested that such an opportunity would not be arriving any time soon.

Stamp, as instructed, was pouring drinks over by the

fireplace. Brandy, by the looks of it. Three of them. I wasn't really a brandy man, but on this occasion it seemed a good choice. I hoped it might sharpen my wits, which were currently blunter than James and Emily combined.

'Who are we waiting for?' My question was directed at Banjo but it was Stamp, treading heavily across the carpet holding three generous measures of brandy, who answered.

'Who do ya think?'

And suddenly, the answer came to me. 'Maeve,' I said. 'It's Maeve, isn't it?'

'Maeve!' he almost spat the word. What sorta name's that? But yeah, Eve-May's running this show.'

As if on cue, a faint draught signalled the opening of another door and I looked up from Stamp's grey face to see Maeve standing at the top of the staircase at the end of the room. It was a Maeve I hardly recognised. Gone was the thin, whey-faced, mousey woman who trod apologetically around The Farts and in her place was a refined woman in her mid-forties, carefully made-up and wearing a beautifully cut, expensive-looking dark-blue trouser-suit and an equally beautifully cut, expensive-looking blonde hairdo.

'Sit down and shut up, Pop,' she said, descending the stairs and walking towards us. 'And Baxter, you're supposed to be keeping control, not hosting a house-party.' Baxter I presumed was Banjo. I wasn't sure if I'd ever heard him use his surname but I guess if he had it wouldn't have been the one he'd been born with. Stamp slumped into an armchair and a brief look of annoyance crossed Banjo's – Baxter's – face. He looked as if he was about to answer Eve-May back but thought better of it. Suddenly, the gun looked slightly less vague. His reaction was interesting. What was his relationship with Eve-May? Were they lovers? She was several years his senior but it was possible. Or was he just the hired hand? Hired hands don't generally think about answering their employers back.

'What's this all about, Maeve?' I asked, deliberately calling her Maeve. I wondered if it might rile her and I was right.

'None of your business, Mr Goody-Gumdrops.' That was a new one. Maeve had rarely spoken in my presence but when she had it had been with a home counties whine. The whine had gone, replaced by a North American twang, though not as pronounced as Mallory's.

'Oh, I think it is, Maeve. Seeing as how I'm sitting here with a gun pointing at me. So I'm hoping this is the part when you tell us all about your evil plans for world domination before tying us up in the cellar and leaving us to die a slow death. If you're thinking the water levels in the Idlebrook might rise up enough to drown us, I'd remind you that this is the driest summer on record, notwithstanding today's rain.' Something similar had happened in a thriller I'd read recently.

'Oh, don't worry, it won't be that slow,' she said. Me and my big mouth. 'Nearly full marks for the rest of it though. But before all that, sister dearest,' and she turned to Mallory, who hadn't spoken since we'd entered the room but was visibly simmering beside me, if her previously snow-white face was anything to go by. It was now approaching a Jontyesque shade of vermilion. 'Perhaps we should introduce ourselves. You were only a kid last time we met. Grown quite tall, haven't you? You didn't get that from darling papa. What comes of having a showgirl for a mother, I guess. Anyway, you've got something for me.'

She was presumably referring to the key, although why she needed it, I wasn't sure. I hadn't yet worked out where the door in the woods was in relation to where we were sitting and, as for what was in there, it could have been a haybarn for Farmer Trickle's Red Herefords for all the clue I had. Anyway, it seemed that Mallory was of the same mind. I could tell by the way she yanked it out of her pocket and hurled it at her half-sister's head. It was a hell of a shot from a sitting position and especially as Eve-May didn't present much of a target; I doubted if she'd tip the scales at much over nine stone. The key, together with its Oxford United key fob, struck her straight between the eyes. She screamed in pain, clasped her hands to her head and staggered sideways into Banjo, who was standing next to her. This was just as well, all things considered, as Banjo had raised his gun as Mallory threw the keys and was about to pull the trigger when Eve-May crashed into him. The bullet took a chunk out of the stone fireplace, missing old Stamp by a hairsbreadth.

I decided it was time for me to stop being an idle bystander (or, more accurately, bysitter), so I attempted to hurl myself at Banjo before he could let off a second shot. I wasn't sure that Eve-May necessarily wanted her sister killed at this point in the proceedings but Banjo seemed to have made up his own mind. Perhaps he was being paid by the dead body. Unfortunately, I'd forgotten three things: my sore shoulder, the fact that I was holding an untouched glass of brandy, and the depth and squishiness of the sofa. The brandy, more by luck than judgement, flew into Banjo's face whilst, embarrassingly, a combination of my shoulder and the reluctance of the sofa to release me from its cushioned grip resulted in me ending up spread-eagled, face-down in the grey pile carpet.

I heard Banjo swear as a quarter of a pint of 45% alcoholic content spirit splashed into his eyes. At the same moment, I discovered I could reach one of his legs from my prone position, so I grabbed it and tugged. Not before he'd managed to fire a second shot though. I had no idea where the bullet had gone and immediately afterwards I had no idea about anything much at all as Banjo landed on top of me and I was thumped painfully above the left ear by what I can only presume was the gun. Everything went black.

24

MONDAY 22ND JULY
PITCHFORKS AND TORCHES

OK, it might not have been the brightest idea I've ever had to throw the key at Eve-May, what with Banjo or Baxter or whatever his goddam name was, standing there with a shooter pointed at me. It worked out pretty good though, all in all.

Eve-May had fallen into Baxter as he fired his gun. I ducked instinctively and heard the bullet whine past and thump into something behind me. It didn't sound like the something was Pop, so, hate the old bastard with all my heart as I do, at least that was something. If he was going to get killed, I wanted it to be me on the distribution arm of that. Looking up again I saw that Sam had taken advantage of the collision between Eve-May and Baxter by cleverly flinging his brandy into his old pal's face. Unfortunately, I could also see the full unadulterated circumference of the hole in the end of Baxter's gun barrel, so I figured the next bullet was going to be hitting me before it reached anywhere else. I didn't have time to say all the shitty things that came to me at that point because Sam, bless him, tried to throw himself into the bullet's path. True, the attempt wasn't all that successful, as he basically just flumped down on the carpet, but I saw him grab Baxter's leg just as he let off the next shot.

Sam had done enough. Baxter fell on top of him and the second bullet came nowhere near me. Unfortunately for Eve-May, it came quite a lot near her. Through her in fact. She was still upright when it hit, although her face was masked with blood from the key and its fob, and her expensive suit was already in need of emergency dry-cleaning. However, the bullet made the dry-cleaning superfluous. The entry hole in her left shoulder was quite small but it would definitely show up were she to try wearing the suit with a white shirt underneath at any posh shindigs, and whilst I couldn't see the exit hole, I suspected it would be a whole heap bigger. She collapsed on the floor. Bearing in mind how loud she'd screamed when the key had hit her, I was quite impressed how silent she was on being properly shot. She appeared to be conscious but relatively harmless, so I looked around to see how everyone else was faring. Pop, amazingly, hadn't moved. He was still sat in his armchair and still had half a glass of brandy clamped in his scraggy old mitt. He wasn't drinking it though, which could indicate the onset of shock, as did the wide, sightless eyes. I looked around for my own drink. I had no idea what I'd done with it. I'd never drunk a sip of brandy in my life but I was beginning to think now would be a good time to start. However, judging by the spreading stain on the arm of the sofa, I'd have to pour myself another one or nick Pop's.

*Unlike Eve-May, Sam **was** unconscious. It looked like he'd been whacked by the gun as Baxter fell on top of him. Already, a vivid purple lump was swelling above his left eye. Of more immediate importance, however, was the fact that Baxter was starting to rise to his feet and was reaching for his dropped weapon. Now, whoever owned the room we were in, basement or not, they had not stinted on the décor. Sitting on a table behind* *the sofa was a sizeable blue and white vase. It looked Chinese, you know, flying dragons and suchlike. Maybe it was Ming, who knows? Anyway, I was merciless. I plucked it off the table and crashed it down on Baxter's head. Bit of a bald spot developing there, I noted, as he fell backwards onto Sam for a second time.*

I picked up the discarded gun. I wasn't sure if I knew how to make it work if push came to shove but I reckoned I was more than a match physically for a wounded Eve-May with or without it. Still, it felt good to hold it.

At that point, I heard a loud banging and muffled shouts coming from somewhere over my head. Either the cavalry had arrived or I had only a short time to learn how to fire the gun if whoever was at the front door turned out to be pally with my half-sister and Baxter.

PITCHFORKS AND FLAMING TORCHES. *That was the scene that greeted me when I opened the front door. Even for Lazytown, I reckoned it was a bit out of the ordinary. True, there were only two flaming torches and I'm not certain that all the forks could be described as pitch but then I'm not from farming stock so I'd have to look that up. It wasn't much of a crowd either, no more than about ten villagers standing on the gravel in front of The Thatched House. So, all in all, it wasn't exactly Transylvania.*

I didn't recognise all of the ten, understandably as I'd set foot in Idleborough for the first time less than a week ago. Lurking in the shadows at the back I made out the rat-like features of Billy the Kid and standing front and centre was the far bulkier Mucker, still wearing galoshes, although this was actually appropriate given the earlier rain. Mucker was holding the bigger of the two flaming torches. Not a particularly well-constructed torch, truth be told; even as I spotted him, the flames were starting to lick at his big, bearlike paw and he dropped the torch and stamped on it. Next to him, I noticed Daisy edging sideways towards another, even fatter guy wearing an old, black Rolling Stones tee who I suspected might be her dad, Dick, although we'd never met. Daisy held neither torch nor pitchfork but Dick – if indeed it was him – had a firm two-handed grip on what looked like a garden rake.

No one said anything for quite a while. I was literally dumbfounded and the deputation on the drive had obviously not rehearsed anything. Mucker finished stamping on the embers of his no-longer-flaming torch and stared at me, an astonished expression on his big, wide face. I guess that was hardly surprising. I'd not known quite what to do with Eve-May – it hadn't seemed like a wise move to just leave her on the floor of the basement room, head wound and bullet-riddled shoulder notwithstanding – so I'd slung her over my left shoulder when I'd gone up to answer the thumping on the front door. She didn't weigh much but even so, my shoulder was telling me this was another thing I probably shouldn't have attempted. Anyway, I could understand that Mucker, Daisy and ensemble might not have reckoned on seeing me standing there with the woman they knew as Maeve wrapped round my neck. I'd managed to lose the beanie hat too, so I daresay I looked a fright, what with the bandage and all.

I guess I'd hoped that I'd find the police on the doorstep but at least it wasn't a crew of gun-toting villains. Even if the sorry collection of villagers – one or two of whom were swaying slightly, having clearly come straight from one of the pubs – had been carrying firearms and not garden implements (and was that a pool cue?), they couldn't have looked less villainous if they'd tried.

So I was glad they were there and glad that Daisy was one of them. She at least had a brain. I smiled at her. 'Hi,' I said. 'If you guys were looking for an after-hours rave, I'm not sure we've got enough drink in.' It was entirely probable that Pop had finished off the brandy by now. *'Possibly we should have specified Bring Your Own Bottle, rather than Bring Your Own Barbecue and Cutlery.'* I was quite proud of that. My concussion might have been wearing off. Either that, or it had returned with renewed vigour and I was just imagining the small crowd in front of me. So when Daisy spoke, it was a relief. It was the first time any of the villagers had uttered a sound and it had started to get a touch spooky.

'Why are you carrying Maeve?' she said. 'And what's happened to her? She's covered in blood.' They were good questions and prompted me to realise that Eve-May was becoming an increasingly uncomfortable burden, so I dropped her on the front step, from which she slid down on to the gravel at Daisy's feet. Amazingly, she still seemed to be conscious although the wound on her forehead was far less serious than the amount of blood on her face suggested. I had no idea how serious the bullet wound was, not being a medical professional, but I guessed if the slug had passed through anything vital, she'd have been a goner by now. Half-sister or not, I didn't care that much but then I remembered she still had a whole heap of questions to answer.

'She'll live,' I said, although I didn't know for sure if that was true. 'Could you call the cops, Daisy, sweetheart, and get them to bring an ambulance with them?' I wasn't confident any of the men with her would be capable of managing these simple instructions, always assuming they possessed cell phones in the first place. Daisy pulled hers out though and dialled 999 which, now that phones are all push-buttony, seems to be a more memorable emergency number than back home's 911, a relic from the days of dial-up telephones when a victim could have died while *you were waiting for the dial to trickle round the full circuit three whole times. My mind was wandering. I shook my head. Maybe I still had concussion after all.*

Daisy put her phone away and took charge. 'They're on their way,' she said. 'Dad, Mucker, take Maeve inside and put her somewhere comfortable.'

*'Doesn't have to be **that** comfortable,' I muttered as they moved forward and bent to pick her up. Daisy turned to me, pushed her glasses up her nose and tried to look stern. 'Now perhaps you could tell us what's been going on, Miss Fillery,' she said. The stern look and "Miss Fillery" indicated that she no longer regarded me in an entirely friendly light and I guess that was understandable. I had after all, opened the door to a house I had no right to be in and deposited their blood-soaked landlady in a heap at their feet. 'And what have you done with Sam?' The villager next to her, a swarthy, pockmarked fella with a fearsome squint and wielding a genuine garden fork, took a step forwards and pointed it, unasked, in my direction.*

'Yeah, who the fuck are you, lady?' he shouted. I swayed sideways as a blob of spittle came flying past. I was beginning to hope the cops would show up soon.

'She's Sam's "friend",' said Daisy, managing to imbue the word friend with more meaning than it warranted. 'She's a reporter for the Stockford Spectacle.*'*

The man with the squint looked like he didn't particularly care for reporters in general and this one in particular. I held my hands up in mock-surrender and stepped to one side to allow the two bulky figures of Mucker and Daisy's Dad to move past me, carrying Maeve uncomfortably between them. Uncomfortably for both her and them, it seemed to me. Indeed, they appeared to be struggling with her insignificant weight a great deal more than I had on my girly lonesome, but then neither of them looked like gym-bunnies. They disappeared into the house and I decided I wasn't going to take a defensive position here. After all, I'd done nothing wrong. I'd been shot myself, I'd been kidnapped at gunpoint by one of their mates and, frankly, I was beginning to wish I'd never set foot in their damn village, which was starting to seem like a flashback to the eighties – the eighteen-eighties that is. Also, Sam was lying downstairs unconscious, underneath the aforesaid mate. Either or both of them could be waking up any time now, and if it was Banjo Baxter first, he might require some more merciless Minging. Where the fuck were those damn cops?

I'd tucked Baxter's gun into the waistband of my jeans at the back and, all in all, now seemed a good time to produce it. So I did. Daisy's face was a picture. Her mouth opened and her round glasses slid down to the tip of her nose. The swarthy guy with the squint and the garden fork took a step back. I wasn't intending to shoot anyone although that might change if there was any more spittle flying about.

'Let's all calm down, shall we?' I said. 'Drop your little sticks and come inside.' I gestured with the gun and Daisy, fork-squint-spittle-guy and the others behind them decided that my argument was suddenly very persuasive. One fork, one rake, one hoe, one pool cue and one no-longer flaming torch hit the deck and, with Daisy leading, they trooped past me into The Thatched House.

Mucker and Dick had taken Eve-May into a lounge on the left of the hallway. This was a room even more expensively furnished than the basement room. There were two more vases of possible Ming provenance on a long, polished wood sideboard and the sofa that they'd laid Eve-May on was so long that there must have been a foot clearance either end of her. The two fat blokes were standing there puffing like they'd never breathe easily again. 'You guys,' I said. 'You'd better sit down before you fall down. The rest of you, stand over there please.' I pointed the gun towards an empty bit of pile carpet – baby blue this time – and then shrugged and placed the weapon on the sideboard between the twin Mings.

'I'm not the villain here, guys,' I said. My voice sounded as tired as I felt. 'That would be my sister here.' I nodded at Eve-May and slumped down in an armchair that was conveniently just behind me. I suddenly felt as weak as a kitten. No more Eve-May carrying for me tonight.

'Your sister?' said Daisy incredulously. 'But that's Maeve.'

'And she'm in Benidorm,' said Mucker, whose thought processes may not have caught up with proceedings yet.

'Look, 'I said, 'I know you've got questions but I genuinely don't have any answers. What I need urgently though is for a couple of you to go down to the basement where you'll find Sam and your pal Banjo, along with my old man. I left Sam and Banjo unconscious but they may be waking up by now. You'll need to have a care. Banjo's not who you think he is. This belongs to him.' I picked up the gun again and looked about for volunteers. There was only one: Billy the Kid, who emerged from the back of the small crowd and took the gun from me.

'Leave it to me, Mallory,' he said and disappeared out the door with a turn of speed I'd never seen him display before. I was slightly concerned as Billy had not thus far in our limited acquaintance given off any air of responsibility or reliability.

'Should someone go with him?' I suggested to the sea of blank, possibly drunk, faces in front of me.

There was a pause of several seconds before Daisy piped up. 'Mucker,' she said. 'Get yourself out of that chair and go down to the basement. See what's going on.' Mucker wouldn't have been my first choice but then my first choice probably didn't live in Idleborough and certainly wasn't in the room. Mucker sighed hugely, heaved himself out of his armchair and waddled out the door, leaving wet, galosh-shaped footprints on the expensive carpet. I'd have gone too but my head was spinning like a carousel now and I felt sick.

As the dizziness expanded, I thought I could just make out the sound of distant sirens.

25
MONDAY 22ND JULY
VASES AND SOFAS

I supposed I must have been unconscious but I didn't know how long I'd been out. All I knew was that if I didn't do something sharpish I'd soon be unconscious again and soon after that, in all probability, dead. As I came to, I was aware of having my throat squeezed, so I opened my eyes to see what was squeezing it. Not a what, as it turned out, but a who, or grammatically speaking, a whom. I don't know if you've ever come round after being out cold but I can tell you it takes a while to get your brain back in gear. And having a bloke who, until half an hour earlier, you'd considered to be one of your best friends, trying his damnedest to throttle you, isn't guaranteed to bring your mind back to its razorlike best. Or whatever level of best it had previously attained.

I was flat on my back on what was admittedly one of the most comfortable stretches of carpet on which I'd ever lain, with Banjo astride me, a look of steely determination in his eyes and a small piece of blue and white porcelain sticking out of his head just north of his leftward steely determined eye. A trickle of blood was oozing slowly from the piece of porcelain, down his cheek and dripping on to me from his unshaven chin. I guess it was the drip of blood on to my face that had woken me. His hands, usually wrapped lovingly around a pint glass, were now wrapped rather less lovingly but no less tightly around my throat. If this carried on, breathing was going to be one of those things fondly remembered from the past.

I tried to shove him off but Banjo was displaying a level of murderous professionalism I had never previously suspected he might possess and was kneeling on my biceps, so it was as if I only had the arms of a T-Rex, too short to reach any part of him to shove. I looked around desperately for something I could grasp that might help me fight back, or at least gain some sort of leverage. There was another shard of blue and white porcelain just within reach, so I inched my fingers across the carpet and grabbed it. That, initially at least, was a painful mistake. The shard was sharper than it looked and I could feel a couple of cuts opening in my palm. Up until now, the blood from Banjo's head had mostly deposited itself on me and not the undoubtedly expensive, pearl-grey carpet but now my own vital fluid was starting to form a small puddle that would likely require a sophisticated cleaning operation to remove.

It took me much longer to think those thoughts than to act. Even so, time was running out. I thrust my right hand with its pointy piece of porcelain up as far as I could reach. Because of my presently dinosaur-length arms, that wasn't in truth very far. But far enough. The porcelain made contact with and sliced into Banjo's left thigh; even his elderly, frankly rather stiff jeans failed to stop its progress. He let out a yell of obvious pain and the clamp around my neck suddenly eased as he removed one hand to feel for the wound. His eyes looked down too, the steely determination now replaced by something akin to the anguish they displayed on that occasion long, long ago – well, last week anyway – in The Bull following the closure of The Farts. All an act, that much was now clear. I freed my hands, reached for his chest and heaved upwards, only remembering my damaged shoulder as I did so.

Despite the sharp stab of pain, it did the trick. I managed to free myself enough to roll sideways, where I collided with a pale-green velvet sofa. Immediately, a positive deluge of blood hit me in the face. At first I thought I must have cut my hand more badly than I'd imagined but then I could see the blood was pouring out of Banjo's thigh. He had, inadvisedly it seemed, pulled the piece of porcelain from his leg. It had evidently pierced what my memory, rapidly returning, told me was the femoral artery. I was far from being an expert but I suspected that not only would the carpet be beyond repair very soon, so would Banjo if something wasn't done to stop the bleeding. Banjo wasn't currently my favourite person, what with the gun and the strangling, but I quite fancied asking him some serious questions and I wouldn't be able to do that if he was dead. I wasn't wearing a belt and neither was Banjo himself, but then I noticed that Harrison Makepeace Stamp was still sitting in his armchair, eyes glazed, as he'd been before all the fighting and unconsciousness had started. There was no sign of Mallory or Eve-May but I saw that Stamp was wearing a belt to hold up his blue chinos. I rolled over, wiping at least some of Banjo's blood off my face with a convenient antimacassar, jumped to my feet with an agility that astounded me, grabbed Stamp's belt and undid it. Even that didn't rouse him from his stupor and, impressively, the half-full glass of brandy in his hand hardly moved.

Pulling the belt from around his over-generous waist took more strength than I expected but needs must. By now, Banjo was lying on the ground, his face white and both hands clamped around his thigh. I wrapped the belt around his leg above the wound, slotted the ends together and yanked hard. The bleeding stopped as though a tap had been turned off. So far so good but we needed an ambulance pronto. I realised I still had my phone on me so pulled it out of my jeans and was just about to dial when I noticed Billy standing over me. He had an altogether familiar-looking gun in his hand and it was pointing straight at my head.

'Drop the phone, Sam,' he said in the weaselly little voice he used when he felt particularly pleased with himself. Actually, it was the weaselly little voice he always used.

Exactly where Mucker appeared from, I have no idea. One minute I was kneeling on the ground over the semi-conscious form of the seriously injured Banjo, with Billy looking eager to make some sort of violent video game grim reality and the next, a size twelve Wellington boot, grey with dried mud, hit Billy square on the back of the head and propelled him over the lime-green sofa behind which he'd been standing. Billy cracked his head on the glass-topped coffee table next to old Stamp's chair. The gun flew in the air and was heading straight for Stamp's unmoving head when I reached across and caught it like it was the most straightforward slip catch in the world. Stamp didn't in truth look too well anyway and it seemed only chivalrous not to let him suffer further injury. Like Banjo, Eve-May and now the flattened Billy, questions needed asking of him.

'You'm all right then, young Sam?' said Mucker,

looming behind the sofa and rubbing his hands together with the air of a man whose job is done and done well.

I heard the faint sounds of sirens in the distance as Mucker plodded, slightly lopsidedly, around the sofa, one foot still encased in its welly, the other adorned with a black sock which might or might not have started its life another colour entirely. Two horny-nailed toes peeped out through a hole with the air of toes who had never seen the outside world before. If they were hatching any plans about making a break for freedom, these were quickly nipped in the bud as Mucker found his ballistic Wellington, flomped down on the sofa, which proved to be of the necessary quality and sturdiness to survive the assault, and pulled it on. This didn't look to be a completely straightforward task and involved quite a lot of swearing, but eventually the boot was back in its habitual place.

Meanwhile, with the sirens getting louder, but still muffled by the fact that we were underground, I was attempting to help Banjo into a more comfortable position. I placed a cushion under his head and raised his injured leg on to an unoccupied armchair, but was worried that if at least one of the sirens wasn't attached to an ambulance, then there was every chance that Banjo wasn't going to make it. He was conscious and moaning slightly, and something told me I should try and keep him awake.

'Banjo,' I said into his face. 'Can you hear me? Don't go to sleep!'

'Don't you'm worry 'bout him,' said Mucker. 'Tha's a nasty lookin' lump on your'm head. You'm need to sit down or you'ms agian' to fall down.' He was right. I'd forgotten all about being knocked out myself by Banjo's gun, which Mucker had recovered from Billy and which was now poking out of a pocket in his old raincoat. I sat on the sofa and glanced around the room. Old Stamp was still in his armchair but his eyes were starting to look less glazed and he was beginning the laborious process of lifting his brandy glass to his lips. I guessed he'd be all right. Billy too. The glass-topped table had survived its collision with his head and Billy himself looked OK, or as OK as a weasely little runt can look. He was lying on his back at Stamp's feet and keeping one ratty eye on Mucker's boots, which were within kicking distance. The sirens above us suddenly stopped wailing. 'Now'm then,' continued Mucker. 'What the fuck'ms been agoin' on 'ere then?'

'Not sure I know,' I said, truthfully. 'It looks like our two pals here haven't been entirely honest with us.'

'Young Billy'm wouldn't know'm honest if they boxed hims ears with it. Banjo, though. You'm sayin' he'ms a bad'un too? And your'm girlie friend's got'm Maeve slung over her'm shoulder upstairs. Says she'm some sort o' crook too.' He scratched his head, a puzzled frown spreading across his wide, grizzled face. It occurred to me he looked more sober than I'd ever seen him, not bad going for a man who, in all likelihood, had spent ten hours that day in The Bull. He jerked a big thumb at Stamp, now glugging brandy like there was no tomorrow and hardly looking like an all-powerful billionaire businessman with a reputation for ruthlessness. 'Who'm this then?' said Mucker. 'The Banker, I'm aguessin'?'

'That's a gentleman by the name of Harrison Makepeace Stamp,' I said. 'He's Mallory's dad but whether he's The Banker too, I don't know.'

'Let'm's ask 'im then.'

'I think you can leave the questions to us, sir, if you don't mind,' came a voice. I looked up. Detective Inspector

Anderson was walking down the stairs, DS Rose a step behind her.

'Questions,' affirmed Rose.

A couple of paramedics trotted past them and headed in our direction and I was aware of a whole group of people, villagers mostly, massing at the top of the stairs behind Anderson and Rose, two uniformed coppers attempting to hold them at bay. Mallory's red hair and white bandage towered over most of them.

IT TURNED out that Daisy had spotted Mallory and me from her bedroom window as we'd made our midnight excursion to The Farts. She'd hurriedly pulled on some clothes and followed us. When we didn't re-emerge, she'd gone to The Bull and rounded up her dad and a few other locals. Whose idea it had been to grab some rudimentary weaponry, no one seemed too sure, and as for what sounded like poor excuses for flaming torches, well, words failed me. After all, they were on their way to The Farts, not Castle Dracula. Anyway, when they'd arrived at the pub, someone I knew only as Squint had noticed lights on in The Thatched House next door and the always locked security gate open. Both those things were so unusual that a decision had been made to divert from the darkened pub and go and ask politely what was occurring at the mysterious house none of them had ever previously been that close to.

Daisy told me all that while an ambulanceman was dressing the relatively insignificant wound on my forehead. I was soon the bandaged double of Mallory, minus the red hair and considerably less photogenic. Banjo and Eve-May – who it turned out had taken a bullet through the shoulder – were whisked off in ambulances under police guard and

Billy was also taken away in a cop car. Most of the villagers were sent home to bed. It was, I realised, getting on for three in the morning but judging by the look on Inspector Anderson's round face, I wouldn't be seeing my own bed for quite a while, and nor would Mallory, Daisy, Stamp or Mucker, all of whom had been told to remain.

We all trooped upstairs, Mallory assisting her dad. I was quite comfortable where I was on the pale green sofa but apparently the basement room was now an official crime scene and needed to be preserved for fingerprinting and other policey, forensic-type stuff. Daisy was deputed – doubtless by herself – to go and find coffee and the rest of us were shown into an even plusher room than the one we'd just left. I slumped down on another sofa, this one covered in some sort of flowery pattern on a white background, I noted inconsequentially. I tried hard to keep my eyes open. The coffee helped.

'Now, who wants to start?' said Anderson, sitting also.

'Yeah, start,' added Rose, standing behind her.

26

MONDAY 22ND JULY
IDENTITIES AND JOBS

It looked like no one wanted to start. For one thing, Anderson's question hadn't been directed at Daisy or Mucker. That left me, Mallory and her old man. It occurred to me that I hadn't heard Stamp utter a single word since Banjo had ushered us all into the basement lounge from the hidden passage, and he didn't look like he was about to begin talking now. Mallory opened her mouth as if to start the ball rolling but then shut it again and looked at me. So that narrowed the starters down to one.

'It was you who told me that Maeve Spaggott was really Eve-May Stamp, Inspector,' I said, rather neatly turning the tables, I thought. 'How did you know that?'

'We were told,' she replied after a few moments' consideration. She held up a pudgy hand, forestalling my next question. 'Jonathan Hardy-Hewitt suggested it to us, so being country bumpkin coppers with nothing better to do, we followed it up. Turns out she didn't bother to hide it very well.'

'So that must mean that Jonty – Hardy-Hewitt – **is** involved in all of this,' I said, sitting forward excitedly. 'And he killed his brother to get the title. Have you got anyone watching the Earl of Northavon? I bet he's next for the chop.'

'Whoa, cowboy,' said Anderson, holding up her hand again.

'Cowboy,' muttered Rose.

'There is one flaw in your argument.' Anderson again. 'The Hon. Jonathan Hardy-Hewitt is dead.'

'No, he's not,' I said. 'He's masquerading as Uppingshott. You said yourself there was something fishy about the supposed Uppingshott's body language. And his sister's. Lady Felicity must be in on it too.'

'In on what? No, Mr Bryant, you're barking up the wrong family tree. Jonathan's dead and we have the DNA to prove it. Who killed him, I'm not sure, but it's looking like it's connected to this place and The Three Pigeons next door.'

'You'ms means The Farts,' grunted Mucker. I noticed that instead of the coffee the rest of us were drinking, he'd managed to acquire a bottle of London Pride. I imagined Daisy had found a stash of beer in the kitchen and didn't want Mucker to be getting withdrawal symptoms.

'Which brings us back to tonight's little bit of merriment,' continued Anderson. 'But before we start on that, Mr Bryant, you still have an appointment with Lady Felicity tomorrow morning.' She looked at her watch. 'Sorry, **this** morning, in about five hours to be exact. We'd like you to keep that appointment. You might help us to fill some gaps. I'm afraid you're not going to be getting much sleep tonight.' She paused. 'Like the rest of us.'

'OK,' I said. I couldn't see me sleeping anyway. 'Back to tonight. There's a secret passage between the pub and this house. That's how Miss Fillery and I got here.'

'Go on,' prompted Anderson. 'We'll come back in due course to what you were doing breaking into the pub in the first place.'

'We were looking for the door I'd found hidden in the woods at the back of The Farts, sorry, The Three Pigeons. But we missed it somehow and ended up under this place, where we came face to face with Banjo pointing a gun at Mr Stamp here.'

'Who's supposed to be in Toronto,' said Mallory, glaring at her father, who finally seemed to be taking a keener interest in proceedings, maybe buoyed by the brandy and coffee and by the fact that he was no longer being held at gunpoint by his elder daughter and her sidekick. Sidekick? I'd long thought of Banjo as **my** sidekick but it turned out he was Maeve's.

'Ah, yes, the young man with the hole in his leg. Hopefully he'll live long enough for us to ask him some questions.' She didn't sound as if she cared too much if he lived past that point. 'To save a bit of time, can you give us his real name?'

'Tim,' I said. 'At least that's what he told us. Banjo's a nickname.'

'No shit, Sherlock. Surname?'

'Maeve – Eve-May – called him Baxter. I'm not sure he ever gave us a surname.'

Suddenly there was some wheezing from the armchair to our right. It was Harrison Makepeace Stamp preparing to come to the party. 'Baxter's his first name,' he growled. 'He's Baxter MacAllister. And he's Eve-May's husband.'

Banjo's assertion that he'd been to Glasgow only once in his life was beginning to look like something else we could add to a growing list of untruths. If he was Scottish, and the name Baxter MacAllister suggested a southward crossing of Hadrian's Wall at some point in his past, then he'd been hiding the accent well. I thought back trying to recall anything that might have given us a clue to his real identity. How had he interacted with Maeve? His wife as it turned out. The truth is I couldn't fully remember. Maeve had been a shadowy background figure to me. Hell, I hadn't even been invited to her wedding, had I? Wait a minute: her wedding. Her wedding to Clem.

'Umm,' I said. 'If Eve-May is married to Banjo – MacAllister, that is – then presumably you can get her on bigamy charges too.'

'At the moment, that's about all we've got that'll stick but I daresay after Sergeant Rose and I have talked to her in a few hours, we'll find something else.'

'Talk,' grunted Rose, and allowed a thin smile to stretch across his broad face.

'Well, try this on for size,' I said. 'She and Clem were supposed to be in Benidorm. She's here, so where's Clem?'

'Don't think for a moment that's not number one on our list of questions,' said Anderson.

So they'd thought about that. Well, if they were only half-decent at their job, then they would have done. 'That door I was talking about,' I said. ' In the woods. Just a thought, but shall we try opening it?'

Mallory held up the Oxford United fob with the Yale key attached. The key appeared to have blood on it. She waved it about a bit. 'Now seems like as good a time as any. Especially as dawn's breaking and we can see where we're going.'

Anderson looked at Rose and Rose looked at Anderson. 'OK, then, well done Mr Bryant,' said the inspector. 'Mind you, if it's where you say it is, we're going to need some heavy equipment to get to it. That greenery at the back of

the pub car park isn't something you can just plod through.'
I assumed her use of the word plod had been deliberate.

'Plod,' echoed Rose, reinforcing that assumption.

And then Stamp spoke again. 'You might find someone else there,' he said slowly. We all looked at him. 'Two people in fact, but one of them long since dead.' He put his grizzled head in his hands and for a moment I thought he was crying. Then he looked up again and I **knew** he was crying; the tears running down his semi-bearded cheeks were something of a giveaway.

'Pop?' said Mallory, moving across and crouching next to him, grabbing his hands in hers. If she hated him as much as she'd suggested, then love and hate really were two halves of the same whole.

Anderson had also risen. 'Who are you talking about, Mr Stamp?' she said, not unkindly. At that moment he was more like a lovable old grandad than a cut-throat business tycoon. He looked up at her. She wasn't very tall so he didn't have to look too far up.

'Madeline,' he whispered. That would be the current Mrs Stamp, I remembered. But he hadn't finished. 'And Jennifer.'

An hour later, I was standing with Anderson, Rose, Mallory and her father next to Clem's immobile old Land Rover at the rear of The Farts. Mucker and Daisy had been dismissed, but there were six other coppers there, two of whom were tooled up. Out on the road, an ambulance was standing by. The rest of the car park was taken up by a yellow JCB, its engine idling, waiting for the go ahead to plough through the thorny barrier in front of us. It wasn't the biggest JCB I'd ever seen but, even so, it hadn't been an entirely straightforward operation manoeuvring the machine through the already broken farm gate – which now lay flat on the ground and beyond any hope of repair – and past the curious dogleg in the side entrance. The JCB had been forced to begin the demolition of the pub a little earlier than planned and there was now a great chunk taken out of the chimney breast around which the entrance to the car park chicaned. I supposed a few bricks – well, quite a few bricks – missing from the already pockmarked wall of The Farts wasn't going to worry anyone, whether or not it ended up as a housing estate; and Anderson had just shrugged her round shoulders as The Thatched House's fence took a direct hit too. The boundary between the two properties was a close boarded eight-foot fence at this point although further on that became a hedge atop a grassy bank. The sun was now peeping over that hedge, and a thin steam was rising from the still wet ground of the car park.

It occurred to me that the ancient Land Rover Defender would have to be moved to allow the JCB to get to the greenery and I wasn't the only one it had occurred to. Sergeant Rose and the four unarmed policemen moved towards it with the obvious intention of pushing it to one side, failing to notice in the faint, dawn light that the vehicle had no wheels and sat atop four piles of bricks. I decided I ought to point out the problem to them before they gave themselves hernias.

'Jesus,' muttered Anderson, before signalling to the JCB driver and pointing at the Land Rover. The yellow beast rolled forward, lowered its bucket and simply scooped the Defender out of its path. It came to rest up against the wall separating the car park from Farmer Trickle's farmyard, crushing four plastic chairs and doing irreparable damage to the Granny's Bobbins pitch in the process.

To everyone's surprise, a smallish hole in the ground was revealed where the Land Rover had stood. The place seemed to be full of unexpected holes. Anderson and I walked across and looked into it, as you would. A short ladder led downwards and the early morning sunlight revealed another tunnel, this one dark, narrow and unsafe-looking, heading off towards the four acres of scrubland with its surprisingly majestic trees.

'Well, that explains how Billy got his tent in there,' I said.

'But how did he manage to shift the old wreck of an auto?' said Mallory, who had joined us. 'He's just a skinny little rat.'

'He wouldn't have had to. He'd have been able to lie down and shimmy underneath it.'

'Well, I'm not going to be doing any shimmying,' said Anderson. 'We'll stick with Plan A, I think. She raised a short arm, and the JCB moved forward again, its claw-like bucket stretched menacingly in front, inches off the ground. It only took a matter of moments to clear a path through the brambles and bushes. None of the surprisingly majestic trees were damaged though, which I was pleased about. I hoped they'd survive whatever was going to happen with the land and the pub. At the moment, of course, we didn't have a landlord and if Viscount Uppingshott truly was the owner of the premises as he claimed, then we could still look forward to the sort of battle we'd originally anticipated before Eve-May Stamp and Banjo Baxter MacAllister had turned things upside down.

I led the way to the first hole in the ground, the one containing the steep steps down to the studded iron door.

The key was now in the hands of Detective Sergeant Rose. Anderson nodded at him and he descended the steps, two armed officers close behind. The rest of us waited at the top, Mallory with her arm around the shorter figure of her father. I cast my mind back an hour.

"Jennifer", Stamp had added to the roll-call of Clem and Madeline, who we might hope or expect to find behind the door. We all looked at each other. It was Mallory who spoke first.

'Who's Jennifer, Pop?'

There was a long silence. It was obvious the old man was struggling to put things into words. He hadn't had the easiest of evenings after all and it sounded as though his present troubles had been going on for a while longer than that. I got up and found some more brandy and passed him a glass; it appeared the house wasn't short of drinks tables, whichever room you were in. He took a big mouthful of the drink and followed it with an even bigger breath. 'Jennifer was my wife,' he said.

I looked at Mallory, whose face was blank. If Stamp had had a wife called Jennifer, neither she nor Wikipedia were aware of the fact.

'Go on, sir,' prompted Anderson, gently.

'When Elizabeth killed herself, I was in shock and I hired a nurse to help me get through the dark days that followed Lizzie's death. Her name was Jennifer. She was a great comfort to me, and we quickly grew close.' He paused. No one interrupted. 'Extremely close. We fell in love and decided to marry. I was still a relatively young man, forty-two, but Jennifer was half my age and Lizzie's family would not have approved, especially so soon after her death. So we married in secret.'

'How soon, Pop?' whispered Mallory.

'A matter of weeks,' said Stamp. 'It was crazy, I knew that, but I was in love.' Again, he paused. 'Still am. Jennifer was the love of my life. We managed to keep the wedding under wraps, but I guess we were never going to hide it for long. We'd planned to stay man and nurse, assistant, whatever, to the outside world for a couple of years and then hold a big, second wedding at the right time. But Eve-May found out. She was already convinced I'd killed Lizzie, her mother, and she went crazy. She came storming round the house. I was out. She attacked Jennifer with a kitchen knife. Killed her. I still don't know whether that had been her intention all along but when I came home, she was still there.'

'Where was all this?' asked Anderson. I presumed she already knew and just wanted confirmation. Wikipedia had placed Elizabeth's death in Stamp's London mansion, somewhere in Hampstead.

'Here, Inspector. Well, not here in Idleberg,' – no one corrected him – 'London. I was spending most of my time over here then. Toronto's my home but you couldn't do a whole heap of business out there. Not in the eighties and nineties anyway.' Not cut-throat enough, I guessed.

'What happened then?' asked Anderson. 'You didn't press charges and it sounds as though Jennifer was airbrushed from history.'

'Exactly that, Inspector,' said Stamp, shrugging. 'Back then, Eve-May was my only child. I couldn't send her to jail. And covering up the murder wasn't difficult. Jennifer had no family and money buys a lot of secrecy. I bought this place and gave it to Eve-May and had a sort of crypt constructed out back for Jennifer. There's a spot for me too when the time comes. So now you know what's behind the door.'

'But that's on land belonging to The Three Pigeons,' I said, remembering not to refer to the pub as The Farts, which would have sounded disrespectful in the circumstances.

'Not so, Mr Bryant,' the old man answered. 'That land has always belonged to this property. The hedge in between is a relatively new construction. It wasn't there thirty years ago. Probably Eve-May put it up.'

'You say you own this house, Mr Stamp,' said Anderson. 'We've been taking a look at the deeds. According them, the property is owned by someone called Jay Spry.'

'You haven't looked far enough, Inspector. Jay Spry is a company, not a person. A subsidiary of Idle Investments Ltd, which is part of Wessex Wayfarer which ultimately is owned by Stamp Inc. Jennifer's surname was Spry, hence the company name.'

Anderson and Rose's faces hadn't expressed any emotion at all of this. I wasn't altogether sure if Rose was capable of emotion although Anderson had shown she possessed a human side. Mallory, however, was understandably shocked. Amongst much else, I guessed she was trying to come to terms with the fact that if her half-sister hadn't killed Jennifer Spry, then Stamp wouldn't have ended up marrying her mother and she, Mallory, wouldn't be here.

So that was not much more than an hour ago. As I watched the three policemen edge down the still-damp, slippery steps to the door, I reflected that, given that Eve-May was already a murderer, there was a very good chance that the late Jennifer wasn't the only dead body we'd find when it was opened. I was glad I wasn't going to be the person to find out first. That would be Sergeant Rose. As he turned the Yale key, I moved slightly to block the already restricted view of the crypt, or whatever it was, from Mallory's eyes. I couldn't care less about Stamp's eyes. If his latest wife turned out to be another victim of his elder daughter, he only had himself to blame for not getting Eve-May locked up in the first place.

The door opened smoothly and the firearms squad coppers, guns in hand, entered first. Rose followed them. We waited above. After thirty seconds, Rose reappeared and nodded at Anderson. She started down the steps, her short legs not enjoying the descent. I suddenly felt an overwhelming urge to see inside the crypt so, not asking permission, I followed her, leaving Mallory and her old man up top with the remaining police officers. As I crossed the threshold, a gun went off at close range. I nearly wet myself. I hadn't been expecting that, although I wasn't sure exactly what I had been expecting. Someone had found a light switch but a thin haze of gun smoke briefly obscured the far wall. As it cleared, I could see two further doors, or rather, gates, comprised of floor to ceiling bars. They looked like the gates to prison cells and as the left-hand gate began to swing slowly open I could see that was exactly what it was. One of the armed coppers had shot out the lock – no Yale keys or Oxford United fobs for this gate – and was now standing back for Inspector Anderson to enter. I stepped forward and peered over her low shoulder.

It was a small room, no more than eight feet by six. There was, obviously, no window and the only light was coming through the doorway, but it was enough to see two people sitting side by side on a plain wooden bench to our left. They were an incongruous couple. Clem, never the cleanest or tidiest man you've ever met, looked and, I have to say, smelt, frightful. I guessed he'd been in this cell for a week and the time hadn't been kind to him. Next to him, dwarfed by comparison, and possibly possessing no sense of smell, sat a woman in early middle age who a few days ago would have looked quite glamorous. Next to Clem she still did. Her blonde hair, which may once upon a time, say last week, have been expensively coiffed, now hung lank and listless over her shoulders and what had until recently been a beautifully cut, white trouser suit was several shades of grubby. This was obviously Stamp's current wife, the usually more fragrant Madeline. She had her hands over her ears following the gunshot to break the lock.

Clem looked at Inspector Anderson and then noticed me standing behind her. 'Youms tooken yourm fucken time, young Sam,' he said.

27
MONDAY 22ND JULY
PALE BLUE JACKETS AND COMMISSION

I hadn't been entirely sure why Inspector Anderson had wanted me to keep my appointment with Lady Felicity Hardy-Hewitt at Stockford Council's Planning Department. It all seemed rather irrelevant in the light of the much bigger picture that had now emerged. OK, the ownership of The Farts was still in question but that would soon be sorted out, presumably in favour of Viscount Uppingshott as he claimed. And then, especially with his younger sister in charge of approving planning applications, I imagined the pub would be no more.

However, questions remained. Clem's letter for one, which seemed to confirm that he'd accepted an offer of a quarter of a million quid for the pub from person or persons as yet unidentified by the rest of us. The pub couldn't belong to both Clem **and** Viscount Uppingshott. Anderson and Rose would no doubt be questioning Clem as soon as he'd had a long shower and a big meal. And secondly, the revelation that The Thatched House was the legal owner of the four acres at the rear meant that it would be impossible to build a viable housing estate unless that extra four acres could be acquired from "Jay Spry", in other words old Stamp himself.

Although Anderson and Rose had yet to formally interview Eve-May and Banjo, the official line of thinking seemed to be that it was they – Banjo probably, given the weight of the study chair – who had killed Jonty. I'd pointed out that his murder could just be a wild coincidence, a burglary gone wrong for example, but as nothing had been stolen from The Manor, and as Anderson didn't believe in coincidences, wild or tamed ('Coincidence,' Rose had grunted with the most sceptical sounding grunt I'd ever heard), my theory wasn't a popular one with the two detectives. They weren't inclined to think that Felicity had any more criminal tendencies than any other Chief Planning Officer but still wanted me to hear her out.

So at nine o'clock sharp, after a quick visit home to shower and change, followed by a similarly brief visit to Stockford Police Station to don a capacious pale blue jacket at Anderson's insistence, I turned up at the council offices. I wasn't exactly at my most chipper, what with lack of sleep, an aching shoulder and the now-purple lump on my head, but I was considerably chipperer than Mallory. She'd wanted to accompany me but Anderson had ruled that out and I'd suggested she get some shut-eye and I'd pop round to her flat following the meeting and after I'd reported back at the nick.

'Good morning, Mr Bryant,' said Lady Felicity, pointing to my head. 'Whatever's happened to you?'

'Walked into a door,' I said briefly. Not original, but I wasn't going to get into a conversation with her about last night's goings-on.

'You'd better sit down,' she said, almost solicitously, and pointed to a couple of armchairs in front of a well-stocked, if rather serious-looking bookcase in her unexpectedly impressive office. I doubted if many other district council planning officers around the country could boast such high-class surroundings. Mind you, it helped that Stockford Council itself was housed in a Grade II, eighteenth century building that was more castle than office block. 'I hear you've suffered a distressing night,' she continued. I wasn't sure who she'd heard that from and, in any case, it had been less distressing for me than for several of the other participants. I didn't for example have a bullet wound in either my thigh or my shoulder and I hadn't had to find my wife sitting in an underground crypt next to the dead body of one of her forerunners. The late Jennifer's mortal remains had been located in the next cell to Clem and Madeline's, in a grave beneath an uninscribed, horizontal tombstone.

'Why am I here, Lady Felicity?' I asked, coming straight to the point whilst remembering my manners at the same time.

'My brother and I need your help,' she said.

That was a surprise. 'I'm not sure what help I can give you. You'd better explain.'

'As I believe you know, Rupert and I are now the freeholders of The Three Pigeons following the unfortunate passing of our brother, Jonathan.'

I don't have a brother, but if I had, and if he'd been bludgeoned to death with a chair, I think I'd describe his passing as rather more than "unfortunate". 'I'm afraid I don't know that,' I said. 'I've only got your brother's word for it. As far as I know, the pub belongs to Clem Spaggott.

That's what he always claimed.' That was a lie. I don't think I'd ever heard Clem claim ownership of the pub, but it had always somehow been implied, and the letter Mallory had found in the trunk seemed to confirm it was his to sell.

'Mr Spaggott was indeed the owner until very recently, when he was persuaded to accept my brother Jonathan's extremely generous offer to purchase the freehold of the premises.'

Ah, now we were getting somewhere. 'I see. And I suppose that on Jonty's death, ownership passed to Viscount Uppingshott.'

'To both of us as it happens. But yes, that is essentially correct.'

'And Jonty wanted to knock it down and build houses.'

'It's obvious, isn't it?'

'And is that your intention too?' A thought occurred to me. 'Pardon me for saying this, Lady Felicity, but is there not just a teeny conflict of interest at play here, you know, what with you being the Planning Officer and all?'

She gave a curious little wave of both hands, rather as if she were giving a demonstration of window cleaning, although I doubted very much if those well-manicured mitts had ever been in contact with an actual chamois leather. 'No, no, no,' she said. 'Absolutely not. The planning department isn't a court of law.' No, I thought, but presumably it was still subject **to** the law. 'However – and this is where you can help us – there seems to be some uncertainty about the ownership of the land at the rear of The Three Pigeons. And without it, constructing the new housing that Idleborough is crying out for would simply not be an attractive enough proposition.'

Every time she opened her mouth she prompted more questions. First of all, Stamp hadn't seemed to think there was any dispute about who owned the land. He had been absolutely clear that he did, via Jay Spry. Second of all, and speaking as an Idleborough resident who prided himself on keeping his nose, ears and eyes close to the ground at all times, I was damn certain that nobody who lived in the village – excepting Squire Jonty, who strictly speaking could no longer be said to be living there – was crying out for the new housing, or at least not the unaffordable, four-bedroom detached properties she undoubtedly had in mind. And thirdly, the help I could supposedly give. I still didn't see it. So I asked again.

'I'm still not sure how you think I can assist.'

'My understanding is that Mr Stamp believes that he owns the land. My late brother, Jonathan, was under the impression that it belonged to The Three Pigeons. As Chief Planning Officer, I have discovered that this is unfortunately not the case' – hello, conflict of interest time again – 'so, as you are close to the gentleman, my brother and I would be grateful for your help in persuading Mr Stamp to consider selling these trifling four acres to us. We would be willing to pay you some very substantial commission.'

Of course you would, I thought. And "trifling four acres"? The two of them stood to make millions on the land, which would be the best part of five acres including the pub itself. However, 'What makes you think I'm close to Stamp?'

'I understand that he is to become your father-in-law.'

I opened my mouth but couldn't persuade any words to leave it. I'd known Mallory for precisely a week and her father about nine hours. One bout of afternoon delight didn't constitute a marriage proposal, not that that was something I was definitely against. 'Where the hell do you get your information from, lady?' I asked, 'A Chinese fortune cookie?'

For the first time, she appeared to be floundering. 'Erm,' she began. 'It was Bax...' and then her lips clamped shut and a faint blush added itself to her already over-rouged cheeks.

But I'd heard enough. I sat back and laughed. 'Banjo told you, didn't he? Baxter MacAllister.' I leant back in my armchair and laughed. She was so deep in the shit they'd be covering the fields with her for months.

'That's not what I said. And even if it was, you couldn't prove it.'

I opened the pale blue jacket that Inspector Anderson had forced on me and revealed the microphone pinned to the shirt underneath. 'I don't have to,' I said.

'It's not enough,' said Anderson, back at the police station half an hour later, as the recording whirred to a stop.

'Enough,' said Rose, apparently contradicting his senior officer, although she presumably understood what he meant.

'What?' I said. 'You heard her. Banjo – Baxter – has been whispering in her tiny shell-like. They're all in it together.'

'There you go again, Mr Bryant. Are you a lawyer?' She answered her own question. 'No, you're not, you're a jobsworth writer of some kind.' That was uncalled for. 'Put you on the stand against a bona fide barrister and **you've** got more chance of going to jail than Lady Felicity and her brother have. Baxter MacAllister, mind you, that's a different matter. My colleagues in forensics think they may have found something helpful in The Manor.' She paused. 'You didn't hear me say that, by the way.'

'Say what?' I said.

'What,' repeated Rose. It was the first time I'd heard him echo anybody but his boss.

So they reckoned they could prove Banjo had been in The Manor. Fingerprints on a study chair? A faint whiff of beer? Neither he nor Eve-May were sounding like criminal masterminds. However, I was still focussing on Lady Felicity. She had clearly offered me a bribe to help her and her remaining brother get their patrician hands on the four acres behind The Farts. I pointed this out to Anderson. 'Sounds like a common-or-garden business arrangement to me,' she said. I started to protest. 'Look, Mr Bryant,' she continued. 'The ownership of The Three Pigeons can be easily proved. If Clem Spaggott sold the pub to Jonathan Hardy-Hewitt, who is now dead, which means the pub passes to his siblings, there's nothing we can do about it.'

'But he was forced against his will,' I protested. 'By Eve-May and Baxter.'

'Probably. Not sure how provable that'll be. And as far as Lady Felicity is concerned, any conflict of interest can be overcome by her temporarily removing herself from the planning process when a decision needs to be made.' She laughed, a barking sound that took me completely by surprise. 'The result of the application might depend on how popular she is with her fellow committee members. But there will be no planning application without the extra land, of that we can be sure. So, either you persuade your girlfriend's father to sell the land to the Hardy-Hewitts and get yourself a nice little bit of commission, or you persuade him not to and you may get your pub back. Mind you, I don't see Viscount Uppingshott as a pub landlord, so in that case, you're back to square one. I imagine they'll try and sell it as a private house. And I doubt if that will prove too difficult. Idleborough must be the only village in the country with four pubs. Most places are lucky to have one these days.'

She was right. Lazytown had already lost nine pubs since the war and one more would be just another statistic. For a moment I found myself wondering how much "commission" Lady Felicity had in mind for my help with Stamp. An attractive little housing estate would be much more visually attractive than the beaten-up old Farts, after all. And we could help arrange for Big Brian to get his beer from Downwycherley Brewery if it meant he inherited the entire clientele from The Farts.

I shivered. What the flying fuck was I thinking of? No, I'd be doing my damnedest to make sure the Uppingshotts never got their hands on the land at the back. I'd need to have a word with Stamp. I imagined he'd be thinking about selling The Thatched House. In another world, I'd buy it myself, but it wouldn't be going for less than a couple of million quid, even without planning permission for the extra land. Even if I had Number 1, Slaughterhouse Cottages to sell, it would be several steps too far for me and as my cottage still belonged to my parents, who were in rude health down in New Zealand, that wouldn't be happening. I supposed I could try and persuade him to give it to Mallory. I'd have a word with her first. I was due to meet her in any case.

I rose and shook hands with Anderson and Rose. The latter seemed to wipe his hand down the side of his trousers afterwards, but I let it go. 'I suppose you two are off to talk to Mr and Mrs MacAllister now,' I said.

'Indeed we are. We're quite looking forward to it, aren't we, sergeant?'

'Forward,' agreed Rose.

'Will you let me know what they say?' I asked. 'Banjo –

MacAllister – was supposed to be my best mate and Eve-May is my girlfriend's sister, after all.' Even I was calling Mallory my girlfriend now. It had been a long week.

'Not a chance,' said Anderson. 'You can read all about it in the *Spectacle* in due course, I imagine.'

'Spectacle,' said Rose.

28

MONDAY 22ND JULY
FLOCKS OF BEES AND INGROWERS

I hadn't been able to sleep. Not so, Pop, who'd accompanied me back to my apartment at just past six o'clock, and who was now out for the count in my spare room. I was curled up on the sofa, curtains drawn against the summer sunshine, thinking. I hadn't been that keen on the old bastard coming home with me. 'What if I throttle him?' I'd asked Inspector Anderson. 'No one could blame me.'

'I would have thought you'd have some questions to ask your father. I know we do but I think I'd like him rested and refreshed before we get on to that. We'll be talking to your sister and brother-in-law first.'

'Half-sister,' I corrected her. And Banjo, my brother-in-law? I shivered at the thought. Mind you, it could have been worse. It could have been Clem Spaggott. I'd only met him once, plonked odorously and untidily on the bench in the underground cell alongside my present mother-in-law, but I'd still take a fraudster and potential murderer over him any day of the week. Although maybe I was being unfair. Sam had, after all, chosen to drink in his less-than-congenial pub for many years when there were three others in Idleborough he could have frequented, so *perhaps there was more to Clem than met the eye. There surely had to be.*

As for Madeline, apart from the temporary damage done to her pride and appearance, she'd seemed none the worse for wear. She'd never been that bright – although marrying into billions of dollars could be construed as a certain sort of brightness – and hadn't fully got to grips with what had happened to her since she and the old bugger had arrived at Heathrow ten days ago. That timescale had been all I'd gotten out of Pop before he'd crashed onto my spare bed. He was still fully clothed. I was quite particular about the men I undressed, and overweight, seventy-two-year-old fathers didn't quite fit the bill. Talking of men who might, Sam had gone home to shower and prepare himself for his meeting with Lady Felicity Hardy-Hewitt, although I couldn't understand quite why that was important anymore. I'd heard Anderson tell him to drop in at Stockford Police Station first but had no idea why.

Madeline had not come back to my apartment. She and Clem, in separate ambulances, had gone off to hospital to be checked out, she accompanied by an attractive young female cop. A potential fourth – or rather fifth – Mrs Makepeace Stamp there, I'd thought, if Pop ever clapped eyes on her, especially with Madeline suddenly looking rather more than her thirty-nine years after a week cooped up next to Clem and no access to washing facilities, let alone beauty parlours. Maddy would definitely have to be on her guard with her guard. I laughed inwardly. Family. You can't choose 'em, can you? Although, come to think, Pop could.

As Anderson had suggested, I sure had a heap of questions I wanted to put to the old man but, glancing up at the clock, I could see it was only a little past nine o'clock so he'd had less than four hours shut-eye. Questions could wait. Sam would be showing up in an hour or two and I guessed I could do with his support when I confronted Pop. Anyways, I wasn't going to be getting to sleep now, so I heaved myself off the sofa, threw open the curtains and headed for the shower. Coffee and breakfast first, slapping the old man about a bit to follow. I remembered it was Monday morning. Jim would be expecting me in the office ten minutes ago. Oh, well, if he needed me, he knew my number, although I guessed my days as an intrepid local reporter were over. It would seem Pop had little more use for me in that role.

*What **would** he want me to do though? How much did I need the reassurance of a hefty monthly allowance nestling comfortingly in my bank account? Did I, indeed, want to go back to Notting Hill? That surprised me. I hated the countryside, didn't I? And that was before it had tried to bump me off. I couldn't see me becoming a fashion queen in Stockford. The locals had only just stopped wearing smocks. Fashion round these parts probably meant dressing in ruffs and crinolines.*

And what about Sam? What feelings did I truly have for him? Or him for me? We'd known each other for a couple of hours under a week. And it hadn't been a week of candlelit dinners and cosy embraces either. Still, that could wait. I'd have to sleep on it. We both would.

In the meantime, I was going to be grilling Pop without the benefit of sleep. The list of questions stretched out before me. How long had he owned The Thatched House? Why was there a secret passage between it and The Three Pigeons? Who had put it there? Pop or Eve-May and if her, when and why? And why had she passed herself off as Maeve and bigamously married Clem? For the land? Surely not. Something to do with Jennifer? None of it made sense.

I took a step back, mentally. It had to come down to money. It usually did where Pop was concerned. Eve-May wanted his billions. Eldest daughter or not, I guessed that she could see she wasn't going to be getting her hands on enough of them to satisfy her, especially since she'd killed the love of Pop's life. Every succeeding divorce would diminish the pot. As would my presence. I shivered. I hadn't given it any thought so far, but it seemed obvious now that I too had been on her elimination list. Remove all the other beneficiaries, make sure Pop doesn't see seventy-three and the money ends up falling straight into Eve-May's pockets.

Or maybe that was Baxter MacAllister putting the thought in her head. Maybe she was just being duped by him. Nothing about the erstwhile Banjo had so far screamed brains to me but perhaps he had well-hidden depths.

TWO HOURS LATER, *that was the first thing I asked Pop.*

I looked at him now, sitting in my armchair and dressed to the nines in a pale-grey suit, crisp white shirt and a military-looking necktie he surely wasn't entitled to wear. At his insistence, I'd packed all the above and more into the world's largest suitcase and lugged it all back from The Thatched House with us. Stereotypically, he'd insisted on pancakes and maple syrup for breakfast, which had meant a quick dash to the supermarket for Sam on his return from his meeting with Lady Felicity and now, suited, booted, showered and fed, he was much more like the old, familiar cross-me-at-your-peril bastard he'd always been.

'I cut her out of the will after she killed Jennifer, but I didn't tell her. I guess I shoulda done 'cos she was madder'n a flock of bees when she found out.' Flock? I knew he was more interested in dollars than wildlife – I'd long since lost count of the tracts of forest he'd had razed and native species he'd given their marching orders – but even so, flock of bees? 'By that time she'd met MacAllister and married him. I thought it was just to spite me. He was a lowlife just out of jail for a stack of store robberies. I thought she'd be grateful I'd not thrown her to the cops after

she'd killed Jennifer and for a while I think she was. It wasn't that easy covering up Jennifer's death, even for me, but we came up with a plan to bury the body in some out of the way spot that no one would ever find and, basically, airbrush her from history.'

'And spots don't come much more out of the way than Idleborough,' said Sam.

'No. Well, if it had been back in Canada, we'd have had thousands of square miles of wilderness to choose from, but over here everybody's on top of everybody else. Jeez, Bryant, how the hell do you Brits live like that?'

That seemed a bit ironic coming from a man who'd only ever seemed at home in a city centre skyscraper, preferably one with his name on. There were at least three Stamp Buildings and two Stamp Towers I knew about worldwide. 'Go on,' I prompted.

'I bought the cottage, built the crypt out back and laid Jennifer to rest inside. Then I had to move on with my life, so I cut off that part of the garden and allowed it to grow wild. I couldn't bring myself to sell the house though and as Eve-May literally knew where the body was buried, I allowed her to use it. I thought she might immerse herself in village life and become a better person.'

'She certainly immersed herself in village life,' said Sam. 'She turned herself into Maeve and married Clem Spaggott.' Mind you, it had taken her a few years. What had she been up to before that?

'Yeah, that I don't get. She was with this MacAllister character by then and between them they must've hatched some sort of crazy plan to get their hands on my fortune. They knew about the change in the will and figured that it would only take three deaths and it would all be theirs. God knows what they thought they'd be inheriting. It takes brains and time to run a company this size. Still, plenty of predators out there happy to buy it off them, I guess.'

'Three deaths?' I said, although I really only wanted confirmation.

'Sure thing, Princess. Yours, mine and Maddy's and, cut out of the will or not, Eve-May would have gotten the lot.'

'They'd have had to kill Clem too.'

'Yeah, seems that way although again, I don't get his involvement.' He looked at Sam. 'I doubt if you'd've missed out either, young feller, seeing as you appear to be joined at the hip to my daughter.' There was a glint in his eye but I couldn't work out if he was OK with the joined-at-the-hip thing – if indeed that's what we were – or not.

Sam pursed his lips. 'So, you, Mallory, Madeline, Clem and me would have been killed and laid to rest in the crypt with Jennifer, and a housing estate built on top.'

'That's a lot of murders,' I said. 'Would Eve-May and Banjo have had it in them? OK, she'd killed Jennifer, but that was in a fit of rage and there's a heap of difference between robbing a few stores and the cold-blooded killing of four people.'

'There's a fifth person too,' said Sam. 'Jonty. Anderson and Rose seem to think they've got evidence pinning his murder on Banjo. But why?'

Pop shrugged. 'I don't know, son,' he said. 'Who is this guy anyway? Jonty, you call him?'

'Squire Jonty,' Sam said. 'The Honourable Jonathan Hardy-Hewitt. How would you describe him? I guess he was a sort of unofficial Lord of the Manor in Idleborough. The police seem pretty sure that the letter Mallory found from Clem Spaggott accepting the miserly £250,000 for The Farts – sorry, The Three Pigeons – was to Jonty. So at the time he was killed, Jonty owned the pub, which then passed to his brother and sister, Viscount Uppingshott and Lady Felicity. I'd originally thought Jonty had killed his brother – his twin – for the title, but I was wrong. It's Jonty who's dead and Uppingshott who accidentally shot

Mallory when she threw a rolling-pin at him in the pub the other day.'

I could see that none of this meant anything to the old man. He'd never had any truck with titles, not unless they came attached to shedloads of dollars, and Idleborough village politics were so far beneath him he'd need a microscope to notice them. The part about the rolling-pin caught his attention though. I had, briefly, explained in the car back to Stockford why I was sporting a bandage round my head but he'd been so zonked at the time, I doubt it had registered. So I went through that part again now.

Meanwhile, Sam had been doing some more thinking. 'Did Eve-May know that the four acres of land containing the crypt was owned by The Thatched House, in other words you, sir?' Where the heck did that "sir" come from? I remembered Pop's use of the word "son" earlier, as well. It looked like conclusions were being jumped to behind my back. I stored that away for future reference. Only one person would be deciding my future, thank you very much, and it wouldn't be either of these two.

Pop thought a bit. 'I don't know,' he said eventually. 'There's no reason she shoulda done, I guess. I bought the place and built the crypt, as I said. I guess I'd separated the land off before Eve-May ever came here. She coulda thought it belonged to the pub like all you locals seem to have done.'

Sam was looking quite excited. 'So, Eve-May thought the land belonged to the pub. She and Banjo were going to kill all of you to get your money and bury you in the crypt. She decided the best way of making sure those bodies were never found was to dump a bloody great housing estate on top of them but she had no money to speak of. Clem owned the land, she thought, so she had to persuade him to sell it for housing. Banjo had been around long enough to know that Jonty would probably be up for buying it. So Eve-May got into bed – literally – with Clem to persuade him to sell.'

'OK, so far so possible, young man,' said Pop. 'But why did MacAllister murder this Jonty fella? If he'd bought the land and agreed to build the houses? It makes no sense.'

I needed to mention something else. 'Where were you calling from when you phoned me, Pop?'

'Which phone call, Princess?'

'Back in May when you sent me to Stockford to work at the Spectacle. Why'd you do that? Did you know this was going to happen?'

'Not exactly, but I heard something odd. I have eyes and ears all over. One or two of them are paid to keep a little bitty check on Eve-May. She'd disappeared from London and showed up at The Thatched House. She'd never used it as much as I hoped she would but suddenly she seemed to be there permanently. I'd thought if you were local, you could take over the eyes-and-ears role for me.'

'You didn't exactly make that clear.'

'No, well, I was just making a start. Get you there to protect the family interests if she started something.'

'Started what?'

'Well, we know now, don't we? I had a sixth sense she was up to something. Experience tells me she wouldn't leave London for long without a very good reason. She's the same as you; you both like good, hard concrete under your feet.'

'If you say so.' I hadn't quite worked out if that still applied as far as I was concerned. 'Last Friday's call. You said you were in Toronto.'

'No, I didn't say that, Princess. You must've assumed. I was in the house with Baxter MacAllister's gun pointing at me.'

'OK. So why did you ask me to look for the key to the door in the woods. The crypt? You know, when you already had a set.'

'Weren't you listening, Princess? Miss the bit where I had a gun pointed at my head, did you?. I had to get you here.' He shook his head and waved his hands around vaguely. 'Not here, I mean. To the house. And not even there. That would have put you on your guard. You didn't know the house belonged to us. So I got you to go to the pub. I knew your young man there had been sniffing around.' He glanced at Sam who had the good grace not to blush either at being called my young man or indeed at the young bit. Still, everyone's young compared to Pop.

Instead of blushing, Sam said: 'Two things, Harrison.' I winced at the "Harrison". I wasn't sure if anyone had had the temerity to call him by his given name since Granma died. Sam didn't give him a chance to object, however. 'First, how did you know I'd been sniffing around? And secondly, what prompted the trip over here in the first place?'

They were both good questions. 'Why did I come over? I come over all the time. We both do. You know that, Princess. Darling Maddy loves the stores and I have a business to run. Your stepmother is of the opinion that Toronto has no stores and there's sure as hell things I can't do in Canada that I can do this side of the pond. And, I've told you, Eve-May's behaviour was worrying.'

'And despite forcing me out here into the middle of nowhere, you didn't trust me enough to find out what she was doing.'

'And what about the other question?' said Sam. 'You know, the one about me sniffing around.'

'Oh, that was what's-his-name, Bill is it? Boy with the ratty face.'

I recalled that it had been Billy the Kid who'd pitched the tent in the woods and had watched Sam find the hidden door to the crypt.

'Billy told you?' said Sam, standing suddenly with a fierce look on his face. 'So Billy works for you? The same Billy who *grabbed a gun last night and had to be wellied by Mucker before he shot me with it?'*

'Calm down, son,' said Pop coolly. 'It aint me Billy works for. It's Eve-May and MacAllister. I just overheard him telling them he'd seen you.'

'But you told me that Billy was working for Jonty,' I said to Sam.

He thought a minute. 'No,' he said eventually. 'I just assumed that. I accused him of spying for Jonty but he didn't actually confirm it. It's odd though. Billy's lived in the village all his life. He's not an ingrower like Banjo.'

'Ingrower?' I said. 'What the heck's that when it's at home?'

'Oh, nothing,' said Sam. 'It's what the locals call newcomers. You have to be at least a third-generation Idler not to be called an Ingrower.' I found myself thinking of toenails and shuddered slightly. We were straying from the subject and there was something else confusing me.

'What was the tunnel for?' I asked. 'Did you have that built, Pop?'

'No, Princess, first I knew about it was yesterday. I guess Eve-May dug it. Doubt she wanted Clem knowing she'd lived next door all the time. Made it easier to keep her double-life secret. How she kept it from him I don't know.'

'Clem was never the most observant bloke,' said Sam. 'But that sounds as likely as anything. Worked for Banjo too. They could just use it to go "home" whenever they liked and use The Farts as their front entrance.

We were just pondering that when the doorbell rang. I looked at Sam. 'I expect that's Anderson and Rose come to talk to your dad,' he said. 'They must have finished with Eve-May and Banjo. Didn't think they'd be this quick though.'

I went to answer it. Sam was right. Anderson and Rose were standing there. Neither of them reached much past my shoulder *height. They looked like Tweedledum and Tweedledee and their expressions were more glum than glee.*

'Something up, Inspector?' I asked.

'You could say that, Miss Fillery. I'm afraid something unfortunate's happened.'

Nothing could be as unfortunate as being murdered though, so whatever it was, I thought the glum looks were a bit over the top. 'You'd better come in and tell us about it,' I said, standing back to let them past. They both took a heavy step forward. For a brief moment, I thought they were going to wedge themselves in the doorway but that only happens in comedies and, at the last second, Rose stood back to let the inspector in first. I followed them into the lounge.

'Good morning, Mr Stamp,' said Anderson in a voice Eeyore would have been proud of. 'I have to inform you that, unfortunately, Eve-May and MacAllister have escaped.'

29
MONDAY 22ND JULY
KIDNAPS AND WINDOWS

'Escaped?' I said. 'How the fuck did that happen? He only has one usable leg and she's got a hole through her shoulder. Weren't they under some sort of armed guard?'

'Apparently, even armed guards have to piss,' said Anderson morosely.

'Piss,' said Rose.

'Eve-May's so-called guard thought she was asleep and went for a short comfort break. Not so short that your daughter, Mr Stamp, bullet wound or not, didn't have time to undress a nurse and borrow her uniform. Next thing you know, she's pushing MacAllister out of the hospital in a wheelchair bold as you like and the nurse is spitting blood and fury at the guard.'

'Is the nurse all right?' asked Mallory, knowing what her half-sister was capable of.

'She'll be fine. Little Irish lass. Walked in the room and got hit over the head with a vase of flowers just as she spotted the empty bed.' I found myself wondering who the hell had sent Eve-May flowers.

'Siobhain?' said Mallory.

'*Gezundheit*,' grunted Rose. It was the first original thing I'd ever heard him say.

'No, I meant, was the nurse called Siobhain?' I recalled that was the name of the nurse who'd been looking after Mallory herself yesterday. She was Irish but if she was still on duty this morning then NHS shift lengths were getting way past a joke.

'What happened to them after they left the hospital?' I said. 'You'd think your guys could catch up with a woman pushing a wheelchair pretty quick.' Old Stamp was shaking his head, presumably in disbelief at the inefficiency of the British police. I guessed that back in Canada, the Mounties would have had a horse in the vicinity on which to give chase.

Anderson shrugged. 'Don't know. Probably broke into a vehicle and drove off. Don't worry, we'll get them. If they try to flee the country, they won't succeed. Of course, it's possible they may come here. After all, if they still have their eyes on your money, Mr Stamp, then all their birds are currently perched in one roost.' In case we hadn't understood, she explained. 'The three of you could still find yourselves dead. We've put a man outside your door, just in case.'

'Hopefully one with a strong bladder,' I remarked.

'Now then, Mr Stamp,' said Anderson. 'I need to have an official word with you, if you don't mind.' Or even if he did mind, I thought. 'So I'll have to ask you to accompany me to the police station.'

'To hell with that, madam,' barked Stamp, who predictably did mind. 'I'm quite comfortable here. And I'm the victim in all this, in case you'd forgotten.' I half expected him to say that the chief constable was an old buddy but I imagined his buddies, if he had any, were rather higher up the food chain than mere chief constables. Anyway, Anderson was as tough as him and his bluster fell on deaf ears. Shortly, he was stamping out of the flat, flanked by the two coppers.

I took a breath and looked at my watch. Lunchtime. 'Drink?' I said, but before Mallory could reply, my phone rang.

It was Daisy. 'Sam?' she said, breathlessly. I could almost picture her round specs slipping down her nose as she spoke. 'Is that you?' I wasn't quite sure who else she expected to be answering my phone but didn't pursue it.

'Yes, Daisy, what's up?' It was clear something was.

'You have to come. They've barricaded themselves in The Farts. It's awful.'

'It always was awful but it did have a sort of rustic charm.' Not the best time to be cracking jokes, I thought as soon as the words were out of my mouth.

'What?' She was understandably confused. 'No, I mean, it's Banjo and Maeve.'

Oh dear. 'What's happened, Daisy?'

'Banjo and Maeve,' she repeated. 'They've turned up and they're in The Farts. And they've got Jeremy. I thought they'd be in prison.'

'Jeremy? Jeremy Jeavons?'

'Yes, and there's some old bloke there too.' A quick think reminded me that Jeremy had been due to meet our ancient MP, Sir Bartholomew Digby, at Digby's stately home for elevenses this morning. I should have done more to keep Jeremy in the loop; a call to update him about last night's events would have been polite and enabled him to cancel his meeting with old Digby. Mind you, what with them both being on the board of Great Mercian Hotels, perhaps he wouldn't have cancelled his mid-morning coffee and cake – or whatever one had for elevenses these days – in any case. Daisy was still talking while I ran all that through in my head. 'What should we do, Sam?' Once again I seemed to be the all-knowing village oracle. I should start charging.

'Are the police there?' I asked. 'I think we should leave this to them.' Anderson and Rose had only left Mallory's flat a few minutes ago so might not be aware just yet that Mr and Mrs MacAllister had turned up back in Idleborough with a couple of kidnappees.

'No. We haven't called them. We didn't dare to. Banjo's upstairs at the window with a gun. He says he'll kill Jeremy and the other man if you don't get over here now with Mallory and her dad. No police, he said.'

How Banjo had got himself upstairs in The Farts with a seriously injured leg could wait for another time. 'OK, Daisy, we're on our way. Who's there with you?'

'Just my dad and Mucker. Oh, no, wait a minute. Big Brian and Ena are coming up the road. Oh dear, Ena's bound to call the police, isn't she?'

'Tell her not to. Tell her I've got it in hand.' I ended the call and looked at Mallory. 'Did you catch that?' I said.

'Some of it. Doesn't sound good.'

'Not good at all. It appears Banjo and Eve-May are holed up in The Farts and they've kidnapped Jeremy Jeavons and our local MP. Banjo's threatening to kill them both if you, I and your father don't take their place. He seems to have got hold of another gun from somewhere.'

'But Pop's at the police station. And, I don't know about you, but I don't much fancy volunteering for my own murder.'

In every book and every film and every television drama

I'd ever seen, the hero (in this case, me) and heroine (Mallory) decide to go it alone and not to call in the police. This maverick approach usually works out all right in the end, often with some inconsequential collateral damage along the way and a minor telling off from the authorities as the credits roll. The hero and heroine kiss, the cops smile ruefully and the villains are carted off to chokey.

But this was real life.

I rang Detective Inspector Anderson on the mobile number she'd given me.

'Stay where you are, Mr Bryant. Both of you,' she said. 'We'll deal with this. We have experts at this sort of thing.'

'In Stockford?' I asked. It seemed unlikely that Anderson would have a fully prepared SWAT team hidden away in a back room somewhere.

'Close enough,' she replied.

'Close,' I thought I heard in the background as she hung up.

'So we stay here then,' said Mallory. 'Does that include the pub round the corner? I'm gagging for that drink you promised me.'

'There are some very nice pubs in Idleborough,' I said.

She smiled. 'I've heard that too. Which one did you have in mind? The Trout does nice lunches.'

'I was thinking more about The Farts,' I said.

I PARKED the car at the cottage and we strolled up the road towards The Farts. A large crowd had by now gathered outside the pub and, having arrived impressively quickly following my call to Anderson, there were several police cars blocking the road from both directions, blues flashing but twos silent. The crowd was largely silent too although I could hear the booming tones of Big Brian from a couple of hundred yards away. I didn't know whether he'd shut The Bull or had acquired some bar staff. I didn't drink there regularly but I'd never seen anybody but Big Brian serving. Mind you, judging by the size of the gathering in front of us, there weren't going to be many punters in either The Bull or the other two pubs. No, on this Monday lunchtime, The Three Pigeons held the attention of everybody in Lazytown.

Big Brian was saying, 'Can't you keep that lump of wood quiet, Pete? I said, shut the 'eck oop, lad.'

It was, inevitably, Pirate Pete who was the subject of this demand. 'Fuck off, fatty,' I heard him say and then, louder, 'Go on Banjo, shoot the old bugger. Worst MP we've ever had.'

Daisy had just begun to protest when there was a loud snapping noise and Pirate Pete's severed wooden head came sailing over the crowd and landed at our feet. I stared at it and it stared malevolently back at me.

Pushing through the crowd, towing Mallory by the hand, I spotted Exhausted Ena, busy scribbling in her spiral notebook, now unhooked from around her neck. 'Hello, Ena,' I said, trying to keep my voice as light as possible for a man who was apparently walking willingly towards his own execution. 'What's occurring?'

She looked up and dropped her biro, apparently startled by our sudden appearance. 'What the Dickens are ye doin' here, youse two?' she hissed. She glanced up at the first-floor windows of The Farts. One of them was wide open. From memory it was the window of Clem's bedroom so seeing it open was a novelty. I could see nobody inside the room but presumably this was where Banjo had been brandishing his gun less than half an hour ago. 'Are ye mad? Yon

Banjo's got a gun and if he sees youse, he'll likely be using it.'

'Yeah, well, that wouldn't make much sense, would it, Ena?' I said. 'He can't go around committing murder and still expect to receive the ill-gotten gains resulting from it. And in any case, he and Maeve are after the big fish, not us little minnows.' I squeezed the not so little, redheaded minnow beside me round the waist. 'Old Stamp's back at Stockford Police Station and I doubt they'll be letting him out of their sight as easily as they did with Banjo and Maeve. Talking of which, is Inspector Anderson here yet?' I glanced around. There were quite a few policemen in high-viz jackets ringing the pub and keeping the crowd back. Not that there seemed much danger of a surge towards the building, the inhabitants of Lazytown being on the whole a cautious lot, bordering on the cowardly. There was no sign of Anderson and Rose but I spotted PC Joe and PC Mum in the yellow-vizzed cordon. Joe nodded at me and his mum scowled. I still wasn't sure what I'd done to upset her.

I couldn't see any armed coppers so Anderson's hidden SWAT team might still have been on its way. 'I havnae seen Anderson,' said Ena, who seemed to have an encyclopaedic knowledge of everybody living in west Oxfordshire, 'but there's half a dozen armed guys showed up a wee while ago. They're all round back. There's been some banging and shouting so could be young Banjo's kicking off in another room.'

'And as far as we know, Jeremy and Sir Bartholomew are still OK?'

'They were, aye, and there's been nae gunshots.'

At this point, Daisy, Dick and Mucker pushed through the crowd in the wake of Big Brian, who was booming, 'Make way! I said give us room, people.'

'You're here, Sam,' said Daisy, breathlessly and unnecessarily. 'Where's your father, Mallory?' She looked around wildly. 'Did you call the police? Banjo said you weren't to. Oh dear.'

'It's all right, Daisy,' I said, holding her by the arms and looking into her eyes. 'Yes, I called the police. This isn't a movie. And if I hadn't, somebody else would have. Now, settle down. Banjo's not going to shoot anyone. The police will have trained negotiators.'

'We haven't, as it happens, Mr Bryant.' Inspector Anderson had crept up unnoticed.

'Haven't.' Rose had crept up beside her.

'No, unfortunately, we can't afford to keep a hostage negotiation team on permanent standby. Police budget cuts, you know.' Anderson shrugged. 'The Met are sending a couple of guys across from London but they won't be here for a while. So, all in all, whilst I did tell you to stay in Stockford, I'm glad you're here. You're MacAllister's pal. I'm sure you won't mind talking to him. Come on, follow me.'

'Hang on, Inspector. I'm a civilian. And in case you'd forgotten, I'm one of the people Banjo's threatening to kill.'

'Do you honestly think that's likely? It's not your money they're after. Talking of which, Miss Fillery, you'd better stay here. Even better, leave. With your height and that hair, you're an easy target.'

'I'm going nowhere,' said Mallory.

'Your funeral,' said Anderson, unprofessionally, turning on her flat heels and walking off through the crowd.

'Funeral,' grunted Rose, grabbing me by the arm.

'Where's Stamp and the redhead?' shouted Banjo through the open window. 'I warned you. The MP gets it first.'

I was trying to work out which room he was in. I wasn't especially familiar with the upstairs layout of The Farts so it could have been anything. Judging by the downstairs, maybe another old tat room. There was no frosted glass, which suggested it wasn't the bathroom, although I doubted if Clem would worry too much about being seen in the nude on those rare occasions he gave himself a thorough wash. Only Farmer Trickle's Red Herefords could see him anyway and they didn't look the type to be easily disturbed by the sight. I caught a glimpse of on old ceiling-height cistern. Bathroom it was then.

There was no sign of Eve-May or the two hostages, nor indeed of the gun. Presumably that was now with Eve-May. I glanced around. There were four armed police in attendance but they were standing well back and looked a bit bored, if I'm honest. Presumably they would become more animated should they be called into action.

'OK, Mr Bryant,' said Anderson quietly. 'This is your chance to shine.'

I didn't have a clue what to say. A degree in media studies doesn't help much in hostage negotiations. Still, I guess I looked a bit gormless just standing there, so I nodded and took a step forward with raised hands. Just in case. 'Wotcha, Banjo,' I said. 'What you been up to then, chum?' These were by some distance the most asinine words that had ever left my mouth.

'Oh, look, it's Mr Stupid again,' said Banjo. This wasn't an entirely inaccurate observation on his part, but still...

'Me, stupid?' I said. 'I think I'm looking at the master of stupidity. If at first you don't succeed, make sure you keep on failing. What the fuck do you think's going to happen now, mate? Let's work it out, shall we? Let's say the police here deliver Stamp and Mallory to you. Oh, and Mrs Stamp too. You'll need her as well, won't you. Your plan's still to kill them so that Eve-May gets her paws on Stamp's dosh? Makes perfect sense. Not. Anyway, that isn't going to happen. None of them are here and none of them are going to be coming here. So, Plan B. What's that? Presumably, shoot Jeremy Jeavons and old Digby.'

'Careful,' whispered Anderson. 'Don't put ideas in his head.'

'Ideas?' I said, loudly. 'Banjo's not had an original idea in all the time I've known him. Even young Billy's got more brains.'

'Fuck off, arsewipe,' shouted Banjo. 'Mr Fucking-know-it-all.' He disappeared briefly from the window and reappeared waving a gun. My plan was working. This left an unarmed Eve-May guarding Jeremy and Digby. Two to one. Admittedly, the MP was pushing eighty and, by all accounts, gout-ridden, and there wasn't much of Jeremy. There was still less of Eve-May though, so I was hoping even the timid Jeremy might try his luck.

Whether he would or not didn't look likely to help me, though, given that Banjo had stopped waving his gun wildly around and was now pointing it directly at me. I hoped the armed coppers behind me were starting to pay a bit more attention and might be considering weighing in before he could pull the trigger, but at that moment there was an almighty commotion and a loud squeal from somewhere behind Banjo and suddenly he was flying through the window to land flat on his face at our feet. The gun disappeared into the thorns at the rear of the car park. Sergeant Rose threw himself on top of Banjo as if he thought he was an unexploded bomb. If he wasn't unconscious before Rose's manoeuvre, he certainly was after it.

I looked up at the window. Mucker's big, round face

appeared, beaming gap-toothedly. 'All rightem, then?' he said.

Behind him I could hear Big Brian booming, presumably at Eve-May. 'Stop squirming, woman, I said stop wriggling. You're going nowhere. I said, it's all over, Maeve, my dear.'

30
SATURDAY 3RD AUGUST
DUCKS AND HOTELS

And that's pretty much it. Mallory had flirted with PC Joe to distract him from his duty guarding the front door of The Farts and that had been doubly successful as his mum had run over to tell Mallory that she "wasn't good enough" for her son, which suggested that she thought no one who wasn't born with royal blood in their veins would be. While that little conversation was going on, Mucker and Big Brian had forced the door and tiptoed – apparently Mucker had removed his Wellington boots upon entering – upstairs, arriving at the bathroom door just as Banjo had snatched the gun from Eve-May and started waving it at me through the window.

Mucker had headed straight for Banjo, seized hold of him round the knees, with no due consideration given to his already injured thigh, and tossed him bodily out into the car park fifteen feet below, whilst Brian had grabbed Eve-May, unfortunately for her, right on the bullet wound in her shoulder, hence the squeal we'd heard.

Leaving Rose and the SWAT team to look after Banjo, Inspector Anderson and I, followed closely by half the village, had burst into the pub and run upstairs to find Big Brian calmly sitting astride a gently moaning Eve-May whilst berating a white-faced Sir Bartholomew Digby – who was slumped on the toilet with every apparent intention of having to use it quite soon and quite violently – about the ever proliferating number of potholes appearing on the Stockford Road, and 'what the bloomin' 'eck are you goin' to do about them, I said, when's they goin' to be fixed then?' Jeremy Jeavons, meanwhile, was calmly washing his hands at the basin in the corner, although judging from the brownish colour of the water, they weren't getting the most effective wash they had ever had.

'Hello, Sam,' Jeremy said. 'I believe this must be one of the most interesting days this pub has ever experienced. I really think we should make every effort to maintain its status.' I assumed he meant keep it open, which had frankly been the whole point of the exercise in the first place. 'I have been having some thoughts about that and was discussing them with my fellow Great Mercian Hotels board member, Sir Bartholomew, when we were unfortunately detained against our wishes by Timothy and Maeve. You and I must have a chat, although now is probably not the best time.'

IT TURNED out that the best time was two weeks later on the Saturday of the annual village Duck Race, something which had completely slipped my mind, what with the events of the past few days. The two of us, along with Mallory and Daisy, were seated in comfortable chairs outside The Bull in the Market Square, where we had an excellent platform from which to view a considerable part of the Duck Race course, with drinks – an unexpectedly pleasant, well chilled

New Zealand Sauvignon for the two girls and me, a cup of tea for Jeremy – replenished regularly by Big Brian himself. Mucker was sitting at an adjacent table with Daisy's Dad, Dick. Mucker looked as happy as a fox in a chicken coop. The village had clubbed together to buy him a month's worth of beer – which equated to six months of beer for most of us – to recognise his heroism in "storming the bastard", as Dick had put it, and disarming Banjo without, quite, killing him in the process. A similar offer had been put to Big Brian but he'd refused on the grounds that if he didn't buy his own beer, he'd soon be out of business. It was a peculiar sort of Yorkshire logic that was lost on me.

I usually took part in the Duck Race myself but Banjo had been one of my partners for the past two years, along with Bob Baker the butcher, so I had temporarily retired myself from active participation and was, instead, due to hand out the prizes to the winners, and indeed to all participants who had successfully drunk six and a half pints of ale and completed the course. In a note of irony not lost on anybody, first prize was a jug of six and a half pints of beer.

'Are you listening, Sam?' asked Mallory who, in deference to another gloriously warm day, was back wearing the powder-blue skirt she'd had on last Thursday week, matched today with a canary yellow halterneck top, neither of which was doing much for my levels of concentration.

'I'm sorry, Jeremy. You were saying.'

'That is perfectly all right, Sam,' said Jeremy. 'As you may be aware, Great Mercian's UK portfolio primarily comprises' – not a phrase I'd be confident of repeating and I was only on my third glass of wine – 'larger, commercial hotels with a minimum of one hundred beds and situated close to major communities and amenities. I believe, however, that a gap in the market exists which is ripe for the company to exploit, especially as more and more people are choosing what I understand to be called staycations.'

I wished he'd hurry up. By my reckoning I'd be required to dish out the Duck Race prizes in less than twenty minutes. 'Where's this gap, then, Jeremy?' I prompted.

'Well, here,' he said, waving an arm around in a general sweep of the village. 'And other similar locations nationwide. I think you would agree that this part of Oxfordshire is particularly pleasant.' In all honesty, I'd always considered it a bit flat and treeless but I could understand its attraction to Ingrowers and visitors, especially with the Cotswolds on the next doorstep but one. Jeremy continued. 'And what does Idleborough lack?' I wasn't entirely unaware of the direction in which his monologue was travelling, so I guessed he wasn't talking about parking, a bus service or a shop that sold stuff you might want to buy.

'A hotel?' I hazarded.

'*Exactement*, Samuel.' I wondered momentarily if Big Brian had spiked his tea. 'To be precise, a small local hotel reflecting the charm and characteristics of the locality.' He paused. He didn't finish with a "ta-dah!" but he might as well have done.

'You mean The Farts, don't you?' said Mallory.

'Indeed I do, Miss Fillery, indeed I do. Both Sir Bartholomew and I will be proposing to our board that we purchase The Three Pigeons to get the ball rolling, as it were. We believe that, in the circumstances, Viscount Uppingshott and Lady Felicity will be only too happy to accept a reasonable offer for the freehold.' It was by now common knowledge that Lady Felicity, under extreme pressure, had been forced to stand down from her position as Chief Planning Officer and had resigned from the local council altogether.

'That's all very well,' I said, 'but you can't turn the pub into a hotel, even a small, charming hotel, as it stands. It's not big enough. You're going to need the four acres at the back as well, aren't you?'

'It's self-evident, isn't it?' He turned to Mallory. 'What do you think, Miss Fillery?'

'It's not up to me, Jeremy,' she said, smiling. 'That land belongs to The Thatched House, in other words to Jay Spry.'

'Which ultimately means your father, Miss Fillery,' said Jeremy, smiling back. This was an entirely new Jeremy Jeavons to me. Gone was the timid barfly from The Farts, replaced by a man fully at home in the world of commerce and big business. Not quite as big business as Stamp's big business, but nevertheless business with a decent heft. 'And, I believe, as the heiress to the estate, as it were, you are in an excellent position to persuade him to sell the land. I should add that our offer would be far more reasonable than that made to the Uppingshotts for the pub.'

I looked at Mallory. She was indeed now the sole heiress to the Stamp Corporation and all it contained, particularly as her father had initiated divorce proceedings with Madeline a week ago. The divorce wouldn't take long. He'd been through enough of them and had enough sway in the right places to ensure it didn't drag out. And that suited Maddy too. A goodly chunk of his fortune would be walking off with her, which is possibly what she'd had in mind ever since she'd first got her scarlet fingernails into him.

'I'll have a word,' Mallory said. 'I dare say he'll be happy to sell the house and the land as two separate lots.'

My heart sank slightly. I hadn't discussed it with her, indeed we'd only seen each other a few times in the twelve days since the showdown in The Farts, but I suppose I was hoping she might want to move into the now unoccupied house. I guessed it was time for a proper conversation about our relationship. Otherwise, now that she no longer had a job at the *Stockford Spectacle,* she might decide she'd be better off back in London. As she herself had pointed out, the western fringe of Oxfordshire was not the best place to pursue a career in fashion.

A loud crash interrupted my reverie. I looked up to see a threesome in the Duck Race, made up of Percy Pocock, Scooby and Postman Pat, all in bright green Orville costumes, who had understandably been trailing along in last place in the race, sprawled in the road outside The Trout, arms and legs akimbo. They had it seemed wobbled straight through the trestle table full of glasses of beer that had been set up outside for the benefit of the participants. Pat had leant over to grab the fullest remaining glass and pulled the other two off their feet. The table and its contents had been thoroughly demolished.

Duty called. I eased myself to my feet and wandered over, pulling a red card from my jeans pocket and brandishing it. 'You're disqualified, lads,' I said. 'Sorry.'

'Thank Christ for that,' panted Postman Pat. 'I've never been in such a crap team.'

'Yer must've been. Yer' the captain of Idleborough Cricket Club, aint yer?' said an adjacent wiseacre in between guffaws.

'Hey, none of that.' I grinned and waved my red card at him too. Then I glanced back towards the tasteless Town Hall on the other side of the square. I could see two trios of "ducks" heading down past the war memorial, beak to beak, a hundred yards from the finish line.

My prize-giving duties awaited.

31

EIGHT MONTHS LATER
FARTHINGS AND GINGER

The opening of the newly re-re-renamed Farthings Country Inn was a subdued affair. Just the fifteen Morris Troupes taking it in turns to jig their stuff in the road outside and a Grand Charity Granny's Bobbins match taking place in the pristine garden recently laid to the rear of the old pub alongside a gravel drive leading to a new car park tastefully placed betwixt a selection of unfelled, surprisingly majestic trees. The old dog-leg in the drive was no more, the external chimney breast having been removed during the renovation of the building; and the eight-foot fence dividing the drive from The Thatched House had also been moved back to allow comfortable vehicular access. Stamp had happily agreed to that before selling the property. Next to the car park, the groundwork had commenced for the block of twelve deluxe hotel bedrooms awaiting construction.

The crypt and tunnel were no more. The late Jennifer's remains had been disinterred and now lay peacefully in a new grave in St Brendan's churchyard.

When I arrived, the massed choir of St Brendan's was

doing a turn preparatory to the opening ceremony itself, the ribbon cutting due to be undertaken by Hugo Granville, star of *Holy Trinity!*

I pushed my way to the bar, smiling and shaking hands with a selection of the great and good of Idleborough and, indeed, Stockford. There was no Clem behind the bar anymore. Instead, he was ensconced in his own armchair next to the open fireplace, beaming at all and sundry. Percy Pocock was similarly seated next to him. There were three people serving. I didn't know any of them but I guessed they would soon become familiar. I'd been told they were living above the shop, so I doubted if it would take them long to become accustomed to Lazytown and indeed the regular patrons of the pub. Inn, rather.

'Dry white wine, please,' I said to one of them, a freckle-faced girl of about twenty.

'That's on the house, Helen,' said Jeremy Jeavons, arriving unnoticed by my side. Next to him was Daisy, wearing a smart black suit, a new hairdo and no spectacles. I peered at the badge pinned to her lapel. "Daisy" it read. "Bar Manager".

'Congratulations, Daisy,' I said. 'You'll be great.'

'Thanks, Sam,' she said. 'It's all worked out hasn't it? Thanks to you. And, er, Mallory, of course.' She paused. 'Will she be coming this evening?'

I shrugged and smiled. It seemed unlikely. I'd messaged her a couple of weeks ago to let her know about the reopening and to offer her, with Jeremy's approval, the free use of Clem's old bedroom, now a comfortable en suite guestroom named Sparrows which, until the new bedroom block to the rear opened, was Farthings Country Inn's only room available for paying guests.

I hadn't seen Mallory for six months. She had decided

that neither Stockford nor Idleborough was for her, especially once she'd accepted her father's offer of a place on the main board of Stamp Inc. Between them, they had also started up Fillery Designs Ltd, based in London Docklands, which she was now running full-time with a workforce of ten. We'd kept in touch for a little while and I'd made a handful of trips to her plush new open-plan apartment overlooking the old docks but it could never last. I was as uncomfortable in east London as she was in west Oxfordshire, and my work was suffering too. My writing had never exactly made me well-off but it had been enough, especially taking into account the not-quite-peppercorn rent of Number 1, Slaughterhouse Cottages, to allow me to live the life I wanted to live in Idleborough. However, my career couldn't take much loss of focus, and travelling up and down the M40, even for a few short weeks, had reduced my creative output to an unsustainable trickle. We hadn't exactly made a decision to consciously uncouple but the trips to Limehouse had just somehow stopped happening.

Another intrusion on my time had been my involvement, as part of a consultancy team Jeremy had put in place once The Three Pigeons had been bought from Viscount Uppingshott and Lady Felicity, and old Stamp had agreed to sell the four acres at the back separately from The Thatched House. Not just to decide how the refurbishment of the new inn should be managed but also to use it as a template for other future additions to the Great Mercian Group's proposed chain of new, small country hotels. Indeed, the Farthings name had been my idea, coming to me in a flash of inspiration after four pints one evening in The Bull, now fully stocked by Downwycherley Brewery. Farthings made it inevitable that Lazytown's residents would soon be referring to the place as The Farts again pretty soon, but either Jeremy and the board of Great Mercian Hotels hadn't grasped the implication of the new name or they had, and were happy to go along with it anyway.

I felt a nudge on my arm and turned to see Stewart Stewart, the new owner of The Thatched House. That had been a surprise. 'Always fancied consorting with the enemy,' he'd said when his purchase had become public knowledge and he'd strolled unexpectedly into The Bull one evening to 'eye up enemy territory', as he'd put it. With a new cricket season looming shortly, I'd already asked him if he was willing to change allegiance from Stockford to Idleborough. 'Don't know, old chap. Anyway, you couldn't afford me.'

'Hello Stewart, made yourself at home yet?' I said now. 'What can I get you?'

He held up a half-empty glass of Prosecco. 'I'll just finish this freeby and then I'll have a large Glenfiddich please. Very kind of you.' Stewart wasn't altogether a bad bloke and the general consensus in the village was that we'd rather have someone relatively local moving into The Thatched House, even Stewart Stewart, than yet another Ingrower, but he could still be a pain. Large Glenfiddich indeed. Nevertheless, I thought I might join him so smiled at Helen the freckly barmaid and placed the order. I hadn't realised they were handing out free Proseccos at the door when I'd arrived and a minor commotion from that direction indicated Mucker's incomprehension at finding a stranger attempting to hand him a tall glass as he entered with an already slightly bewildered expression on his large moon face.

'Wha's this then, fizzy piss?' he said, backing away and almost knocking over Daisy's Dad, Dick, who had entered right behind him. Fortunately, they both remained on their feet; untold damage could have been done to the newly refurbished bar had the two behemoths toppled over.

I called across. 'Hey, guys, come here and I'll get you a proper drink.' Like The Bull now and The Farts up until last summer, Farthings was also a customer of Downwycherley Brewery. Jeremy had been quite insistent that any group contracts Great Mercian had for the supply of alcohol to its premises should not apply to Farthings. As he'd said, he wanted to continue coming here himself of an evening and to be surrounded by friends when he did. I didn't think it polite to point out that I'd never actually seen him partaking of any of Downwycherley's products nor that most of the regulars of The Farts would not necessarily call Jeremy a friend. I hoped the latter situation was now changing though as, without him, there would be no pub, even if it was now designated an inn, for them to return to.

I glanced down at Mucker's feet as he and Dick wandered across to the bar. Gone were the Wellington boots, replaced by a sturdy pair of brown loafers with Velcro fastenings. A few of us had got together to buy the new footwear for him and not just because he could hardly wear wellies into Farthings but also because all the other establishments were beginning to get fed up with them, particularly Beatrice Balthazar. He had rejected all shoes with laces on the grounds that they were 'too fiddly for me fattem fingers'. I can't say he looked altogether comfortable in the loafers he'd finally accepted – a possible cause of the near tumble at the door – but it was early days.

'Like what they've done with the place then, gents?' I asked as they lovingly wrapped their paws around pints of

Old Bedstead. They glanced around as if they'd only just noticed the altered surroundings, but before either of them could reply there was a polite cough from the far end of the bar, where the choir of St Brendan's had now finished regaling us, and Jeremy Jeavons was preparing to address the crowd. 'Speak up!' some wag shouted before he'd even begun, and the ensuing ripple of laughter seemed to relax him.

'Welcome, everybody,' he started confidently. 'I'm delighted to see so many of you here, not just former regular patrons of The Three Pigeons but others who may well have never dared set foot in the old pub at all.' Another ripple of laughter.

'I've never heard him sound so self-assured,' came a murmur from behind me. I hadn't noticed her arrival although, six feet tall with the same familiar mass of red curls, it's fair to say most other people probably had. The bump may have caught their attention too. It was, after all, quite sizeable.

I looked at it. I expect I had my mouth open, not necessarily the sort of cool, calm look I might have gone for had I been given fair warning. In the background, Jeremy was still talking and another ripple of applause signalled his introduction of Hugo Granville to perform the official ribbon cutting. There even was a ribbon, I noticed, hastily strung across the front door between the Prosecco table and a coat stand that was another new addition to the decor.

'Aren't you going to say anything?' asked Mallory. I wasn't sure what to say. She was evidently very pregnant. I'm not a midwife but I doubted she had long to go.

Daisy's Dad, Dick broke the ice in inimitable style before I could come up with anything coherent, sensible or, most importantly, polite. 'Put a few pounds on, young missy, I'd say. Feedin' you well down in London, are they?'

'Hello, Dick. Hi Mucker. Yes, that's right. Eating for two, you might say.' She looked at me. 'OK, Sam, I'll give you a start. Yes is the answer. I'm wondering how you'd feel about a ginger son?

THE END.

Afterword

Like all little-known authors, Steve relies heavily on word-of-mouth and readers' reviews to spread the word about his books. If you have enjoyed Lazytown (or, indeed, any of his other books), please leave a review (or just a rating) on Amazon or Goodreads. These really do help bring the books to the attention of new readers. Thank you.

https://www.stevesheppardauthor.com/

ACKNOWLEDGMENTS

And thanks go to:

The brilliant Justine Gilbert for her immense assistance in getting this book out in the world; to Jennie Rayment for not allowing me to give up; and Rob Sheppard for his helpful comments on the original draft.

Also, Christine Hammacott at artofcomms.co.uk for the fabulous cover.

Finally of course, thanks to all my family and friends for their continued support of my efforts ('What? **Another** book? Oh, all right, go on then.'), especially those who happily enjoy village life in West Oxfordshire.

About the Author

Steve Sheppard was born in Guildford and spent nearly forty years moving around Surrey before running out of places to live there and moving to Buckinghamshire and thence to Oxfordshire, where he spent a quarter of a century in a quirky village which was honestly nothing like Idleborough.

Having written his first book, Steve felt it was time to move again before the paparazzi caught up with him, and decided to head back to his roots. However, he forgot to stop when he reached Guildford and ended up in Hampshire.

Steve has spent his whole life trying to discover the secret of how to become a fully-functioning adult. He has so far failed. One thing he has learnt is that he ought to have tried writing a book forty years earlier than he did, although he also now realises that he should have become a celebrity first, as this would have made selling it much easier. As well as ***Lazytown,*** he currently has three comedy spy thrillers to his name: the Dawson and Lucy Series, all published by Claret Press: ***A Very Important Teapot*** (2019) set in Australia, ***Bored to Death in the Baltics*** (2021), not set in Australia and ***Poor Table Manners*** (2024), which takes place in Cape Town. These feature a fairly hapless hero and a considerably less hapless heroine, together with varied supporting casts, most of whom are not who they claim to be. The books have been read by approximately a million fewer people than Steve might have hoped. Despite this, a fourth Dawson and Lucy title is on the cards.

The Dawson and Lucy Series:

A Very Important Teapot

Bored to Death in the Baltics

Poor Table Manners

Printed in Dunstable, United Kingdom